ZANE PRESENTS

Slippery When WET

Dear Reader:

Cairo has done it again; no surprise to me. *Slippery When Wet* is a collection of steaming hot novellas that will have you making booty calls, late-night sex drive-bys, and putting ice everywhere but in an actual glass to try to cool yourself down. I am sure this book will do extremely well since my *Purple Panties* books caused an uproar as well. Passion and sensuality are universal and there is something extremely arousing about women getting it on with each other. And you do not have to be a lesbian, or even a female, to enjoy reading about it.

So sit back, light a candle, pull out your favorite toy—inanimate object or breathing human being—and prepare to be stimulated beyond where your own imagination could ever take you. Cairo's imagination will take it to the next level, and then the next level, and then even the next level. He is a beast when it comes to spinning eroticism in an entertaining fashion. *Slippery When Wet* will have you wanting to experiment with some new things, no matter who you are.

As always, thanks for supporting Cairo and the other authors under Strebor Books. We strive to bring you the most cutting-edge, out-of-the-box material on the market. You can find out more about our other titles on www.zanestore.com and you can find me on Facebook @AuthorZane or Twitter @planetzane. My direct email address is zane@eroticanoir.com. Please shoot me an email and let me know what you think and make sure you check out all of the rest of Cairo's books as well.

Blessings,

Zane

Publisher
Strebor Books International
www.simonandschuster.com

ZANE PRESENTS

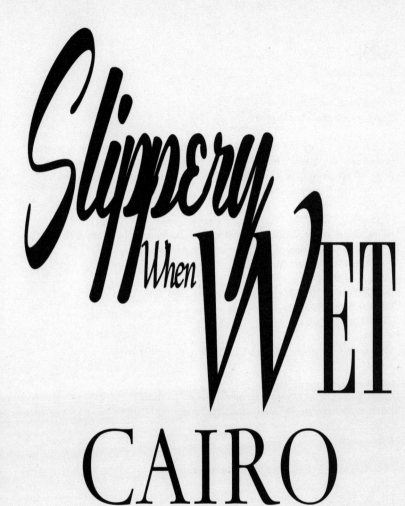

Slippery When Wet

CAIRO

SBI

STREBOR BOOKS

NEW YORK LONDON TORONTO SYDNEY

Strebor Books
P.O. Box 6505
Largo, MD 20792
http://www.streborbooks.com

ISBN 978-1-59309-435-5
ISBN 978-1-4516-7843-7 (e-book)
LCCN 2013933641

First Strebor Books trade paperback edition November 2013

Cover design: www.mariondesigns.com
Cover photograph: © Keith Saunders/Marion Designs
Interior photograph: © Dan Bannister/ShutterstockImages

10 9 8 7 6 5 4 3 2 1

Manufactured in the United States of America

ACKNOWLEDGMENTS

Aiight, my freaks, I'ma keep it real wet 'n' slippery for ya. Eight books in and I'm still bringin' the heat! I think y'all gonna really enjoy *Slippery When Wet*. Whether you swing that way or not, there's a story in this joint that's sure to wet even the "straightest" chicks' drawz! So get ready to wet them fingers, them toys, or whatever else you use to get off wit' 'cause it's 'bout to be a whole lotta fuckin' 'n' suckin' goin' on!

To the sexually liberated and open-minded: Thanks for continuin' to wave ya freak flags, ridin' this hot, *nasty* wave with me, and gettin' down with the juice. Let's keep it wet, keep it sticky, and always keep it ready! The Cairo Movement is here to stay!

To all the Facebook beauties 'n' cuties and cool bruhs who make this journey mad fun: Real rap. Y'all my muthaeffen peeps! Thanks for vibin' with ya boy! And, uh, run me some of them sex tapes y'all got hidden. I wanna watch!

To my peeps, Flenardo Taylor, aka, Freknardo, the freak-nasty poet: Yo, playboy, real spit. I 'preciate how you stay showin' me mad luv, spreadin' the word 'bout my joints to ya peeps, and constantly biggin' me up. You already know what it is!

To all the silent-haters, closed-minded & sexually repressed peeps who ain't ready for the heat, yet somehow still find themselves sneakin' off somewhere to read my joints on the low, rollin' their eyes 'n' suckin' their teeth, while pressin' their sticky thighs together, tryna keep them drawz from gettin' wet. Buckle up, *muhfuckas*...this one's gonna set ya ass on fire!

To Zane, Charmaine, Yona and the rest of the Strebor/Simon & Schuster team: As always, I hope you all know how much ya boy appreciates the never-ending luv!

To the members of *Cairo's World*: Uh, yeah, yeah, yeah...I already know I tol' y'all in my *Big Booty* acknowledgments that I was gonna stop neglectin' the other side and keep the flames *turnt* up for y'all and I haven't. Well, uh, yabba-dabba-doo... don't do me, goddammit! I'ma get it together real soon. ☺

And, as always, to the naysayers: Here's another joint for you to pop shit about. You already know it's because of you that I keep it raw, hot 'n' oh-so *nasty*! Keep juicin' the haterade, my peeps. It keeps me horny and keeps me strokin' out that hotness! Lick them fingers or keep it movin'. Either way, I ain't goin' anywhere!

One luv—

Cairo

Juicy Fruit

One

If I don't get me some dick soon…

"My pussy's sooo fucking horny. I wanna fuck," I mumble out loud as I step inside the chrome elevator and press the button for the second floor. The elevator doors shut, and then it begins its descent down to my secret rendezvous spot. I step back further into the elevator, glad I am the only one inside. *I want someone else to play in* (and with) *this wet coochie.* A hard dick, a wet mouth, a long tongue, a big toe, fingers…I'm so fucking horny that right now I don't give a damn what it is being pushed inside of this hot slit as long as it's attached to another live, breathing human being. Because being single *and* forever horny is not it!

I wanna fuck, damn it!

Oh sure this whole self-induced celibacy thing was/is my idea. Shit! But, when you're used to being fucked down every day—for almost a year, then go completely cold turkey, it starts to take a toll on you. And, baby, trust. Having no dick in my life is killing me *slooooowly*. And believe me. I have been enticed to go on an all-out fucking spree. But I refuse to give into temptation. I rebuke the power of good, hard dick, and what it has done to me over the years. It's fucked me silly. It's dragged me into drama. It's had me believing bold-faced lies. It's had me moving in men who expected me to take care of them. Oooh, good hard dick has had me settling when I knew better. And the list goes on.

So after my last fiasco of a relationship, I made a conscious decision to stay away from men and all of their bullshit until Mr. Right comes along. Because, up until now, I've had more than enough of my share of Mr. Wrongs, starting with Mr. Dead Wrong and ending with Mr. All Wrong All Along. I could write a book on how trifling some of these sorry-ass men are. But I won't. And I'm not going into the New Year bashing or harboring any ill feelings toward men. I mean. I know I'm a good catch. I own my own home. I have excellent credit. I'm educated. I'm supportive, encouraging, and loving. Bottom line, I'm a damn good woman. And, yeah, maybe I do need to lose fifty…okay, seventy-five, pounds or more. Mmmph. That's what my ex told me the night before he told me he was tired of fucking "a big girl." Really? The nerve of that insensitive bastard! Then to add insult to injury, he added, "I'm not in love with you, anymore."

"Oh really?" I had replied, stunned. "Then why are you with me?"

He stared at me as if I'd asked him one of the dumbest questions he'd ever heard. "Damn. You really gotta ask? Because you give good head. And the pussy's good."

I blinked. After all I had done for him, he had the audacity to part his lips with that shit. Sorry, but that answer was it for me. Realizing that he thought I was only good for sucking his dick and fucking him felt like someone had stabbed me in the chest a thousand times, and left me for dead. I was stunned for several minutes, digesting his words before I finally came to my senses. Right then, I climbed out of bed and helped him pack his shit, then showed him and his big, black dick to the door.

Yes, I'm a *big girl*, as that asshole called me. But I'm not fat-nasty with it. In fact, I'm a beautiful, thick-hipped, big-boned, cocoa-brown woman who embraces every inch of her one-hundred-and-eighty-five-pound frame, proudly and boldly. And any man who can't appreciate me, or my dangerous curves packed with ass and 36 double-D titties, can go straight to hell. Fuck 'em!

I'm a size sixteen, okay. And I wear it well. And you'd think any man in his right damn mind would want a woman who has a long tongue, deep throat, and a wet, juicy pussy that loves to fuck. You'd think a man would want a sexy, full-figured bombshell who has some meat on her bones rather than chasing behind some skinny, anorexic bitch you see running around starving herself half to death. Mmmph. Not Maurice, that's for sure!

So thanks to him, it's been eight months, three weeks, four days, eleven hours, and forty-seven minutes and fifteen excruciating seconds since I've sucked a dick, fucked a dick, or been fucked over by a dick. I guess that last part is a blessing. No…it *is* a blessing!

Still, I can't say I don't miss being touched and caressed and held. That I don't yearn to have this smoldering fire blazing between my legs pounded out by something other than a dildo. But I made a promise to myself that I would not give out any more of this pussy to another man until I'm swept off my feet by someone who can appreciate a full-figured woman who has her shit together instead of being intimidated by her. So, until then, I will suffer through this aching between my thighs alone— stress-free and drama-free, and continue to take matters into my own hands until something, or someone, worthwhile comes along.

I press my legs shut, discreetly rubbing them together as I eye the surveillance camera. I slyly pinch my right nipple. If there wasn't someone on the other end of the lens watching me, I would pull my skirt up over my hips and finger-fuck myself right here in this elevator. I glance up at the flashing light as the elevator descends. *16, 15, 14, 13, 12, 11*…hoping like hell it doesn't stop on any of the floors until I get to my destination. The woman's bathroom, with the single stall and sink, tucked in the far right corner of the second-floor lobby. The one I use religiously—or the one up on the twentieth floor when it's not already occupied, like now—to masturbate in. Most of the folks here at Sci-Tech take three or four smoke breaks throughout the day. Me, I take what I call *masturbate* breaks. I love cumming, all over my fingers, all over my toys, then licking them clean. I love the taste of my own pussy. *10, 9, 8, 7, 6…*

Still…my pussy's hungry for a good fucking. And no matter how many times I masturbate, I can't ever seem to take the edge off for any longer than a few hours before I'm back at it again. Stroking my clit, then easing one finger, then two fingers, then three, inside my horny cunt before replacing them with my most faithful, trustworthy travel companion—the Trojan Twister Intimate Massager—with its four twistable positions and eight settings. Oooh, yes. With two double-A batteries, this little gadget brings me quick relief during the day while I'm at work until I can get home to ride down on one of my many dildos.

I slip my hand down into my Dooney & Bourke, feel around for the satin pouch, then sigh with relief. *Something's gotta give, soon. But this'll do for now.* The elevator stops on the fifth floor. I suck my teeth as it opens. In steps Viola from Procurement. All gussied up in her Sunday's best, bringing in with her the lush peachy scent of Heat by Beyoncé. This gossipy bitch doesn't know the difference between church wear and business attire. Today, she has on a brown, ankle-length skirt and a long, matching suit jacket with rhinestones on the lapel. I roll my eyes. All she needs is the handkerchief with the lace trim, the gloves, and wide-brimmed hat to match and she'd be church-ready. Heathen-ass ho!

"Good Morning, Ava," she says, smiling wide, bright and phony the minute the door shuts. "Happy New Year."

Okay, be nice, Ava. It's the New Year and you promised yourself you were going to leave old resentments in the past. Yeah, but I also said if I didn't have anything nice to say to someone that I would simply not say anything to them at all.

I take a deep breath. "Oh, hey, Vee. Happy New Year to you as well."

"So, where you off to first thing this morning? Isn't your office up on the eighteenth floor?" She glances at her watch. "It's not even after ten yet, and you're already prowling the halls."

Don't let this bitch get to you!

I tilt my head. "And here it is at the top of the New Year and I see you're still worshipping in the House of Messy," I shoot back, shaking my head. "First day back to work and you're *already* minding everyone else's business, except your own."

She grunts, dismissing me. "So how you been, Ava?"

Okay, I see this trick wants to purposefully get on my nerves first thing this morning. "I'm beautiful, thanks." I don't bother asking her how she's been; I don't care to know. It's obvious. Stuck-up and wound up real tight.

She gives me the once-over, and smirks as she turns to face the mirrored wall of the elevator. "Um, how's your girlfriend doing? You know"—she pats her thigh, keeping her stare forward—"that rough-looking girl with the dreads who works up on the twentieth floor in Tech Support. The two of you always seem so cozy together in the lunchroom."

I give her a confused glare. But I know exactly whom she's referring to. Starleesha Wilkerson—well, Star for short. She's a lesbian. Not that I have anything against lesbians; I don't. But this ho does. Her moral compass doesn't allow her to embrace another's sexual preference, which in layman's terms translates to her being an opinionated, homophobic bitch!

"I don't have any *girl*friends here. But if you're talking about Star, how about you ask her yourself since you seem to be so concerned. I don't keep tabs on her."

The elevator stops and opens on the third floor. "I see the way she looks at you."

I frown. "And what exactly are you implying?" I narrow my eyes, placing a hand up on my hip in a combative stance.

"You ain't foolin' no one," she snidely says over her shoulder.

I blink, taken aback, as the gunmetal gray doors slide shut.

Two

I'm not a lesbian…

My skirt is hiked up over my hips, my panties somewhere down around my knees. I am squatting over the toilet, stroking myself with eager fingers. "Mmmm…" I moan, imagining her slithering tongue nestled between the folds of my wet pussy as I toss my head back and shut my eyes. She is nameless and faceless, my dark chocolate lover. But she visits me in my fantasies quite often. My clit is sucked into her mouth, being pulled at, coaxed out from its hiding place, swelling in size; its tip sensitive and alive, shooting decadent sensations through my entire body. I am bucking against her face, grinding on her mouth, wanting to scream as I reach my first wave of an orgasm.

No, I am not a lesbian. I am curious.

"Oooooh yes," I murmur as my imaginary lover delivers delicious tongue strokes across my clit, along my swollen lips, and into my saturated slit. Juices ooze out, wetting my fingers. I turn on my vibrator, roll it over my clit and gasp. Teeth bite into my nipples, one at a time, pulling and stretching them. The low hum of my silicone friend heightens my arousal, pushes my urges and imagination to unchartered limits as I replace sticky fingers with it, plunging into my wetness. "Oooh, yesss…"

I slip my fingers into my mouth, suck and slurp and lick, sliding my moist tongue in between each finger, savoring my nectar.

Imagining my juices are her juices. That I am tasting my first pussy, my tongue easing out of my mouth, licking at her nub as she places her hand on the back of my head, slamming my tongue into her pussy. "Oh, yes, fuck me, baby…mmmmm…" I hear my imaginary lover whisper.

My fantasy fuck, my delicious secret, my invisible lover all wrapped into naughty deeds. Her tongue, her fingers—in my pussy, my ass—caressing my clit, pinching my nipples. She tells me to turn around, to get on my knees, then slides a very thick, eight-inch pink dildo into my slippery slit.

"You want that big pink cock? You like how that feels stretching your pussy?"

She rapidly pushes it in and out of me, slapping my ass every so often.

"Oooh   yeah…uh…uh…mmmm…uh…mmmph…aaah…oooh yeah…fuck yeah…yeah, yeah, yeah…mmmph…"

"You wanna taste your pussy?" She pulls the dildo out of me, glides it over my lips. *"Open your mouth, suck your pussy off that big fucking cock…"* She jams the dildo down into my throat. *"Gag on that cock!"*

"Ooooh, mmmph…" Gurgling sounds escape the back of my throat as she stretches my neck open. She's shutting off my airway and I am getting dizzy. Mercilessly, she stuffs my throat, reaching under me and pinching my clit. I suck and slurp and gag, moaning and groaning. She slaps each ass cheek. My pussy is wet…so very wet!

In my mind's eye, her tongue slides across my puckering asshole and I feel myself melting, creaming all over my vibrator.

"Oh…Ohhhh," I whisper. Imaginary hands cup my ass, squeeze and slap it. My lover's breath hot against my ear as she tells me how badly she wants me, needs me. How eager she is to touch me, please me, be pleased by me.

Another moan escapes me.

"Pull your ass open. You want it in your ass and pussy? You wanna be fucked by two huge cocks?"

"Yes, baby…give it to me in my ass…stuff my pussy, boo…"

The pink dildo slick with spit is pushed against my asshole. I feel it pressing up against my tight, hungry hole, its head slowly prying its way in. Methodically, she works the head in. I gasp.

"Relax," she whispers, then bites my left ass cheek. She hands me a beige, fleshy, eleven-inch dildo, commands me to suck it. To wet it up real good, then slide it into my overheated pussy. I do as I am told, moaning.

"Oh yes…"

Another inch of thick silicone dick is pushed into my ass as I am stretching my pussy, filling my slit with goodness. I buck my hips. My eyelids flutter. Sweet agonizing bliss shoots through my body. I am in the midst of coming.

"Oooh, yeah…you like it in your ass, huh?"

"Yes, yes…oooh fuck, oooh fuck…"

Mouth open, eyes closed, I let out a low moan. My fingers quickening over my clit as I bury my travel companion further into my soaked pussy. Its vibrations sending delicious chills along my spine. I run my tongue over my parted lips. My silicone buddy probing my pussy, delving into wetness, twisting around clutching muscles. I grip the handicap rail to steady myself as my knees buckle. The cold steel cooling my warm hand. I slowly pull out my vibrator, roll it around on my clit, then ease it back inside of me. I turn it onto its highest setting, causing ripples of delight to turn into waves of pleasure. I am coming and coming and coming. Nonstop, surges of hot juices splashing out of me.

I picture my lover clamping her warm mouth over the mouth of my gushy pussy and sucking my juices out.

"Oh yes, oh yes, oh yesssss…" In my mind's eye, my thighs lock around my lover's face. I ride her tongue, fast and hard. Her grasp tight on my hips, she devours my pussy until I coat her taste buds with my honey.

I pull my vibrator out of my soppy wet cunt, then slide it into my mouth, licking and lapping along the sides, savoring my juices.

"Oooh, your pussy tastes so good," I hear her say in between licks and slurps. Her tongue flicks my clit. *"You like that?"* I gasp the moment I place the tip of my vibrator back on my engorged clitoris. I close my eyes as I massage my clit with the vibrator imagining it's my lover's tongue. I whimper softly. Over and over, I stroke my clit. Its low hum pulsing through my pussy until I can no longer take it.

I spread my legs wider and slip the tip of the vibrator into my pussy, teasing myself before plunging it deep inside of me.

"Yessssss…"

"You want me to fuck you with my tongue?"

I moan as my eyes flutter open. *"Yes, fuck me. Oh, God, Oh, God, Oh, God…yesssss…mmmm… I'm coooooooming. Yes, yes, yessss…"*

My pussy squirts as someone knocks on the door, distracting the tingling in my pussy, disrupting the pulsing in my clit. "Hello?" a male voice inquires. "Is everything all right? Are you okay in there?"

"Uh…y-yeah," I squeak out, trying to pinch back the squirting of my hot juices. "Uh-ooh. I…"

"Are you sure everything's okay? Hello? Ma'am?"

I clear my throat. "I'm fine. Be out in a minute," I manage to say in spite of the shuddering of my walls. I ease my vibrator out, clicking it off, before sliding it into my mouth and sucking it clean.

My knees are wobbly. But I make every attempt to steady myself so that I don't topple over. I slip two fingers into my pussy, then scoop out the remaining bit of my juices and slide my fingers into my mouth, licking my lips when I am done. Satisfied that I have scooped out all that is left of my orgasm, I reach into my bag and pull out a packet of feminine wipes, then wipe myself clean.

A few seconds later, I am pulling my panties up, straightening out my skirt, then washing my hands. I stare at myself in the mirror. *Girl, your horny ass needs to get laid, fast. You're too damn fine not to have someone in your life handling all of this good, fat pussy.*

Three

"Sci-Tech, Ava speaking."

"I miss you," the voice on the other end says, causing flashes of what used to be to run through my head. I quickly shake the thoughts, rolling my eyes.

"Why are you calling, Maurice?"

"I was thinking about you, and wanted to hear your voice; that's all."

I laugh. "Oh, really? We haven't spoken in eight months, and now—out of the blue, you're suddenly interested in hearing my voice. What, them skinny bitches aren't working out for you?"

"C'mon, Ava, baby. Don't do me like that. I know I fucked up."

I tuck the phone into the space between my cheek and neck as I scroll through my emails. "Okay, you fucked up. Glad you realize that. Now, what do you want?" This fool has the audacity to say he wants to see me tonight. Please. I'll let my pussy freeze over in hell first before I ever let him sniff, lick, or stick this juicy hole again. "Uh, not. No, thank you. You had your chance, Maurice. And there's no second chances being given out over here."

"Don't you miss what we had, baby?"

I frown, deleting various emails, then opening my spam folder. "No." Yeah, it's a bold-faced lie; there are times that I do miss him. His touch, his kisses, his dark, delicious dick hitting the bottom of my pussy and stretching its walls; I miss it all. And I am pissed

at him, at myself, for him being the cause of my cunt slowly
churning out cream. But *no* is all he is deserving of after how he
ended it, wanting to fuck some nondescript skinny bitch over me.

"You don't mean that." His voice dips dangerously low. "I know
you miss me, baby." My pussy responds, coming alive. I swallow.
"I wanna see you."

"That's too bad." I press my thighs shut. "I'm no longer available to you, Maurice. So do us both a favor and don't call my job
again."

"I was really hoping we could still be friends."

"Maurice, I want you to listen to something, okay?"

"Yeah, I'm listening."

Click.

Fucking asshole!

He calls right back and I have to threaten to get a restraining
order against him if he doesn't leave me the hell alone. I hang up.
Less than a minute later, my phone is ringing again. It's another
outside call. I'm annoyed that my phone's caller ID isn't working. I know it's him so I snatch the phone up on the third ring
and give it to him real good. "Listen. I told you we have nothing
to say to each other. Call this number again and I will have your
monkey ass charged with harassment. Now stop calling my
motherfu— "

"Whoa, whoa," the voice on the other end says. "Who pissed
in your bowl of Cheerios today?"

I am immediately embarrassed. "Ohmygod, who is this?"

"Girl, it's Kara. And remind me to never get on your bad side."
She chuckles. "Long time no chat. Happy New Year to you."

Kara—or Karalyn, used to work down on the tenth floor in
Logistics before landing a government position down in Bethesda,
Maryland over a year ago. Although we weren't BFF's, we're

friendly. She's someone I would go out to lunch with, or meet up after work for an occasional drink. And I liked her enough to want to stay in touch, which is a rarity for me given the fact that I don't usually do well befriending other women. But there's something different about Karalyn—I mean, Kara. She always kept to herself. And like me, kept her personal life private. The only thing any of us knew about her personal life—and that was by chance—was that she was married and had no children. Other than that, she kept it strictly professional. And I liked that about her.

"Ohmygod! I'm so sorry, girl. I thought you were…mmph. Never mind. Happy New Year to you, too. It's good to hear from you. It's been ages since we've talked."

"Yes, it has." She tells me she's spent the last six months working over in Afghanistan training. That she returned to the Sates about two weeks ago and had been thinking about me. "Hence the reason for why I'm calling you. I was wondering. What are you doing this weekend?"

Hmmm, let's see? Aside from playing in my pussy and OD-ing on red Velvet cake and vanilla bean ice cream the entire weekend, it's not like my life is one big social calendar. I haven't been out on a date in months, nor have I had a vacation since the one I took with Maurice last summer to the Margarita Islands, which I practically had to beg him to go to. I glance at my computer screen. "Um, nothing really. Why? What's up?"

"I was hoping you'd say yes to coming up to my cabin in the Poconos this weekend. I haven't been there in months and really need to get up there to check on things. I thought maybe we could have a girls' weekend, just the two of us."

What the fuck? Is this chick serious? What the hell I look like going up to some winter cabin with another woman—*alone?* She's cool and all, but not like that!

"Look, before you say no," she adds, sensing my reservation. "Think about it. I have some bottles of Moscato already on ice, and the liquor cabinet up there is fully stocked with any other liquid pleasures you might want. We haven't talked in a while. We can sit around the fireplace, snacking and drinking and watching old reruns of *Desperate Housewives*." I chuckle, surprised that she remembered how much I love that show. "And it'll give us a chance to get caught up. Besides, judging by the way you answered the phone a few minutes ago, it sounds like you could use a little getaway."

Well, she's right about that. Still…

"I promise you, it'll be a very relaxing, refreshing weekend; for the both of us. And who knows, maybe you'll want to keep coming back."

I smile at the thought of having somewhere else to go instead of staking out the malls for clearance sales, or being cooped up in my house, staring at the walls, eating myself into another dress size. "Okay, I'm sold. When and where?"

"Oh, great," she says, sounding a bit too overly excited. *But why?* "Girl, you have no idea how you've made my day. I look forward to seeing you." She gives me the address and directions. I tell her I will work a half-day on Friday, then head up. We talk a few minutes more, then disconnect.

At six o'clock, I shut off my computer, slip into my coat and prepare to leave for the day. "Miss Wilson," Erica—one of the administrative secretaries, stops me, carrying a huge floral arrangement in a crystal vase. "These just came for you."

I raise my eyebrow in surprise. "For me?" Erica hands me the vase. There's a white envelope in the center of it. I open it. Give me another chance? I'll do whatever it takes. i miss you. Maurice.

I tear the card up, then hand the vase back to her. "No thanks. You can toss these." I walk off, ignoring the young assistant's curious look. "See you in the morning."

The rest of the week flies by uneventful. I become immersed in briefings and reports at work, then spend an hour and a half each night at the gym right after work so that by the time I get home—around eight, I am too exhausted to do anything else besides shower and then hit the sheets. So Friday rolls around faster than I had hoped. For some reason, I feel nervous. And I've been tempted a few times to call Karalyn to cancel. But then I think about the alternatives, and decide against it. *Hell, it's the New Year and I promised I would spend it doing and experiencing new things. So I might as well get started now.*

At twelve P.M. sharp, I am pulling out of the employees' parking garage. With my overnight bag already packed and in the trunk, I stop at the Exxon down the street from the job. Gas up, then head up Interstate 280 toward Interstate 80, heading westbound.

Four

"So, do tell," Karalyn says, moving around the *L*-shaped granite counter. We've eaten lobster and shrimp dishes she's whipped up. And have spent the last several hours getting caught up with each other's lives while listening to her vast collection of music. Surprisingly, Karalyn has been extremely chatty. She's told me that she and her husband, Kenneth, have been divorced for the last six months, partly due to his infidelities and, mostly, to her not being happy in the marriage. She said it felt like she was suffocating. Now the conversation has shifted over to me. I sip my wine, eyeing her over the rim of my glass as she reaches for her glass of wine, then takes a sip. It's close to eight o'clock in the evening and we've already finished off two bottles of Moscato, now working on our third. And, yes, my guard and hair have both been let down. I'm feeling good. "What happened between you and ole boy, anyway? What's his name?"

I sigh, shifting my weight onto the stool I'm sitting on. "Maurice."

She snaps her fingers. "Yeah, that's right. Mister Fine. Mmmph. Anyway, what happened or *didn't* happen to cause this breakup?"

I toss back my drink. "What else you have besides wine? I need something a little more stronger than this."

She chuckles, pointing over toward a room off of the kitchen. "There are a few bottles of Ciroc and, I think, I have some Bombay, Tequila, and Remy in the cabinet as well as out in the pantry. And you still haven't answered the question."

I get up from my seat and head for the bottles of liquor, feeling tipsy. "I'd rather not talk about him."

"I thought the two of you were madly in love."

"Please. So did I. But that one-way love affair has since been derailed." I walk back out with a bottle of peach Ciroc.

She guzzles back the rest of her wine, then sets her glass on the counter. "So what happened? What changed?" She reaches over and grabs a handful of grapes from off a ceramic platter and pops two in her mouth.

I roll my eyes, cracking open the bottle. "Girl, long story." I walk over to the fridge and pull out a tray of ice cubes, then locate a can of pineapple juice she has in another cabinet. Now in the back of my mind I know I probably shouldn't have any more to drink. And I definitely should probably stick with the one and not switch over to something else. But, tonight, I feel like pushing the envelope to the edge. I feel like letting my hair down and simply being in the moment. *And I'm sure I'm going to pay for it in the morning.*

Karalyn stares at me, tapping her nails against the granite. "Well, are you going to keep me waiting? Spill it. I wanna know what happened between you and Maurice?" I pull out a clean glass from out of the cabinet. She tells me to grab her one as well. She's decided she's had enough of the wine for one night.

"Say when?" I say as I pour vodka into a glass over three cubes of ice. She waits until it's half-full, then says, "when." I add a splash of pineapple juice, then hand her the glass.

"Aaah, yesss. Now this'll kick it up a notch," she says, taking a sip.

I grin. "Glad you like."

"I definitely do. *A lot.*" She eyes me over the rim of her glass. "How about we take this into the living room so we can get a little more comfortable?" She stands, stretches, then takes another sip of her drink. "You sure know how to make a simple drink taste delicious."

"Hey, what can I say?" I tease. "I'm good at whatever I do. Trust."

"Oh, I'm sure you are. And I can't wait to find out *what else* you're good at." The statement drips with innuendo. My face suddenly feels flush with embarrassment.

She laughs, walking off into the living room. "Relax, girl. I'm only teasing."

"Oh," I say, not sure if I am relieved or disappointed that she's, uh, *only* teasing. I've never looked at Karalyn or any other woman—other than my faceless imaginary lover—in a sexual way. So the fact that I have to restrain myself from practically leering at her perky D-cup breasts, her ass in skintight jeans, or her sumptuous lips is way beyond me. I blame it on the alcohol. Blame it on being in need of a good fuck.

Karalyn turns to me. "Sooo, you *coming* or not?" The word *come* sounds soft and sexy the way she says it. It lingers in the air between us. It's hidden meaning teasing me.

I grab the bottle of vodka and walk toward her. "I'm coming, geesh."

She laughs. "Then hurry up 'cause I wanna hear all about your breakup with Mister Fine. Don't even think I forgot."

I roll my eyes up in my head, following behind her. "Girl, I already told you. Long story." I set the bottle on the table, then take a seat down on the opposite end of the sofa from her. "I need a refill."

"We have a whole bottle of vodka and the entire night." She takes my glass from me, her delicate fingers gently grazing mine. Heat shoots through me. I shift in my seat. She fills the glasses with Ciroc, then tops it off with peach juice, then hands me mine.

I take a sip eyeing her as she fixes hers, then sits a few inches away from me.

I raise my glass to her. "Not bad." Now it's her turn to tell me how she's good at everything she does. She emphasizes *everything*.

"Now, give me the short version of how Mister Fine broke your heart so we can spend the rest of the night drinking and doing *whatever else* comes to mind. Or we can simply sit and do nothing at all, except finish this bottle off."

I smile. "Sounds good to me. Long story short, I loved Maurice more than he loved me. Hell, I loved *him* more than I loved *me*. But the icing on the cake for me was when that motherfucker said I was too fat."

"Fat? Is he serious? There's nothing *fat* about you, girl. Oh, he's a fucking idiot! Mmmph. He actually called you *fat?*"

"Well, not exactly in those words. But that's what it sounded like when he decided to tell me while I was sucking his dick that he wanted—no, needed—his space. That he was no longer attracted to me. Translation, I want a skinny bitch."

"That bastard!"

"Yeah. Tell me about it. It's a good thing he didn't fuck-up my self-esteem too bad, but imagine how I felt hearing that shit with a mouthful of his cum. I felt like I had been punched in the forehead for grazing the head of his dick with my teeth." I shake my head. "I should have known something was wrong when he stopped going down on me, then eventually no longer wanted to have sex as much."

She gives me an incredulous look. "He did what? Stopped giving you head? That's a no-no. *And* you were still sucking his dick?"

I give her a dismissive wave. "Chile, among other things." I take a sip of my drink. "I was that man's whore in the sheets. Anything he wanted sexually, I gave it. I'd let him slip his dick out of my pussy, pull it out and suck it clean, then let him run it all up in my ass with no questions asked. Why? Because he was my man and I was willing to do whatever I needed to in order to keep him satisfied. But whenever I asked him to eat my pussy, it was always some half-assed tongue lap. Then when he stopped doing it altogether and I asked him about it, he said it was never really his thing, but only did it because he wanted his dick sucked."

Karalyn sips her drink, listening intently.

I shake my head, thinking back to the last time Maurice and I made love—no, fucked. His wide, delicious dick a pleasurable fit, stretching and filling me. A sweet ache building up deep in the wells of my cunt, swelling my pussy lips. I gasped as he dipped his hand between my thighs, arching my back and spreading my legs to give him more access to the back-shot view of his cock sliding in and out of me. It's presence brushing up against my G-spot. My free hand fluttered to my breasts. Pinching my nipples, rolling them between my fingers. I slammed back on his dick, bouncing and clapping my ass around the base of him, nearing myself to an orgasm. But then he gripped my hips, digging his nails into my flesh, and started banging deep and hard into me while letting out a long, low groan.

Then, after a series of short, jerking thrusts, it was over. He had cum.

And I was left teetering on the edge of an orgasm of my own, my pussy whimpering and pulsing for release. All I needed were a few more deep strokes and I would have spurted a stream of hot juices. But Maurice had already slipped out of me, rolling over onto his side, then through heavy-lidded eyes, telling me goodnight as he pulled the covers up over him. There was no half-hearted kiss on the lips or cheek. No feeble attempt at trying to pull me into his arms. Nothing.

But that wasn't the first time he had taunted me, getting off before making sure I'd gotten off, too. It had become a pattern. One I ignored up until that night. "Wow. Um. I know that's not it, is it?"

He shot me a look over his shoulder, frowning. "Yeah. I'm good."

"Well, I'm not," I huffed, snatching the covers back. "I didn't cum yet."

"Whose fault is that? You better go pull out one of them toys and go finish yourself off. Next time, make sure you get yours before I do."

And with that said, he turned back over on his side, yanking the covers back up over his head. I was stunned and pissed all in the same breath. I couldn't believe his response to me.

I press my thighs tight, remembering how good his dick was. Too damn bad he wasn't any good.

"That selfish bastard!" Karalyn hisses. "That's one of the reasons why I divorced Kenneth. He was so disconnected from what I needed sexually. And I don't really think he cared as long as he got his." We both take sips from our glasses, knowingly. "I know why I stayed with Kenneth for as long as I did. Because I wanted my marriage to work. But why did you put up with Maurice for as long as you had?"

"I simply accepted it. I wasn't ready to let go. I thought things would get better. And I wanted a ring so I didn't make a big deal about it, even though I felt...I don't know. Rejected in a sense. After awhile sex with us became routine, like it was a chore that he needed to hurry up and get finished with. For me, it became a desperate mission to keep him. Sometimes I'd wonder if it was me."

"Girl, hush. It definitely wasn't you. He sounds like he was a selfish bastard. Good riddance to his trifling ass. He did you a favor."

She holds her glass up toward mine. They clink together.

"Exactly. I'm so over him and any other emotionally bankrupt asshole. I'm sick of the games, and all of their fickle ways. Girl, I'm so done with stroking a man's super-sized ego. I'm done with 'em." I don't realize how that sounds until it's fallen out of my mouth. As if I'm done with the male species forever, and ever, Amen. "Anyway, that's the past. I'm eight months free of that mess. And I have no intentions of going back to it. Right now I'm happily single and doing me."

Karalyn smiles. "Girl, good for you." She reaches over and swipes a strand of hair out of my face, her fingertips lightly brushing against my forehead. "He didn't deserve a woman like you, anyway. You're a beautiful woman who deserves so much better, Ava. You deserve to be with someone who's going to appreciate you, love, and cherish you." A surging heat sweeps through me as she says this. I shift in my seat, attempting to ignore it.

Conya Doss has been playing in the background. And when her track "Don't Change" pours out into the room, Karalyn and I quietly slip into our own mental zones, sipping our drinks and bobbing our heads to the beat, getting lost in our thoughts.

It's 3 A.M., when I finally slide between the sheets of the queen-size bed in Karalyn's guestroom. My head spinning from the liquor, I close my eyes and squeeze my thighs together as I run a hand over my hardened nipples. I let out a low moan as I pinch them.

What is going on with me? Why exactly am I here again?

My fingers slip down between my thighs, imagining Karalyn's hands touching me, teasing me, seducing me.

I don't fall asleep until almost five in the morning.

Five

The next evening, Karalyn and I are sitting in the living room. We've spent most of the day lounging around her cabin, talking, drinking bottles of wine, and listening to music. And I am surprised at how comfortable I am around her.

Rahsaan Patterson's "Feels Good" is playing. The fireplace is lit. The mood is…intimate. And I should be concerned. But I am not. Still, I am taken by surprise when Karalyn reaches over and grabs a stuffed shrimp from off the platter set in front of us on the coffee table and holds it, perched between her index finger and thumb, to my lips. "Open your mouth. Eat it." Her words come out hot and thick like molasses. I clamp shut the sweet stickiness that has already started to seep between my legs. I shift in my seat.

She sees my expression and laughs. "It's only shrimp I am trying to feed you." Her eyes gleam. "Or would you prefer I feed you some*thing* else?"

I blink, lifting my hand to take the shrimp from her.

She shakes her head, pulling her hand back. "No. Use your mouth."

I am both turned on and taken aback by her dominance. My pussy clenches as she presses it to my lips, coaxing me. Karalyn feeds me the shrimp. I close my eyes and take it in one voluptuous bite.

"It's good, isn't it?"

I refuse to meet her eyes as I chew.

I can't believe I'm sitting here doing this.

I reach for my glass and take a sip. "Yes." Without thought, I lick my lips. "It's delicious."

"Like you, I'm sure. So when's the last time you had your pussy ate?"

I almost choke on my drink. "Ohmygod, I can't believe you asked me that."

She shrugs. "Well, tell me. How long has it been?"

Too long!

I let out a nervous chuckle, wondering why I'm not more uncomfortable with this. Wondering why it doesn't matter that I am sitting here with another very attractive woman who's clearly flirting with me.

I put my glass to my lips, then toss back my drink. "It's been months."

She eyes me. And for a split second, I think I see amusement flutter in her eyes as she licks her lips. But I can't be for certain. Shit. After the last four drinks I've had, I can't be sure about much of anything that's going on right now, especially about why I'm feeling so…horny. "Can I ask you a question?"

I nod. "Sure."

"You ever been with another woman?"

No, but I've fantasized about it. Of course I don't share this tidbit.

"Have I ever been with a woman, how? *Sexually?*"

"Yes."

I shake my head, reaching over and pouring myself another drink. My throat suddenly feels as if I've gulped down sand as my heart thumps in my chest. I'm nervous, but not in an uncomfortable way. "No."

"Would you ever try it?"

I pause and look at her, trying to figure out where this line of questioning is heading. I twist in my seat. "No. I doubt it."

Okay, yes, I've masturbated—multiple times, to the thought. And, okay, truth is. Some—no, all—of my best orgasms have been as a result of those fantasies. Still, that's doesn't mean I'm willing to openly admit it to her or anyone else. And it definitely doesn't mean I want to live them out. *Or do I?* I mean, what if I like it? What if I want it again? Would that mean I'm a lesbian? "I don't knock what anyone else does," I push out, shifting my eyes from hers. "But I'm not gay."

"I didn't say you were. I'm only asking if you'd ever wondered what it would be like to be with another woman. And would you ever consider it?"

I look at her. "I'm strictly dickly. I mean, right now I'm sick of men. And, yes, I've temporarily banished them from my bed and my life, but only for the moment. I'm still very much in love with the feel of a hard dick plunging inside of me."

My cell rings. I pull it out of my front pocket and glance at the screen. It's Maurice. *Speaking of the devil*! I press IGNORE, then turn my phone off.

Karalyn takes a slow, deliberate sip from her drink, kicking off her shoes. I glance down at her neatly polished toes. "Well, maybe you should think about giving it a try before knocking it."

"Oh, I'm not knocking anything," I assure her, shifting in my seat. I glance at her full, sensual lips. Swallow. "You already know I subscribe to the philosophy of live and let live."

She shifts her body toward me, tucking her leg beneath her. She flashes me one of her dimpled smiles, and I almost forget about the throbbing in my cunt. Almost. Her coffee brown eyes take me in, and she flashes me another toothy grin.

"You know. I've always felt this special connection between us. And the one thing I've always liked about you is your open-mindedness. You have a free-spirit that I have always been attracted to."

Blink. Blink.

All of sudden, I'm feeling myself starting to overheat, instead of being put off by what she's said. Perhaps it's due to the Ciroc, or it could simply be from the fire burning in the fireplace. Or maybe it's the way she's looking at me—intense and probing, that has caused the temperature in the room to rise. Whatever it is, it has me starting to sweat, literally and figuratively. Karalyn's brown, doe-shaped eyes have now become slanted slits that seem to be leisurely undressing me, peeling back layers of clothing and inhibitions.

"And if it were up to me, I'd have my tongue buried in your pussy right now."

"I-I…" I stutter, trying to regain some level of composure. But she has struck a match to a secret yearning, one I have never considered exploring…with her…until this very moment. And now I feel a slow burning flame of desire starting to spread. My cunt smoldering with curiosity and lust.

"All I'm saying is, you might find being with another woman to be an enjoyable experience. I know if I had the chance, I'd make sure it'd be one you'd never forget. And one thing I can promise you, you definitely wouldn't have to ever worry about *me* not eating your pussy. I'd love to be your personal pussy eater."

Instantly, my cunt moistens. And I imagine the slip-slide of her fingers in my cum-slick pussy. Her gaze heightens my arousal and curiosity, causing my clit to pulse between my thighs, hungry for a mouth, the flick of a tongue.

I gulp back my drink.

"Do you enjoy having your pussy eaten?" she asks, dangling temptation in front of me, purposefully trying to pry open Pandora's box.

I reach for her drink, laughing it off. "Oh no, girl. No more of this for you tonight. Obviously someone has had a little too much of the devil juice." I set her glass on the table in front of me.

She reaches over and takes her glass back. "I'm not drunk."

"Well, clearly you're *not* in your right frame of mind, either." I let out another nervous chuckle. "Obviously you must have a little more than Ciroc in that drink that has you saying stuff you'll regret in the morning."

She shoots me a look. "I don't live with regrets. I'm very much aware of what I'm saying. Life is too short, Ava. You're a beautiful, sexy, vibrant woman. And if you haven't figured it out yet, I'm a lesbian."

I am not sure if I should be surprised by this news or not. I have known Karalyn for six years and, although I could never flat-out put my finger on it, I always sensed there was something more to her cool, calm demeanor. She'd always kept her personal life private. And I never felt the need to pry. I still don't. It was always speculated by the nosey bitches at the job that Karalyn might be a lesbian or, at the very least, bi since no one had ever seen her with a man. They'd say she had an invisible husband since no one had ever met him. But I never gave it much thought. I simply assumed she was a tomboy who threw on a dress and heels and some lipstick when needed, but was most comfortable in sneakers, jeans and a T-shirt.

"Ohmygod," I say, gasping and feigning shock. "And here I thought you were just flirting with me."

She laughs. "I am. Shamelessly, I might add. But I'm also very serious. I'm attracted to you, Ava. And I've wanted to make love to you ever since the moment I laid eyes on you."

My mouth drops open. "I'm really flattered. But I—"

"Listen, before you shoot me down with rejection, let me say this. I'm not telling you all this to try and put you on the spot. This has been something I've wanted to say to you for a while, but didn't have the courage or the nerve to until now. Hope I haven't offended you or made you feel uncomfortable by sharing this."

I swallow, shaking my head. "No, no...not at all." *But shouldn't I be? A woman just sat here and told me she wants to eat my pussy and fuck me down. Shouldn't I feel something, other than turned on?* "I mean. Yes, I'm a bit surprised that you'd confess all of this to me, but I'm definitely not offended. Or uncomfortable."

I've actually enjoyed it!

Oh, and by the way, I finger-fucked myself to sleep last night with thoughts of you fucking me.

"I'm not into women like that," I say, hoping it sounds convincing. But shit. Who am I fooling? In all honesty, I've found myself at times glancing at certain women and wondering what they'd look like naked, trying to imagine what it would be like tasting them; or them tasting me.

Karalyn scoots over closer to me. "I know you're straight..." *Am I really?* "And I know you're probably not the least bit interested in being with another woman. But, if you were, I hope you'd let me be your first."

"I'm not a lesbian."

She smiles. "I never said you were. Having one sexual experience with a woman doesn't classify you as gay, or automatically make you a lesbian. All I'm saying is, think about it. No pressure. No worries."

I swallow. "Wow. I really don't know what to say."

Umm, hello! How about hell no! How about no thank you!

"You don't have to say anything," she says, pouring another

drink for herself. "Just think on it while I go hop in the shower." She stands up and removes her shirt, tossing it on the sofa. She unzips her painted on jeans, then shimmies out of them, leaving them on the floor. I struggle to keep my eyes off of her dimpled, honey-colored ass half-wrapped in a pair of see-through red lace undies that are riding up in her crack. She has a nice ass. I shift my eyes as she bends over, her ass cheeks practically in my face as she reaches for her drink.

Ohmygod, this bitch is real brazen!

I can smell her cunt.

Excited.

Or is that mine?

I fight the impulse to lick my lips. I gulp down the remainder of my drink, swallowing down the urge to cup her ass, to kiss it, to lean in and inhale her. She has piqued my curiosity. My arousal's heightened. And now I'm…I'm ready to try some new things.

Ohmygod, what is going on with me? No more drinks for me!

Karalyn walks off, unlatching her bra, then dropping it on the floor. "If you want to experience what it's like to step over into the other side," she says over her shoulder, "come join me in the shower. And I promise you, what's done in the cabin will stay in the cabin." With that said, she whisks off down the hall, leaving me sitting here flustered. And my pussy a sopping wet mess!

I don't believe this. I shake my head, pouring myself another drink. I gulp it back, along with my nerves.

Girl, look at you all scared! Isn't this what you've wanted? Isn't this what you've spent the last three years fantasizing about? Well, now here's your chance to experience everything you've ever masturbated thinking about firsthand.

I slowly lift myself up from off the sofa, feeling lightheaded from the drinks, Karalyn's proposition, and the anticipation. I walk down the hallway, half-talking myself out of going through with it. But my curiosity, and yearning desire, get the best of me. And before I come to my senses I am already slipping out of my clothes, leaving a trail behind me; my shirt, my jeans, my bra, my panties all abandoned.

Six

And here I am.

Standing.

Heart beating.

Breath quickening. I am trying to work up the nerve to push open the door and step in, knowing that once I do there is no turning back. I glance down at my feet. Right outside the bathroom door are her panties. Bright red with black trim. Without thought, I pick them up. Hold them in my hand, staring at them, realizing I am oozing juices out of my slit. I shiver, having the sudden urge to sniff them. To bury my whole face into the silken fabric and inhale her scent, sneaking a whiff of her essence. I close my eyes and inhale, deeply. Breathing in everything she is. Sweet. Musky. Wet. Hungry arousal. Her lusty aroma clings to my nostrils, causing my clit to throb. The folds of my own sex swelling with eagerness.

I pull in a deep breath, then push the door open. I stand transfixed at the silhouette behind the sliding glass door. She is watching me watching her. And for a split second, my mind drifts into fantasyland.

"Sooo, are you going to play Peeping Tom," she says, slicing into my salacious thoughts, "and stand there, gawking, or are you going to come join me?" She laughs.

I blink. "Huh?"

She slides back the shower door and is standing in front of me. My eyes trail her body, then fix on her dark brown nipples, wet and soapy, standing at attention. She repeats the question. A knowing smile comes over her face as she slides the bar of soap over her nipples, down her stomach, then between her thighs.

I step in, naked and ready. We are standing face-to-face, the spigot and my pussy both spurting; the spigot, warm water; my pussy, warm juices as she lathers my body with a loofah sponge. She tells me to turn around so that she can wash my back. I do. Her hardened nipples press into my back as she reaches around to palm my breasts and rub my nipples between her thumbs and forefingers. I gasp.

"You like that?"

My voice gets lost in the kneading of her slender fingers as they work my nipples, causing a moan to escape from somewhere deep within me. She grinds her pussy into my ass, nibbling on the nape of my neck, then sucking on my earlobe.

"I'm going to make you feel like no man has ever," she whispers into my ear, inching a hand down my stomach, then dipping between my thighs. I gasp, again. "I've wanted you for so long, Ava. I can't wait to feel this pussy. To taste it. Make love to it."

I moan as she feverishly works her fingers over my clit, gyrating my hips in sync to her strumming fingers. "Oooooooh, yes…"

"You like that?"

I respond with a low groan.

"Ooooh, your pussy's so wet, Ava…"

"Mmmmm…"

She turns me back to face her, showering me with passionate kisses as she continues to play with my clit. Her mouth goes to my left breast, sucks in a nipple, twirls her tongue over it, then moves onto the right one, doing the same thing. Heat races through my entire body. Her touch is soft and sensual. My body shivers as she gives each of my breasts equal attention, licking and sucking and nibbling, while skillfully manipulating my clit and pussy with her fingers. I have never experienced an array of intense feelings like this in my whole entire life. My whole being responds to her touch.

She...this, is driving me crazy. I don't know how much more of this feeling I can take before I explode. Before I scream out at the top of my lungs. "Ohgod, please, Kara..."

"Please, what?" she replies in a throaty whisper, eyeing me seductively.

"Eat my pussy."

She licks a trail down the center of my chest, down to my stomach, dipping into my navel before inching her tongue further south until she lands on my spot. She wraps her hands around my ass and presses her nose against my clit, before pulling open my lips and sliding her tongue into my heated cunt.

I gasp. She pulls her tongue out, then sucks my clit into her mouth, licking me with the wide, flat surface, then rolling her tongue and flicking it with the pointed tip. She does not stop until I shudder out an orgasm.

The hot wetness of her mouth mingles with the sizzling heat and moisture of my excited pussy, causing me to feel lightheaded. I am on the brink of coming again. I reach for her and pull her up to me, desperate to taste my wet sex on her tongue, her lips. I have always wondered what it would be like kissing another woman. And now I know. It's like...heaven. Maybe it's the fact that this secret fantasy is taboo that has me feeling like I'm floating on clouds. Maybe it's the way her fingers caress my clit, then fuck my pussy that has me wanting this feeling to go on forever.

Her lips find mine.

"Oh, Kara…" I lift one leg up and wrap my arms around her neck as she grinds her wet pussy against mine. Clit to clit, a searing bliss courses through every inch of me, exposing me to a sensation I never imagined. Her tongue finds its way inside my mouth.

"Can I make love to you?"

"Yes…oooh, yesss…"

"You gonna give me that juicy fruit?"

The question catches me off-guard. I open my eyes, giving her a confused look. "Huh?"

Her right hand slinks back between my legs. Her voice is a whisper. "This fat, wet pussy. Your juicy fruit." She gently rubs my clit with her thumb, presses on it. Her eager fingers finding my pussy lips as she continues to tease the tip of my clit with her wet thumb.

I shudder and nearly cream all over her probing fingers. "Ooooh…"

"Let me taste your juicy fruit, Ava."

A moan escapes me. "Mmmmmm."

"You want me to lick that sweet pussy?"

I hump her hand. "Yesss. Please, Kara. Ohgod, yes…lick my pussy. Stop teasing me."

Her fingers slip out of my valley, tormenting and teasing my now empty pussy. She kisses me again. Then, as quick as her fingers were gone, they are back, moving inside of me. Two fingers become three, then four, stretching my cunt, searching my treasures, sending heated lust coursing through my entire body. I don't know how much more of this I can take before I explode. Her delicious four-finger fuck is pushing me to the edge of an orgasm. The walls of my pussy spasm as she pulls a nipple into her mouth, then gently licks, sucks and bites down on it.

"Ohgodohgodohgod…yes, yes, yes…work my pussy…oooh, yes…"

"You want me to slide this tongue in that pussy? Taste your juicy fruit?"

I whimper as her fingers slip out of me again, escaping my cunt's clutches. Karalyn knows exactly what she's doing. Knows exactly how far to bring me before taking me over the cliff. She smiles, thrusting two fingers back into my weeping pussy. My body is pressed against the cool, wet tiles.

I wind my hips on her hand, forcing my mouth onto hers, biting down on her bottom lip as I come on her fingers.

"I want to taste you," I say, reaching between her legs, searching for her own wetness. The words ooze out like hot lava, thick with lust and desire. I am beside myself. Caught up in the heated moment. Tasting another woman has never crossed my mind... until now.

I kneel down between her legs. Her pussy is shaved. The tattoo of a black dragon's head with red flames shoots downward toward her clit. I breathe her in. The scent of her sex sends a pulse through me as I inhale, then lick her clit. I lick and lick and lick, twirling my tongue around her engorged nub. Pleasuring her in the same melodic way I enjoy pleasuring myself, soft gentle strokes that quicken. I glance up at her and have to fight the urge to press my mouth to her cunt. Her lips are brown and puffy. Her clit begs for attention. Instinctively, I lick it, flick it, lap it lovingly. I have tasted my own juices many times. Have imagined licking my own pussy many times. But tonight, I am savoring the pussy of another woman for the first time. The sweet, tangy taste clings to my tongue. Karalyn begins to moan and purr and rotate her hips. I lick her pussy as if it is my own. I often fantasied, but never imagined eating another woman's pussy would be like this...so good. My wet, hungry tongue sinks chin deep into her quivering pussy. I am getting lost in her. Her taste. Her smell. Her body.

"Yeah, that's it, baby," she coos as she threads her fingers through my hair and begins thrusting against my tongue. "Oooh, yes…get it, baby…lick that pussy…aaah… Ohshitohshitohshit…" her wide hips buck. "Right there; just like that…I'm coming… ooooh, yesssss…"

Ohmygod…I'm eating another woman's pussy! And I'm enjoying it. I'm really enjoying it!

Her body shudders as she climaxes into my mouth. I, too, bring myself to climax, creaming all over my fingers. Karalyn and I finish our showers, satiated and full—for the moment.

Hours pass as we make love over and over, drinking and giggling like two schoolgirls who share a dirty secret. When we have finished ravishing each other's bodies for the third time, she pulls me into her arms, both of us basking in ecstasy's afterglow. We lay here, marinating in sweet bliss for what seems like forever before either of us finally speaks.

"Are you okay?" Karalyn asks, concern laced in her tone. She strokes my cheek, then leans in and kisses my hair.

I nod, nestling deeper into the crook of her arm, then drifting into a deep, well-needed slumber.

The next morning, I open my heavy-lidded eyes to Karalyn sucking and kneading my breasts, her tongue thoughtfully twirling around each nipple with equal attention. Her eyes flicker up at me. "Good morning," she says, releasing my nipple from her mouth.

"Good morning." I stretch and yawn. "You sure know how to get a girl's juices flowing first thing in the morning."

She grins, slowly trailing a finger along the center of my breasts, then down my stomach. "I hope you don't mind. I decided to get a jumpstart on breakfast."

"Oh." I gasp as her finger presses up against my clit. "Oh, yesss…" I swallow, feeling arousal pierce my clit. I spread my legs. *Oh, God, what have I gotten myself into? Shouldn't I feel guilty, even badly, for what happened between us last night?*

Isn't what the two of us are doing wrong?

Hmmm…then why does it feel soooo fucking good?!

Karalyn is now between my legs. Her soft lips close firmly around my clit, her tongue swirling rhythmically over it. I shut my eyes tight and rock my hips against Karalyn's thrusts. "Oh, God, this feels so…good. Ooooh, please don't stop…mmmm… Oooh, yesss…I love the way your tongue feels on my pussy… Ooooh, yess…mmmm…"

I glance down at Karalyn between my thighs, my arousal surging through my body as I watch her. I lose myself in uninhibited groans and grunts of pleasure as Karalyn whimpers. Her short, uneven breaths keep me encouraged, urging me to me come— heavy and loud—as she swirls her tongue over my clit, sucking and licking.

I clutch the sheets. Shriek. Thrash my head from side-to-side as I inch closer to climaxing. Tightening my thighs around Karalyn's head, I quiver with delight as my hot, creamy juices erupt into her warm, eager mouth. She's taken my body to heights of pleasure I never knew possible. Oh, yes. Her lips, her tongue, her fingers, have made love to every inch of my body. And, I know, that this will be one weekend—one experience, I shall never be able to forget.

Seven

For weeks following my cabin rendezvous, I throw myself into my work, trying desperately to forget those two passionate, sex-filled nights in the Poconos. Not because I didn't enjoy the experience, but because I want more. Karalyn touched me in ways no man has ever touched me. She opened up desires I've kept hidden for years. And no matter how hard I try to block that weekend out, I find myself savoring the memory of the way her body felt against mine; the way her clit pressed against mine; her nipples in my mouth, mine in hers; the way our slick, pulsing pussies humping and were pumping into each other; two opening slits of wet, greedy desire, leaking sweet, sticky juices.

I can't stop replaying the way Karalyn attentively, lovingly, lapped my swollen lips, tongued my slit, then devoured every part of my pussy. The way she kissed me with tender sweetness, slowly, with so much intensity and passion that I felt like I would melt into the sheets as liquid heat spurted out of me. I have made myself cum over and over, reliving the experience. But I don't want her. I want…that feeling again—with a man. I want, no I need, a man to handle my pussy the way she did. Lovingly.

And that's exactly what I hoped would happen when I agreed to go out on a date with Jarrod. Jarrod and I started working at Sci-Tech around the same time—about twelve years ago, but we never really said any more than an occasional hello to each other whenever we'd run into each other. However, that all changed last summer when he was transferred over to my department. So for the last six months he's been pursuing me. However, I wasn't interested. Until now...

Until Karalyn reopened a door to a dormant sex life I thought I had sealed off. Karalyn did this. I allowed her to. Now, I want to be touched and licked and fucked, from head to toe. And I'm willing to break my promise—the one I made to not fuck anyone else until Mr. Right came along. Well, Jarrod may not be my Mr. Right for a future. But he's my Mr. Right for right now.

We have finished a delicious meal at Negril's in the Village. Now I'm nursing my third coconut martini; Jarrod's on his second Red Stripe. And the more I drink, the sexier he starts to look. Not that he's an unattractive man. On the contrary, Jarrod's dangerously fine. A pretty-boy with flawlessly smooth skin and thick wavy hair.

Muscular arms.

Chiseled chest.

Big hands.

Big feet.

My god!

And here I sit, staring this cocoa-brown man with the deep dimples and smoldering brown eyes in his face, sharing a cozy table for two, forcing myself to stay in the moment. Not that being here with Jarrod is a bad thing. It's just that my mind keeps wandering back to my weekend at the cabin with Karalyn. I can't seem to shake it. I can still feel her hands on my flesh. The way they journeyed over my body, kneading my breasts, my ass. I can still feel her lips pressed against mine; her tongue searching my mouth, my pussy, my erect nipples. Her wet pussy on my tongue, her clit pulled into my mouth, I can still taste her. Can still feel her warm body against mine, her pelvis grinding into mine—our clits slipping and sliding against each other's, swelling with excitement, aching for release. I can smell her. Her wet, excited pussy stained on my senses.

She has been burned into my memory.

Damn her!

I'm not a lesbian. I love dick!

Then why is your pussy soaking wet, thinking about face-fucking another woman?

I bite down on my bottom lip.

"Did I tell you how lovely you look tonight?" Jarrod says, cutting into my scandalous thoughts.

I blink my attention back to my date. He is staring at me. Lost in my dirty images, I was absentmindedly staring at his lips but now I'm blushing back my embarrassment as I realize that he is returning my gaze with the same intensity. "Huh?" He repeats himself, causing me to smile. I bat my lashes. "Um, let's see. Not in the last"—I glance at my watch—"forty minutes you haven't."

He laughs, causing his eyes to sparkle. "Hey, what can I say? I'm a sucker for a beautiful woman." He reaches over and squeezes my hand. "And you, Miss Ava Wilson, are one helluva beauty."

My face heats. And, surprisingly, I find myself getting extremely turned on by the direction of our banter. Thoughts of Karalyn are quickly evaporating, replaced by naughty notions of Jarrod's mouth and tongue sucking on my sensitive nipples that have been swollen with lust for most of the night, threatening to poke holes through my lace bra had I not been trying to conceal my arousal by keeping an arm folded across my chest. Images of Karalyn's legs up over my shoulders and my face pressed between her smooth thighs are now replaced with me grinding my cunt on Jarrod's tongue. Fucking his face, riding his lips. Visions of me climbing underneath this table, unzipping his pants, then fishing out his dick and sucking the cum out of it, draining his balls until they shrivel up like two sunbaked prunes have replaced the ones I was having of Karalyn and me performing fellatio on each other in the sixty-nine position. She atop of me while my arms wrap around her hips as I pull her pussy into my mouth, burying my eager tongue into the back of her slit.

I wonder if he has a big dick.

My pussy tingles.

I collect my thoughts, taking a slow sip of my drink in an attempt to squelch out the fire burning between my legs. I see myself leaning over into his lap while he drives me back to his place, unbuttoning and unzipping his pants, sliding my fingers into the slit of his underwear and pulling out his cock, then taking his dick in and out of my throat, sucking him with an animalistic fervor I hadn't known existed inside of me until now.

Damn her!

Damn him!

I eye Jarrod, teasingly. "And compliments, Mister Denson, *will* get you *every*where."

Which is exactly what I'm hoping, I muse, pressing my thighs together. Thus far, the conversation between us has been safe— work, hobbies, travel, what we like to do in our spare time, stuff like that. But as the alcohol courses through my body and heats me and the images of my weekend with Karalyn take up space in my head, I'm feeling more bold and daring. My horny pussy is ready to be fed some dick. All the same, I can't help but feel my panties moistening.

Oooh, yes…I'ma take this fine black man home and fuck the shit out of him. I'm long overdue for some hard dick!

Oh, God, I hope he can fuck!

Jarrod winks. "That's exactly what I'm hoping. I am *more* than willing to be at your service." He leans up in his seat, resting his forearms up on the table. "So, is that an invitation for what's to come?"

I grin slyly. "Perhaps. The night is still young. Let's see what happens *after* dessert."

"Better yet." He wriggles his thick eyebrows up and down. "How about we blow this joint, head back to my place, and make our own dessert?" The invitation is coated with thick desire. My pussy throbs at the sound of it, causing the sticky dampness between my legs to make me feel mischievous and slutty. I slip off my heel, then extend my leg out, resting my foot in his lap.

The look on his face is a mixture of shock and pleasure. He glances around the cozy, candlelit restaurant. I have caught him off-guard. He slyly inches his crotch forward, spreading his legs, welcoming what's to come.

"Sooo, tell me, Jarrod." I purr, eyeing him seductively as I massage his crotch with the ball of my foot. His dick is long and thick. I smile to myself. "Are you seeing anyone? Do you have a wife and kids hiding away somewhere at home no one knows about?"

He chuckles, mindful to keep his voice low as he shakes his head. "Whew…um…damn…" He tries to keep his composure. He presses his legs shut around my foot. "No, no, none of the above. No wife, no chil…dren. And I'm definitely…not seeing anyone at the moment. And you are making this…*very* hard to think and talk."

"Ooh, I like it hard. Nice." I feel his dick thicken and stretch the fabric of his pants against my foot. "Mmmm," I tease, licking my lips. "Very nice." I let my manicured toes knead his aching bulge as his eyes sweep across my swollen breasts. He gazes at my hardened nipples, then zooms in on my cleavage ready to spill out of my low-cut blouse.

I should feel guilty for flirting with him; for using him like this. But my screaming pussy is wailing and begging for a good fuck, demanding that it gets stretched and gutted by a hard black dick. And, tag...he's it.

Still, I have always prided myself on never, ever, mixing business with pleasure. And I definitely have never shit where I eat. Office romances very seldom work out. Neither does having a one-night stand with a colleague—usually. But, lately, seems like I've been going against everything I stand for, like sleeping with Karalyn, for one. And now this.

I can feel my juices seeping through my purple lace panties, oozing down around my pussy, staining my designer skirt. I am relieved it's a chocolate brown. The last thing I need is to be embarrassed by a big, round wet stain on the back of my skirt when I stand.

I knew I should have worn a liner.

He licks his lips, grinning suggestively. "You sure know how to get a man to *rise* to the occasion."

My mind flashes to the steamy shower I shared with Karalyn a few weeks ago. A decadent ache pulses through my clit, remembering the way her touch set my pussy ablaze.

I blush.

"Ava, what the hell is wrong with you?!" I scold in my head. *"Here you are out having dinner with this fine specimen of a man, and you're sitting here thinking about another woman licking your pussy when you should be thinking about him fucking you from the back with him palming your large swinging breasts and pinching your thick, hard nipples while you throw that ass back on him, trying to fuck the skin off his hard dick!"*

Your pussy needs to be fucked!

And have you not forgotten you have a big dick under your foot, hard, *and obviously more than* ready *to fuck you?*

"I always aim to please, Mister Denson."

"Is that right?" I simply smile, now using both of my feet to massage his dick. Jarrod pulls in his bottom lip. He grunts, cutting his eyes around the dining area, then locking his eyes on me. "You're something else, Ava. You sure…mmph…you don't wanna head out now?" He slides a hand underneath the table, caressing my right foot, then pressing his legs shut. His dick has gotten bigger…longer, if that's even humanly possible.

He tosses back his drink. Then tells the waiter he'll have another when he comes to our table to check to see if there is something else he can get for us. "Anything for you, ma'am?" the waiter wants to know. I tell him no, not at this moment. A few seconds later, he walks off. I watch as he crosses over the room, then descends down the stairs toward the bar area.

"You still haven't answered my question," Jarrod says, giving my foot a relaxing massage under the table. I have to fight myself to keep from moaning.

I tilt my head coyly. "And what question was that?"

He grins. "Do you *always* aim to please?"

I pull my foot back from his lap, then slip it back into my heel. "I'll give you the answer to that when I return from the ladies' room." I stand up, smoothing the front of my skirt out, hoping there isn't a puddle of bliss left in back of me. Jarrod's lustful stare lands in the center of my crotch, then sweeps upward to meet my gaze. He pulls in his bottom lip.

I am convinced he smells my warm, wet cunt wafting from under the hem of my skirt. He knows innately that my pussy juice is seeping out, flowing between my legs. He licks his lips, then grins as if he knows that I know that he knows. "I'll be back in a sec," I say, sauntering off toward the steps that lead to the main level of the restaurant, maneuvering my way around tables and waiters toward the bathroom.

Once I finish, I wash my hands, then stand in front of the mirror, fumbling through my purse for my tube of lipstick. When I find it, I carefully reapply a coat over my ripe, warm ready-for-a-night-of-dick sucking mouth. *And clit, too, so it seems.* I shake my head, blotting my lips, then blowing a kiss to my image in the mirror before heading back out to my date. *Fuck for the night is more like it.* As I am about to reach for the handle, the door swings open, almost slamming into me. I instinctively jump backward.

"Oh, excuse..." My mouth drops open and her eyes lock on mine. I am surprised. *Oh no! Please don't tell me this woman is really some certified nut who's stalking me!* "Kara, what are you..."

Without a word she grabs me, cups my face between her warm hands and kisses me, cutting me off and pushing me back into one of the opened stalls. She kicks the door shut. Her mouth is on mine, her tongue slipping into my mouth. *Oh, God!* Her lips are soft and so damn juicy. Her hand slides down my back, finding their way to my ass. She palms it, holding me tightly against her grinding pelvis. I moan and gyrate my hips into hers. My pussy already throbbing and slick from all of my previous lewd thoughts.

"I wanna eat your pussy," she says, reaching under my dress, grasping the waistband of my moist panties. I feel like I am teetering on the edge of deception being here with her—her fingers working my clit over—while leaving Jarrod sitting out there with his hard dick practically ready to burst through his pants.

"Wait...wait," I say breathlessly, trying to pry her hands from off of me. "You still haven't told me what you're doing here."

"I'm here having dinner with a friend," she says, grinning. "I saw you when you walked by our table. And now I'm ready for my dessert."

I blink. "And what's that?"

"You." She pushes me up against the stall door and snakes her tongue inside my mouth. A shiver of arousal snakes up my spine as her body presses into mine. She pushes my panties aside to feel my wetness.

"Oh, God, no," I protest, concern in my voice. "What if someone walks in?"

"Then we'll give them a show. Do you want me inside of you, Ava?" Her lips press against my ear. She trails her hand along my quivering thighs.

Oh, God!

"Uh, um…"

"Say it. Tell me you want me."

I am so very conflicted. Her hand is now pressed to my clit over my panties, and she's kissing my neck. I let out a soft moan, tilting my head back to give her access.

God, her hands and lips feel good!

"I…want…mmm…wait…I…we…can't do this."

"Yes, we can. And we will. Say you want me."

"Not here."

"Yes. Here. Right now." Another soft moan escapes me as she loops her fingers into my Vickies and fingers my secret. My clit responds to her touch. "Let me taste this wet pussy, Ava."

"Oh, God…Oh, God…"

"God can't help you. Only this hot tongue can."

She plunges her fingers into my slickness. I shut my eyes and throw my head back, lifting a leg, planting my foot up on the toilet paper holder.

Girl, get a grip of yourself!

We're in the women's bathroom, for Christ's sake! What if someone walks in and catches us?

"I just want a taste of this wet, juicy fruit." My thighs shake as she strokes me, working her fingers in and out of my dripping cunt. "You like that? You like the way I play in your pussy?"

I moan. "Oh, God, yesssss."

"Let me lick your pussy. Then you can go back out there with lover boy, who is very handsome by the way."

In my head, I hear myself pleading for her to stop. I hear myself telling her *no* over and over, trying to pull her hand from between my wobbly legs. This is what I imagine myself doing. But it isn't real. What's real is that I am in a bathroom stall with another woman, enjoying the way her lips feel on mine. Loving the way her fingers feel on my clit, in my pussy. This shouldn't be happening. But it is. And it feels…so *fucking* good!

I am not a lesbian!

"Oh, yesss…ooooooh, yessssss…"

"C'mon, Ava. Let me get a taste of this pussy. The sooner you give me some, the sooner you can get back to your table. I know you don't wanna keep lover boy waiting. Tell me you want me to eat your pussy so I can let you get back to him."

Her fingers ease out of my slickness. She puts them to my lips. I open my mouth. Allow her to slide her fingers in, tasting me on them. She slips her fingers from out of my mouth, then puts them in hers. Sensually, she sucks and licks them, turning me on more.

I have allowed all of my good senses to get drowned in lust. I feel her hands inch their way back to my hips. Feel my panties slip down over my thighs. Trance-like, I step out of them. I know I am not in my right mind. But I don't give a damn! I am horny!

So fucking horny!

"Eat my pussy," I say in a throaty whisper.

She grins, inching downward, squatting as she pushes my legs apart, spreading them wide. She wastes no time devouring my pussy with her hot, wet mouth. I bite down on my bottom lip to keep from screaming with pleasure as she feasts on my sex, sucking the folds of my pussy lips...licking my clit and pulling it in with her teeth...dipping her tongue into my hot, sticky hole.

I am not supposed to be enjoying this...her tongue and mouth all over my pussy, but I am. "Oh, God, yes."

She pulls her tongue out of me, grabbing my hips. "Turn around. I wanna eat this sweet pussy from the back." I do as she's asked. My ass jiggles in her face as she grabs each cheek with her hands and shakes. She slaps it again. Tells me how she loves the way my soft, juicy ass quivers in her hands. "Pull open your ass for me."

I reach in back of me, and pull open my cheeks. No man has ever eaten me out this way—with skillful precision. Karalyn's tongue work is breathtakingly superior. Yes, I've had my share of some great pussy eaters, but what Karalyn is doing to me with her mouth and tongue could quickly become an addiction.

"Oh yes...mmmmm...eat that pussy, baby...oooooh..." I wind my hips. Bounce my ass up on her tongue. "Get that shit...oooh, yessss..."

Karalyn has my whole body overtaken by lust. She has me saying shit I am sure I will regret saying when it is all said and done. When her lapping tongue goes from my slippery slit to my asshole, I buck my hips and start speaking in tongue. "Ooohfeelso goodooooohfeelsooooogoodoohoohoohooh...getitgetitgetitgetit..."

Panting and moaning, my juices flow out into her mouth like

a roaring river. She gulps and swallows every last drop, then gives my clit a long, lingering kiss, then stands up, leaving my cunt starving for more.

Gasping as she gazes at me, my eyes lock onto hers for several stunned moments as she slowly licks her glistening lips, then kisses me—sharing her tongue and my sticky nectar with me.

As always, I taste delicious.

Five minutes after Karalyn leaves the bathroom, I return to my table where Jarrod is still sitting, glancing at his watch. He looks up at me. "Oh, there you are. I didn't know if I should dial Nine-One-One or not. I was starting to get..." he frowns, concern etching over his face. "Is everything all right? You look flushed."

No, I'm not. My pussy is wet and wide open and aching to be fucked.

I place a hand up to my forehead. "Yes, I mean, no." I fan myself. "I'm a little hot"—*yeah and very bothered*—"that's all. Let's say we skip dessert and get out of here." *So you can finish up what Karalyn started.* "I really like the idea of us making our own dessert."

He grins, standing up. "The check's already paid. Let's go."

Eight

"We need to talk," Karalyn says, brushing past me the minute I open the door. Her tone is as icy as the weather outside. I'm not surprised to see her. It's been two weeks since I've last seen her. She looks beautiful wrapped in a full-length fur. "I want to know why you've been avoiding me?"

I shut the door behind her, pulling the belt to my robe tighter around my waist. "I haven't been avoiding you. I've been busy."

She whirls around and faces me. Hand on hip. "If you're going to lie to me, Ava, at least make it a believable one."

She's right. Although I haven't flat-out ignored her emails or text messages, I've purposefully avoided talking to her on the phone, in fear that hearing her voice would make it more difficult than it already is to stay away from her. Like hot, melted Godiva chocolate drizzled over Häagen-Dazs ice cream, I've come to realize Karalyn's dangerously addictive. And, after our steamy transgression inside the bathroom stall at Negril's, she's a guilty pleasure I'd rather not become hooked on—if I can help it.

Besides, I've sort of been casually spending time with Jarrod the last few weekends. Okay, I'm using him. That night after our dinner date, I went back to his place and ravished every inch of his thick, dark chocolate pole. A part of me felt guilty knowing my ravenous desire for him was sparked more out of necessity than actual yearning. Karalyn—her mouth, her tongue, her fingers—

caused that. Caused my pussy to cry out in desperate need to be fucked, deep and long and hard. That night, Jarrod delivered—well, I might add. He fed my pussy passionate strokes of pleasure. And, I've slept with him three more times since.

In hopes of forgetting.

Yet, my mind still sweeps through snapshots of Karalyn's nakedness. The opening of her cunt, pink and glistening, pulled open—ready for my tongue and fingers. I had never eaten pussy, or sucked on a clit, before her, but hers—her sex, was warm and sweet and luscious. The tangy taste was tantalizing. I savored every drop of her, licking and lapping her up. Her clit pulsed in my mouth, slippery with juices. It's an experience I will never forget.

And no matter how hard I try to block what we shared out, I am still reminded of my own nakedness beneath hers. Our slick clits grinding and sliding against the other's. The light flutter of her tongue over my nipples, over my skin—trailing down and over my body. The way her soft hands cupped my ass, pulling me into her with need and desire—heated images that keep me wanting more.

Her eyes are on me, but for some reason I can't bring myself to look at her. I shift my weight from one barefoot to the other, trying to contain the beating butterflies in my stomach.

She unbuttons her coat. Underneath she is wearing a long black sweater dress over black leggings with a pair of black leather riding boots. "Have I done something to offend you?"

I shake my head. "No. Not at all."

"Then what is it? Are you feeling guilty for allowing yourself to experience and enjoy what we shared?"

I shift my eyes from her knowing gaze.

Her eyes narrow as she slips off her coat. "So now you're questioning your sexuality, aren't you?"

"No," I say, crossing over into the center of the room, keeping a safe distance between us. I can smell her. Her perfume and her pussy—two distinct intoxicating scents. A pulse beats heavy in my throat as I swallow. "I'm not questioning anything. I know who I am. And I know what I like."

"And what is that, Ava? Who are you?"

Confused.

"I'm not a lesbian."

She cocks her head to one side, eyes glistening with amusement. "Who said you were?"

"Well, no one," I say, indignantly.

She eyes me. "Look. I'm not here to throw myself on you or try to convert you into becoming some card-carrying, flag-flying lesbian. But I know that neither that weekend in the Poconos together nor the mini-tryst we shared in the bathroom stall has whet your curiosity. You want more. And there's so much more I want to give you."

"Look, Kara. I really like you. And I'm glad we…you know. Did what we did. But I'm not interested in being in a relationship with a woman."

She laughs. "And I'm not asking you to be in one. I'm not trying to marry you, hon, so relax. I want to *fuck* you, Ava, frontward, backward, sideways, and in every other way imaginable. I want to push your imagination to its limit. Give you the sexual experiences your curiosity seeks."

My lashes flicker as I stare at her. Just in those words, she has managed to heat my pussy. My mind travels back to the cabin, then inside the bathroom stall. Flashes of the way her fingers and tongue teased my dripping slit, then slid into my pounding wetness—spreading me. Fucking me—invade my mind. "What we shared was great. And I thank you for the experience. But I can't—"

"Is your pussy wet?"

"Excuse you?" I stare at her, disbelieving.

"C'mon, Ava. Don't play coy." I shiver as she stalks toward me, lust flooding her eyes. "I can smell your wet pussy from here. It misses me, doesn't it?"

Embarrassment warms my cheeks. I swallow. My throat becomes suddenly dry. My clit throbs. My pussy feels thick with juices. I stand rooted in horny need as she reaches between my bare thighs, moaning as her fingers peel open my swollen petals, then plunge inside my pussy. Somehow, I have suddenly become a slave to her, to the erotic desires she's unleashed within me. She smirks, satisfaction painted across her lips. "You're soaking wet like I knew you'd be."

I close my eyes as she strokes me, two fingers, then three fingers, moving in and out of me. My pussy swallows her fingers as she goes deeper, squeezing them. "Give me that pussy, Ava...come all over my fingers for me..."

I moan.

This woman has me feeling like I am going to lose myself all over her hand in any moment. My breathing changes. I am on the brink of coming. She's found my spot—again, causing my whole body to vibrate. The juicy entrance to my cunt sucking and clenching around her knuckles until I am creaming; my pussy swallowing more of her hand as I come.

"You want me...?"

Oh, God!

She's pushing into me, into that hot spot deep inside of me, pleasuring, swimming toward the surface slowly cresting to a wave. I am riding her fingers, riding this feeling...of heat and wet yearning.

I moan. "Yes."

"Yes, what?"

"I want…you," I say, feeling lightheaded as my breath catches in the back of my throat. My climax takes me by surprise, blazing through me like a wildfire as she plucks at my clit, then plunges back into my soaking wet sex. Heat radiating through my cunt, scorching the edges of everything I am with a dark pleasure I never knew existed within me. Kara strums my pussy with her fingers, bringing me to sweet euphoria. Taking me to a whole new place of bliss.

I let out a low deep moan, shuddering and clutching her hand between my thighs.

She withdraws her fingers and brings them up to my lips. I open my mouth and suck her wet fingers like a sex-starved junkie. She brushes her lips against mine. Her tongue slips gently in, then out before she teases my lips with small licks, then bites, pulling my bottom lip into her mouth. Wetness floods over my pussy lips as her heated tongue finds its way back into my mouth. The kiss brief, but intense. I am breathless as she pulls away, lazily drinking me in with her gaze. Then slowly licking her lips.

"The smell of your cunt makes my mouth water. I want to ravage you. Eat you up." She leans into me, her tongue tracing the shell of my ear. "I'll be back for brunch on Sunday."

It's a whisper, hot and enticing. It's message clear. She slips back into her mink, spins on her heels and walks out the door, leaving me standing in the middle of my living room—my body trembling, my pussy still quivering.

What in the world have I gotten myself into?

Nine

Three days later, Karalyn whisks through the front door of my two-story home carrying three grocery bags filled with fruit from Wegmans. She had called late last night and said she'd be stopping over today, but hadn't given a specific time as to when she'd arrive. I assumed it would be later in the day. But here she is.

I shut the door behind her, fastening my robe belt tighter around my waist. "What's all the fruit for?"

A wicked grin forms on her lips. "Breakfast." She lightly brushes her lips against my cheek, then sweeps a loose strand of hair that has fallen into my face behind my ear. She traces her finger over my cheek. "God, you're a fucking beautiful, sexy woman."

I blush as she walks toward the kitchen, leaving me standing in the center of the room, stunned. I quickly follow behind her. She sets the bags up on the countertop, then removes her mink. I take it and hang it in the hall closet. When I walk back into the kitchen, she's already made herself at home, moving about my kitchen as if she's been here many times before. She looks over at me, smiling. "Have you eaten?" I tell her I have. "Then I guess that's more for me."

I eye her as she starts slicing fruit. Karalyn looks sexy in her black, one-piece jumper. I try not to stare at her high, round ass as she flits around my kitchen, washing and slicing fruit.

"Have you had your shower, yet?"

I shake my head. "No. I was getting ready to hop in when the doorbell rang."

"Well, how about you go freshen up. Don't put on anything; just your robe."

I eye her curiously. "What exactly are you having for breakfast?"

Karalyn's full lips curve in a devilish smile. "*You*."

At that very moment, everything inside of me heats with desire and want and need. I am too weak with lust to turn down the invitation. I go and shower, anticipation coursing through my veins.

My mouth waters and my pussy tightens as Karalyn saunters over toward me carrying a large, white ceramic bowl filled with sliced mango, peaches; huge, mouthwatering strawberries; pineapple wedges; and, huge market-fresh cherries in one hand. And a bottle of Dom Pérignon in her other. Then she goes back to the counter and retrieves two other smaller bowls, then ambles back over to me.

I am propped up on the counter, a towel beneath me, my legs spread wide. I am eager and ready. Karalyn sets the bowl of fruit and champagne down beside me. She grins down at me. "You're beautiful. I've been starving for you all week."

I attempt to say something, blushing. But the thoughts in my head become jumbled words; incoherent sentences the minute she steps in closer and her mouth is on mine, her tongue searching. She tastes like champagne and chocolate. Sweet and intoxicating.

She steps back, her gaze full of lust and heated promise. "I'm so hungry."

"What are you hungry for?" I whisper, my lips quivering.

Her finger traces the slit of my pussy. "You."

I gasp. Every nerve ending in my body comes alive to her touch. Again, no man has ever made me feel this kind of energy, this kind of want.

"Open your mouth."

I lick my lips, then slowly open my mouth. She rubs the juicy flesh of a mango slice across my lips. I flick my tongue out to taste it, and she pulls back teasing me. She slides it over my nipples, then brings it back up to my lips. She slides her fingers and the fruit into my mouth. I curl my tongue, licking and swirling it around and around the fruit, pretending it's her clit. Wishing it was her clit. Sensual heat ripples through me at the thought of having her pussy pressed against my lips, my own greedy tongue eager to tease and taste her. I suck in the mango, then chew, savoring its sweet, sticky juice.

Kara presses her lips to mine, slipping her tongue into my mouth. Her hand covers my pussy. In seconds, two fingers plunge into thick wetness to find the swell of my spot. I gasp, breathless.

"OhmyGodohmyGodohmyGod," is all I mutter as pleasure ignites every fiber of my body and places me on the edge of ecstasy. Kara pushes her three fingers into me until they can't go any deeper. The rhythm of her probing fingers coaxing me toward climax. "Oh please…mmmph…ooh…"

"'Oh please', what? What do you want, Ava?"

"Uhh…your tongue."

"Where?" She nips at the lobe of my ear. The heat from her breath causes my cunt to clench. A wave of carnal need slams me, hard.

"Uhh…mmmm…"

"Tell me where, Ava. Where do you want my tongue?"

"On my pussy, my clit. Uhh…"

She kisses her way down to my taut nipple, drawing it into her mouth, sucking and licking it until I am panting. I roll my hips, meeting her hand, clenching the fingers fucking me good. A river of pleasure flows out of my pussy.

"You're so fucking wet, Ava," Kara says, gazing into my eyes before lowering her head between my thighs to tongue my clit and suck it into her mouth. I surprise myself, screaming out her name as my orgasm rushes out onto her tongue. She keeps her mouth covering my slit, sucking and lapping out the rest of my climax. Finally, she lifts her head and kisses me, letting me taste my own sweet need.

Oh, God! My whole body aches with want, with desire. I don't know how much more of this tongue and finger dance I can take.

"We're not done," she murmurs between kisses. "We have a whole bowl of fruit to be eaten. And I will not stop until we have devoured every piece."

Next she feeds me a strawberry. I bite into it, savoring its tart juice. She pulls it away. Slides the half-bitten piece of wet fruit along my collarbone, the center of my chest, then over my nipples. I can already feel another patch of slick moisture between my legs as my body tingles with excitement. My areolas thicken with want—for her tongue, her mouth, to suckle, to nibble, to lick. I am drowning in the sensation, flooding in aching need.

I reach for her, try to push her head down between my legs…

"Lick my pussy," I beg. I am more desperate than ever for release. I lift my hips off the counter. "Mmm…eat my pussy."

Karalyn grins. "Not yet." She reaches for the bottle and slowly begins to pour champagne down my collarbone, over my breasts, dribbling the cold bubbly over my hard nipples.

I gasp at the cold sensation, then moan when her warm mouth wraps around my right nipple, then my left. Her wet tongue slides over my skin, licking and lapping up every drop of champagne from my skin. Then she reaches for a pineapple, squeezes it in her hand and drips its juice over my lips, then my nipples, before gliding it over my clit.

I moan again as she thrusts two fingers between my pussy lips and ducks her head in between my thighs to suck my clit. Her fingers focus on tickling my G-spot, and her tongue laves my clit, swirling over it this way and that until my body convulses and my pussy spasms around her probing fingers, clutching and pulling them in deeper.

"Oooh, oooh, ooooh...mmmm...oh yes..."

"Cream on my fingers for me, Ava, baby...give me all that sweet pussy juice..."

Her fingers are hitting my spot, opening the floodgates. I arch my back and scream as a wave of orgasms gush out of me. My pussy melts around her hand. Karalyn quickly removes her fingers, then opens her mouth and catches my spurting juices. I buck my hips as her lips wrap around the mouth of my pussy and she sucks what's left out. I am spent.

No man has ever...my breath gets caught in the back of my throat. My mind is swirling. I can't let this woman turn me out. But I am afraid it may be too late.

I eye Karalyn lustfully as she waves her cum-slick fingertips beneath her nose and savors the heated scent of my cunt. She grins, inhaling deeply. "Mmm, I love the way your pussy smells. And"—she sucks the tip of each of her fingers—"I love the way you taste more, like sweet, ripe fruit. Close your eyes."

I lean my head back and shut my eyes, trusting her in a way that I've never trusted another. I shiver as she glides something cool and wet and sweet over my lips. She tells me to lick my lips. It's another pineapple wedge. She glides the juicy fruit over my breasts, circling each nipple with it until they harden. I moan as she slides the piece of fruit down my stomach, then dips it into my navel. She swirls it over my clit, then brings it up to my lips. She pushes the fruit into my mouth. I chew and moan as her tongue twirls around each nipple.

I open my eyes as she's reaching into the bowl and retrieving a sliced peach. She repeats her journey from my lips to my nipples, along my stomach, into my navel and then...my pussy. I gasp as she slides the peach into my dripping slit. It's coolness causing my insides to shudder. Next, she reaches for another pineapple chunk, again staying the course along my body, gliding it over my clit. Its sweet juices cascading down into the crack of my ass. She slides her tongue into the center of my ass cheeks, then laps around my puckering hole before pushing the pineapple in.

I gasp.

My skin gooses pimples as my pussy goes up in flames.

"Hold it in, Ava." She lightly presses her wet fingertip against my anus as her mouth covers my cunt. She licks and licks and licks, her tongue rolling over and around my clit. My ass stuffed with pineapple. My fingers find their way into her hair, entangling themselves around strands of her hair. I thrust against her tongue as she sucks the peach into her mouth. Then her tongue laps around my asshole, urging out the pineapple wedge. She sucks it into her mouth. She lifts her head, chewing the fruit, then leans up and kisses me. Savoring the sweet and tangy mixture of fruit and my pussy and my ass, their juices intermingled, I groan in ecstasy.

"You taste so delicious, Ava." Her lips are on mine, again. She is squeezing strawberries into her hand, mashing them up against my pussy and clit.

I am moaning.

Her head is back between my legs. Her lips and tongue devouring my clit and slit.

"Oooh, Kara…mmmmm…you make my pussy feel so good. Oh, God, yessss…"

Her fingers find my spot.

My thighs quiver and shake.

"Uhhh, ooooh…mmmmm…ohgodohgodohgodohgod…"

I come in crashing waves against her tongue, against her fingers. My whole body trembles. My pussy convulses as Karalyn eats me, licks me, teases me, devours me…sucking my pussy and clit in loud, juicy slurps.

I toss my head back, savoring the moment.

No, I am not a lesbian.

No, I am not a lesbian.

I repeat this over in my head. Try to convince myself. Clouded by moans and groans and loud slurping sounds.

Oooh, she eats my pussy so fucking…good!

Oh, God…sweetJeezus…her tongue feels delicious!

I arch my pussy up toward Karalyn's mouth. Grip the edges of the countertop. "Oh, yesssss…eat my pussy…mmmm…"

My gasps become louder.

"Whose pussy is this?" Karalyn wants to know. Her fingers inching their way into my sticky ass. Her tongue flicks back over my clit. "Is this my juicy fruit, huh?"

I wind my hips, whimpering. "Eat my pussy. Oooh, pleeeeease."

"Tell me whose juicy fruit this is?" She finger-fucks my asshole, sliding another peach inside my pussy. I am losing my mind. No, Karalyn is driving me out of my mind. "You like that?"

"Yesssssssss!" I scream, feeling another orgasm pooling its way out of my cum-and-fruit-soaked cunt.

"Whose juicy fruit is this?"

"Yours! Oh, God, yessssss… It's all yours…uhhhh, oooooooh…"

"Good girl," Karalyn says. Her tongue slips into my mouth. She sucks my bottom lip into her mouth and I can taste the juices of the fruit and my pussy. We share a long, heated kiss filled with burning passion and desire. She pulls away and stares at me. A smile stretches across her face. "One of these days, I'ma fuck you real good, Ava." I blink. "But for now, I'ma eat the rest of this sweet, juicy pussy." Her head ducks back between my legs. Her hot breath tickles my clit as she slips a strawberry into my slippery slit. "Now come all over my tongue."

Her mouth covers me. I feel the hot, slick wetness of her tongue as it slides across my pussy. I hear her slurping the juices that dribble out of me, fruit juice, cunt juice. Her tongue darts inside of me fishing and probing out the piece of fruit until she has it in her mouth. She lifts up, chews it, then leans in and kisses me, sending me over the edge all over again. I whimper and moan, my cunt contracting around Karalyn's fingers.

She reaches for two strawberries, crushes them into her hand, then feeds them into my pussy, slowly…purposefully. She pushes two fingers into me, churning pussy juice and strawberries with twisting fingers. She slides more crushed strawberries into my already juicy cunt.

"Mmmmm, this pussy is so wet…I wanna get lost in this pussy."

I let out a moan.

She sucks my clit between her soft lips as she finger-fucks me, taking me to a place of ecstasy beyond my wildest imagination. I grip her head between my thighs and scream.

Breathlessly, she's hovering back over me, offering me her fruit-stained mouth. I slip my tongue into her mouth, greedily sucking on it as if it were a dick. "I'm going to come…" I gasp against her lips. And in a rush, I come over and over.

No, I am not a lesbian. Yet, I am loving the way Karalyn handles my pussy. Oh, God...mmmmph...hands down, thus far, my best orgasms have been with her. And I can't wait to see what it's like to be fucked by her.

She leans over me, her eyes delving into mine. Her pillow-soft lips settle over mine, pressing lightly. The tip of her tongue flicks, but when I part my lips to welcome her kiss, she pulls back, cupping my cheek.

Silence.

Intense staring.

Telepathically, she knows. She sees it through the windows of my soul. Forbidden desire has become a burning need. *She* has become my yearning, my guilty pleasure.

No, I am not a lesbian.

Oh, God! But...

"I'm still famished," she finally says, slipping her hand between my thighs and licking her shiny, silken lips.

I spread my legs wider, push Karalyn back down between my thighs, arching my back and pushing my cunt into her mouth—welcoming her back to her feast.

My sweet, juicy fruit.

Sweet 'n' Sticky

One

Our pussies are wet with cum. The sweet, muskiness of hot, sweaty fucking clings to the air around us, thick and intoxicating, as Celeste—my most recent sexual conquest—rubs her golden-brown pussy between my smooth, chocolate-brown thighs. Clit-to-clit, hips bucking, we're grinding to a hot, nasty beat filled with low moans and grunts. Our sweat-slick bodies have become one, our cunts dissolving into a steamy river of passion as we buck against the tides of orgasm. Our rhythm and breathing quicken as we near euphoria.

I whisper into her ear. "Oh, God, yessssss…cum for me…"

Mentally, I had been fucking her all morning. From the moment my loving husband walked out the front door of our sprawling Tudor estate at four A.M.—with his Balenciaga briefcase in one hand, and Tiaga leather Louis Vuitton carry-on in his other—and sped off in his 750Li heading en route to the airport for a business meeting in Los Angeles, I began spinning the web of seduction. Text messages filled with the promise of dipping my tongue into her pussy, followed by probing fingers plunging into her tight asshole. Celeste loves ass play. Loves her asshole stuffed with fingers and toys. She's my kinky, little sex freak.

My secret pleasure.

And, yes, I am living a double-life. One I've carefully kept hidden from Aaron—my very wealthy, attorney-husband whom I've been happily married to for the last ten years.

Am I living a lie?

No. I'm living my truth. I love my husband. He is my everything. I love all that he represents—the epitome of success. I love his strength and masculinity, his devilishly handsome looks, and his deliciously thick, black dick. And I love the way he makes my body feel when he makes love to me. But, I love pussy, too. I love the femininity of what a woman represents. The curve of her hips, the endless slope of her ass, the dark nipples that swell and harden like chocolate Kisses when aroused. I love the way her cunt warms and wets when excited. Love its sweet, musky scent. Love the way it melts in my mouth and all over my tongue and fingers. Love the way my tongue rolls over her clit and swells as she arches her back and explodes into my mouth.

Yes, I have the best of both worlds. And I have no intentions of *ever* leaving my husband for another man *or* a woman. He completes me—well, ninety-five percent of me. I know he should be all I need. And he is…for the most part. Still, Aaron would never understand that, although he is all I will ever need in a man, there's that five percent of who I am that craves the touch of another woman. Telling him, or him finding out is not an option. I am not willing to risk losing him, or my lifestyle. Aaron is the only man for me. And he's the only man I will spend the rest of my life with.

So I keep my guilty pleasure secret. Keep both worlds separate.

And this month's desire is Celeste—a five-foot-seven, half-Dominican and half-black bombshell beauty with round, brown doe-shaped eyes wrapped around long, lush lashes. I am only attracted to beautiful, feminine, well-kept women, like myself. My last lover was the spitting image of Halle Berry. The one before her was a Stacy Dash look-alike. And the one before her bore a remarkable resemblance to Sade. God, she had some good pussy.

Over the years, my bed has been filled with an assortment of gorgeous women, with insatiable sexual appetites, who fuck the shit out of their husbands, spend their money, and secretly crave the comforts of being with other women. Women who love pussy as much as I do, but have no intentions of ever leaving their husbands.

We have our own little secret society of wet, horny pussies, eager to please and be pleased by each other. "Oooh, yessss, Miasha," Celeste moans, bringing me out of my reverie. "Fuck my pussy, my love. Fuck me good..."

Her pussy moves against my hand, swallowing my fingers. Her breath catches. She is on the verge of coming, again. Her body shakes. I remove my fingers from her slippery hole, licking my fingers clean, then slipping my tongue into her mouth. We kiss, long and hard. I reach for her breasts and pinch her nipples, then roll them between my fingers. She moans. I moan as her fingers explore my own breasts. She tongues my nipple while cupping my pussy.

I am on fire.

She climbs on top of me and we grind our pussies together, moaning and bucking and fucking and screaming out our passions at the top of our lungs. We are lost in the cacophony of sounds. The muffled squeak of mattress springs, the slap-slap of sweaty skin, the swish-swish of juices, the grunts and growls; all parts of the chorus to our lust-filled song.

I am coming.

She is coming.

Our bodies shuddering as ripples of pleasure become waves of abandon, crashing against the lining of our walls, forcing their way out into rushed squirts.

"Eat my pussy," I demand in a raspy whisper as she slowly lifts off me. I remain on my back, lift my legs and spread them into a V-shape. Celeste's lips curl in a half smile.

"You must have read my mind."

"Yes. I know how you love this pussy, cum-filled and sticky."

She lowers her body down between my legs, her breasts lightly brushing against my skin. Her tongue circles my clit as her fingers find their way inside me. I surrender to the wave of sensation, coming against her hungry mouth. I pull her up toward me and lick my juices from her lips while allowing my hand to slip between her thighs. Her wetness pours down over my fingers like warm rain.

"Mmmm…oooooh… Ohhhhhh, Miasha…"

Our lips meet, tongues swirl around the others. Slowly, I pull away. Tell Celeste to get on her knees. She smiles. Turns over, then inches down toward the foot of the bed, getting on all fours. She has a firm and round ass that tapers down to beautifully toned thighs. She arches her back. Presses her head into the luxurious 1800-thread-count sheets that smell of mint and jasmine.

I slap her plump ass cheeks, then part them. Her fat pussy lips shimmer in wetness. Celeste gasps as I slide two fingers, then three, into her cunt. Her legs widen. Her hips buck back against my hand, her pussy hungrily opening—taking it all, demanding more, staying in sync to the swift movements of my hand. She grinds and winds. She hisses and moans. Soon she is coming. And I am slurping at her pussy. Gulping down her warm cream.

"Oooh, yessss…get it-get it…mmmmm…Oh, God!" Her body shudders, then jerks as I latch on to her clit, still pumping my fingers into her pulsing slit. The mouth of her pussy clenches my fingers, pleading for more. I slip in a fourth finger, sliding my hand in and out of her in a sawing motion. "Oooh, ooooh…uhhh… mmmm…"

"Give me that wet pussy," I whisper. "Cum on my fingers… that's it, that's it…give it to me…"

Licking and sucking her, the scent of our horny cunts float around us. I devour her. Then change position. She is now on her back. Her thighs spread, knees bend, as I clamber on top of her and straddle her face. Her long, curled tongue stabs into the center of my hole, darting in and out as my fingers splay open her lips and suck her clit. I ride her face, her mouth, her tongue. Her legs clamp up around my back. She bucks her hips upward, offering me her pussy—all of it. And in one greedy swallow, I take her pussy into my mouth. Gobble her up. Our moans and gasps fill the room.

We are both up to our eyeballs with unadulterated pleasure. My hips jerk against Celeste's face. Her hips buck against mine. She brushes my pussy with long fingers, stroking my thick wet lips, then massaging my slick clit. There's a deep throb in my pussy. I am on the verge of exploding. My stomach tightens. My grunts and groans signal to my lover my satisfaction. I feverishly suck her clit, fingering her pussy. Celeste cries out under me, latching her mouth over the roof of my cunt until it spurts out a sweet, sticky cream.

"Oh, God, Oh, God…" Her body thrashes about. She is filling my mouth with her cum, slick and plentiful. I continue sucking her until she has emptied her pussy. I swallow her warm, wet stickiness, then roll over onto my side, spent.

"That was heaven," Celeste purrs, sitting up and licking my cunt juice from her fingers, then her lips. "You sure have some sweet, sticky pussy."

I smile, grasping her face in my hands. I kiss her lightly on the mouth. "So do you." My hand finds its way between her thighs, tracing a finger over the swell of her lips. She's so slick and warm that I am tempted to drop to my knees and serve her a tongue-fuck, but I resist the urge. Instead, I caress her lips. Tickle and tease them. Her hips gyrate. I continue my finger play until her ass churns and her pussy juice flows. She is so wet with want, and desire. She's greedy, as I am.

"Finger me," she whispers. Her cunt greets my fingers warmly and wetly as I sink two in. "Ohhh, yes…"

With my free hand I massage her breasts, my mouth alternating from one thick, dark nipple to the other as I finger her pussy. She moans, her hand now reaching between my thighs. She has found my own wetness and allows her probing fingers to be drenched in my juices, my cunt sucking her in knuckles deep.

And for the rest of the morning we make sweet, passionate love until we are both speechless, and paralyzed, and blinded by heat from the intense pleasure of multiple orgasms.

TWO

Five hours later, I'm sprawled out across my king-size bed naked, basking in the afterglow of my romp in the sheets earlier. I'm satiated and filled with bliss. I lick my fingers and touch my clit in afterthought, grinding my hips into my hand. Ten minutes into my foreplay, the phone rings as I am about to cum. I gasp, reaching over to grab the cordless on the nightstand.

"Hey, beautiful."

I smile. "Hey, sexy man. I take it you've landed safely."

"Yeah. I'm headed to the Biltmore now. How was your morning?"

I glance over at the French-cut panties tossed up on the nightstand, a sweet reminder of this morning's tryst. A smile forms on my lips as I reach over and bring the white lacy cloth up to my nose. I inhale deeply. The musty smell of Celeste's cunt still lingers in the crotch of her panties. As I toy with the silky material, I push two fingers into my wet slit, remembering the way the garment stretched over her ass, hugged her hips, and captured her cunt. Its bold imprint stained by seeping juices and the wetness of my mouth as I tongued her slit through the fabric. A moan slips out from the back of my throat, reveling in the way she tasted.

"It was deeee...mmm...lightful..."

He chuckles. "Oh yeah? Is that right. And what made it so delightful, baby?"

"Mmmm…playing in my pussy."

"Mmm, nice. I like that." His voice dips dangerously low and deep. "Is that what you're doing now?"

Aaron loves it when I masturbate. He loves hearing me moan. He loves the smell and sound of my wet pussy. And he loves watching me more. "Yessss."

"Damn, I wish I could see you finger-fucking that pretty pussy. You fucking that pussy for Daddy, huh, baby?"

I grunt, slowly moving my fingers in and out of me.

He lowers his voice to almost a whisper. "Yeah, baby. Give Daddy that pussy. I wish I were in back of you right now, fucking your brains out, slamming you deep with all this hard dick."

"Oooh, yessss…fuck me with that big, black dick. Give it to me, baby…ooooh…"

"Damn, baby, you got my dick hard as hell."

"Mmmmm. I love your big, hard dick. You wanna slam it all in my tight cunt? Make me squirm and squeal from being fucked fast and hard by you." My fingers go knuckles deep inside my slit, rapidly stroking my spot. "Oooh, I want you to fill my cunt with your thick cum, baby…"

"Open them pretty legs, baby. Let me see that wet pussy…"

I imagine Aaron's driver eyeing him in his rearview mirror as he strains to keep his throbbing cock trapped between his boxers and his designer dress pants.

I reach for my cell, spread my legs wide for him and snap a picture of my wet pussy, open and ready. I click SEND. I imagine Aaron in the backseat of the Town Car that has picked him up from the airport, now transporting him to his hotel, with his large hand pressed into his crotch. His dick thickening at the thought of my pussy splayed open by wet fingers.

Aaron knows I'm his freak. But he also thinks I am his perfect, little trophy wife. If only he knew how naughty I am when he's gone. If only he knew how many pussies and tits and assholes my tongue has caressed. If only he knew how many warm, wet mouths have caressed mine. How many tongues have lapped at my clit and swirled in and out of my holes. The mere thought of him finding out frightens and excites me.

"I sent you something."

"Good," he says. "I'd love the real thing."

"Me too."

"You drive me crazy, woman."

"I know I do."

"Look. We're pulling up into the hotel now. I'll call you after I get checked in. I love you."

"I love you, too," I say softly.

"Keep that pussy wet for me."

"I always do."

Ten A.M. the following morning, I am walking into one of the most lavish day spas in the tri-state area—The Pink Kitty, an exclusive "for wealthy women only" spa—for my monthly spa treatment. From their five-thousand-dollar Evian baths to their exclusive Bee Venom and Umo 24-carat gold facials to their diamond and ruby manicures and two-thousand-dollar-an-hour Pink massage—The Pink Kitty not only caters to the pampering needs of its wealthy clientele, but provides other deliciously decadent services that feed the libido and quenches one's thirst for secret lesbian trysts.

Every woman who walks through their doors walks out refreshed, relaxed, and glowing from erotic release. With its soothing music, soft pink lighting, pink walls, plush pink carpet, pink floral arrangements and white Italian leather sofas and pink leather cubes for seating, The Pink Kitty surrounds its clients with femininity as scantily-clad female hosts, or servers, mill about ensuring each card-carrying member is being handled with the utmost care as they sip on the finest champagnes and herbal teas while nibbling on imported caviar or strawberries coated in the richest, sweetest, darkest chocolate in the world while they mull over an extensive list of spa services.

Today, I am foregoing the traditional spa treatments and finger-and-toe-sucking manicures and pedicures offered for something a lot more sexually gratifying. Their signature Pink-Six is what I have come for, and will be *coming* from. Three women, three sets of hands massaging and kneading and caressing every inch of my body with special attention being focused on stimulating my clit & G-spot, and flooding my pussy with pleasure. For eighteen hundred dollars, I will be given an hour-and-a-half worth of titillating, toe-curling orgasms.

Ooh, there's nothing like a day at The Pink Kitty.

"Miasha, darrrrling," the mocha-colored, latex-clad salon manager—a very sexy Korean and black woman with perky breasts and a well-toned body, purrs as she greets me with cheek-to-cheek air-kisses. "You look fabulous as always, darrrling."

I smile, stepping back to take her in. "Ooh, and so do you, Lakita." I eye her from head-to-toe. Lakita Lee is drop-dead gorgeous. At fifty, she doesn't look a day over thirty, thanks to an array of aestheticians and plastic surgeons she keeps on speed dial. I smile, taking in her attire. She's wearing a short, pink latex dress with a pair of thigh-high latex boots. My gaze locks onto her plunging neckline, showcasing her double Ds, then eases down to her pierced navel. The diamond necklace around her neck sparkles brilliantly underneath the glow of the lights. She slowly turns. The back of her skintight dress has two cutout holes, giving me full of view of her plump ass. She has a curled pink tongue with a cherry on its tip tattooed on her left cheek. "Oh, my. You look good enough to eat."

I reach for my second flute of champagne as she turns back to me, tossing her glossy black hair over her shoulder with the flick of her head. A sly grin curves her pink-painted lips as she slinks a hand up her dress. "Oh, I am, darrrling." She brazenly dips a slender, manicured finger into her honey-pot. My mouth and pussy start to water as I shamelessly watch as she stirs her juices. A slight moan escapes her mouth as she eases her finger out of her slit, then places it up to her lips. "Mmmm, yummy. Perhaps I'll give you a sample a little later."

I lift my flute. "To endless possibilities."

She takes a flute from a sterling silver tray as a sever waltzes by. "And never-ending orgasms."

"Ooh, I like the sound of that."

Our glasses clink.

Three

Thirty minutes later, after twenty minutes of luxuriating in the sauna, I am stepping out of a steamy shower into my personal chamber—one of many individual rooms assigned to clients to ensure their privacy—wrapped in a luxurious pink robe, being greeted by a gorgeous, naked woman with, smooth chestnut-colored skin, standing in a pair of red ankle-strap stiletto Louboutins.

Her hair is cut short and sassy with streaks of blonde highlights. Her breasts are full with large, thick, pierced nipples. There's a large, round bed in the center of the room. Large oil paintings of pierced tongues, labias, and clits done in hues of pinks and purples adorn the hot pink walls. "Hello, Miasha." She greets me with a slight Spanish accent. "I am Anya, one of your masseuses for today. You can remove your robe, then lie down on your stomach."

I smile, untying my robe.

Her sparkling green eyes drink in every inch of my Pilates and gym-sculpted body as my robe slides off my shoulders and drops to the floor. She licks her lips, keeping her gaze on me as I walk over to the bed, crawl onto the middle of it, then lay on my stomach.

My body shivers in eagerness as the mattress dips from the weight of Anya. She hasn't even touched me, yet, and my pussy lips are already quivering. I inhale her spicy scent, pressing my aching clit into the cool white sheets, wanting…no, needing, instant relief.

"Relax," she says, her breath warm and tickly on my flesh. "You have a beautiful ass." She softly brushes a hand over each cheek, then lightly grazes her fingertips over them. I moan. "It's so soft. I can't wait to slide my tongue in it. Spread your legs."

I gasp as she inches between my thighs, drizzling warm, scented oil over my skin. Her soft hands melt into my flesh, massaging the kinks, gliding all over—neck, shoulders, back, ass, hamstrings, calves, soles of my feet, then back up again. Her warm, oily hands leave my body slick. She parts my ass cheeks, mounts me, then grinds her clit onto my tailbone, her breasts pressed flat against my back.

"Oooh, the crack of your ass feels so good on my clit. I'm gonna cum into your crack and then lick your ass." I wind my hips. The heat from her pussy warming my ass causes sparks to ignite between my own legs. She reaches under me, cups a hand over my own throbbing sex and fingers me.

"And your pussy's so wet."

"Oooh, yes." I match her thrusts, humping and pumping. I can feel her heartbeat thumping, racing with intent, against my back. She is on the verge of climax. "Yes, come on me. Oooh, yes, let me feel your hot juices splash on my ass and drip down into my asshole. Oooh, yesss…give it to me…"

She grunts. Her fingers rapidly dip in and out of my slick heat as she rides my ass, grinding her clit into me as if it were a dick. I clench my thighs and ass cheeks together. She keeps humping me until her body trembles and warm cream creeps out of her pussy, and slides into the crack of my ass. She trembles for a few seconds, catches her breath, then lifts up from me, sliding down between my opened legs and pulling open my ass. Her warm tongue slithers in a line up my crack, licking up and down, lapping up her juices. Then she slowly circles my asshole with the tip of her tongue.

I bite into my bottom lip, surrendering, giving into the intense sensation as she works her heated tongue into my asshole. My hips begin to pump, slowly grinding my clit into the mattress.

"Uhhh…oooh, yes…"

My moans begin to echo around the sparsely furnished room as an orgasm swells, then gushes out of me.

"Turn over," she says low and husky, her voice thick with desire. "It's time for you to get your money's worth. Are you ready?"

I turn over on my back, my heart racing, my pussy pulsing. "Yes. Give it to me. All of it."

I draw my legs up to my chest and clasp the back of my knees, spreading open my cum-sodden cunt and giving the sexy Latina ample access to my sweet treasure. With eager fingers, she spreads open my lush, swollen lips and plunges her tongue inside.

I moan, arching my back. As she's swiping my clit with her tongue, my pussy starts to contract. I murmur softly, pinching my own nipples that have suddenly become hard, brown pebbles of excitement. Hot cream trickles out of my cunt, her curled tongue darting in and out, in and out, to retrieve it.

She sucks my clit like it's a piece of hard candy, teasing it with the tip of her tongue. "Oh, yes…suck my clit…mmmm…oooh…" I grab her head, clenching my thighs so she can't move.

"Mmmm," she moans into my sex, licking, lapping, dipping and darting her tongue, swirling it all around my center. "Your creamy pussy tastes so…sweet."

She sticks a finger in, then another, into my wetness. My eyes flutter close. Oh, god, I love the sounds of my wet pussy being fucked by fingers. "Mmmph…give me another…"

"Are you sure?"

"Yes. Give me more. Oooh…"

She fucks me with steady thrusts, gliding in and out of me in swift, slippery motions. Two fingers become three, three fingers now become four. I gasp and whimper, enjoying the sensation of having my pussy stretched. I can feel another orgasm building. I moan in my throat as my cunt clamps around her hand.

"That's it, beautiful. Come for me. Come all over my fingers…"

"Uhhh…ooooh…mmmmm…aaaah…"

She nips at the pillow softness of my cunt lips, then bites down. I growl, clutching the sheets, reaching for Anya, thrashing as my orgasm crashes over me, snatching my breath. I gasp. She nips me again, then using her tongue to lave the sting.

I pant and scream, nearly out of my mind. My cries of pleasure coming from deep in my throat egg her on, encouraging her to keep stroking my spot.

"That's it, Miasha. Give it to me…" She clamps her mouth over my pussy and sucks, her tongue wildly slathering my clit, then dipping into my sea of wetness; the waves splashing over her hand, her fingers, and her mouth.

"I hope you've saved some for us," a sultry voice says from the opposite side of the room. I crane my neck to glance over at the door to see who *us* is. But I don't see anyone. The door is still shut. No one has walked through it.

But there is another entrance. One in back of us, over in the corner. I assumed it was a door to a closet, but it isn't.

"Oh, there's a whole lot more," Anya says, looking up from between my thighs, her lips soaked and shiny from my juices, slipping three fingers inside of me, probing my pussy until she finds my spot. I cry out. "And she keeps coming and coming and coming."

"Sounds delicious," the voice says.

"Yes, it does," another voice chimes in.

I don't see who the other women are until they converge onto the bed, bringing with them vanilla- and peach-scented skins and aroused cunts.

"Hello, beautiful," a tall, dark chocolate woman with dark brown eyes, shiny smooth skin, and short, curly hair says. "I'm Isis." She's on the left side of me, while her counterpart—a short, thick-hipped, cinnamon-coated woman with small breasts, is on my right.

"And I'm Jasmine," she says, leaning forward and wrapping her plump lips around my right nipple. Her tongue swirls over it, causing me to gasp, while Anya goes back to devouring my cunt and Isis lightly tugs my left nipple between her teeth. Both women have a hand between their own spread legs as they suck my breasts, squeeze them, rub my erect nipples against their lips, then stuff each breast back into their mouths and lick while Anya fingers me. Isis and Jasmine both slide two of their wet fingers into my mouth, stretching it open, sharing their tangy juices with me. I lick and suckle and moan as I savor their decadent essence.

I writhe in ecstasy, the heat of passion boiling through my veins as I reach for Isis and Jasmine, my hands and fingers searching between their legs for warmth and wetness. They both moan when I find it. Spirals of tingling sensation pulse through my cunt, curling, swirling.

Anya reaches under me, cups my ass and squeezes it, sucking my pussy lips.

"Mmmph...ohhh, yes..."

Anya's tongue finds the center of my ass. She laves it, tongues it. And instantly I become a trembling, whimpering mess of hungry need. And then it is there...her finger. Pressing up against the puckering rim; its tip pushing inward.

Oh yes!

My muscles clench, then relax as her finger inches in. She works my asshole, her warm, wet mouth latched onto my clit. It hurt, her finger in my ass, but it also felt good, so very good. I moan, writhing and begging and pleading.

"Yes, oh, yes..."

Isis and Jasmine continue ravishing my breasts while I finger their pussies. Anya pushes a second finger in and searing white heat blazes through me. I arch my back. She scissors her fingers, stretching my heated tightness. My hips lift into her thrusting and sucking and tonguing. She finger-fucks me and sucks my clit until I come again and again and again.

Eventually each woman takes turns eating my cunt, fingering my cunt, lapping my cunt lips, sucking my clit, coating their lips and tongues with my juices as it spills out of my slit.

"Eat her pussy good, Jasmine," Anya urges, flicking her tongue over a nipple.

"Uh, uh, uhhhh…I'm coming…ahhh…"

"Yeah, come for us, beautiful," Isis coaxes, pinching my other nipple.

I buck my hips. Let out a loud, piercing groan.

"Oh, we're not finished with you, yet," Isis says. "Roll over. I want to taste you from the back."

Breathlessly, I roll onto my stomach, inch up on my knees. Isis gets in back of me and buries her face in my ass, licking my tiny, tight hole, then snaking her tongue to my pussy lips. Jasmine leans over me and slaps my ass cheeks, then pulls them open. Isis tongues me from ass to cunt, probing, thrusting, licking, teasing, and tasting my juices. Jasmine slips a finger into my ass while Isis replaces her tongue with two of her own fingers, arching them and pressing against my G-spot. She massages the pulsing flesh as Anya dips her head under me and sucks my clit, sending an electrifying jolt through my whole body.

I moan louder.

They devour me, seducing me, their gluttonous tongues ravaging every inch of my body, my sticky sex, until I am drifting into sweet, heavenly bliss.

Four

Two days later, Celeste and I are back at it again. Her husband of six years, an investment banker, has left for a business trip to Singapore. Although I am still floating—and pleasantly exhilarated—from my time at The Pink Kitty, I am always up for a rendezvous in the sheets with Celeste. She is free to play for the next two weeks. Unfortunately, I only have until Friday evening to indulge my libido however I desire before it's back to my life and wifely duties as Mrs. Aaron Simmons. Then I will fuck my husband with an urgent need, with reckless abandon, like there's no tomorrow. Something I happily do.

Until then...I smile, arousal gnawing in the pit of my belly, feeling Celeste's gaze on my nakedness. I spread open my legs. Pat my pussy—a welcoming signal for her to taste it. Cover her hot mouth over it, then fuck the cream out of it with her tongue.

"Come lick my pussy."

Celeste gets down on her knees and makes her way over toward me in a seductive crawl. Catlike and sleek, she eases toward me, her tongue flicking in and out of her mouth.

I pull at my nipples. Smack my pussy. Then pull open brown lips to reveal the fleshy pinkness, wet and willing.

The heat from her mouth tickles my clit as she positions her face between my legs and speaks into my cunt. "Ooooh, I love this pretty pussy." She inhales it. Breathes in its peachy fragrance. "Mmmm...it smells delicious."

She laps it. Her talented tongue gathering the slick cream that begins to seep out, languidly teasing my pussy.

She kisses it, lightly.

I toss my head back. Shut my eyes. "Mmmm…stop teasing me."

She kisses it again.

I moan.

She slides her tongue in. She is French-kissing my pussy, her tongue sweeping the insides of my walls. My muscles clamp shut around her thick tongue. "Oh, yes…mmmm…eat my pussy…yesssss…oooh…mmmm…" I palm the sides of her head and fuck her face. Grind my pussy deep and hard onto her mouth. My breath quickens. I am nearing my first climax. I coax her to swallow up my pussy. "Oooh, yes…like that…mmmm…put it all in your mouth, baby…you want me to cum all in your mouth…?" She latches on, moaning and groaning while sucking and licking and slurping. She eats my pussy with growling enthusiasm. Greedily, shoving and stuffing her tongue chin-deep inside of me. "You love my pussy, huh? You love eating this wet pussy?"

She grunts, pulling my clit into her mouth.

A sweet burning heat rips through my inner walls, causing my stomach to tighten. I buck my hips. Pound my pussy up into Celeste's mouth. "Oh yes, oh yes…I'm commming…oooooh…mmmmm…"

Celeste removes her mouth and buries three sleek fingers into my cunt, twisting and pumping them rapidly in and out. I yelp. My chest heaves. My clit throbs.

She keeps fucking me…deep and fast.

I am surrendering to her, to this…the sensation of being licked and being fingered. Cunningly, fiendishly, Celeste manipulates her fingers to take me to the edge with just the right amount of pressure and movement.

In and out.

She smiles triumphantly as she probes and massages me, my body beginning to shudder.

"Uhhh…mmmm…yes, yes, yes…uhhhh…"

"That's it…give me that sweet pussy milk."

Her wet thumb glides over my clit.

I am humping her hand.

"Oooh, oooh, oooh, oooh…"

Fingers become replaced with her tongue, darting frantically in and out, flicking around my center.

"Ooooh, yessssss…you love the taste of my cum? You want me to nut all in your mouth, all over your tongue?" she groans. "Here it comes…I'm coming…"

"Yes, baby…give me that sweet, sticky nut…oooh…come for me…"

Coiling my fingers through her hair, I clamp my thighs around her head and fuck her face, humping and humping and humping.

Oh, God…I am losing it!

My legs spread open, again.

Deliberate fingers—one, two, three, find their way back inside of my wetness.

The swishing sounds of my cunt become louder than my own breathing.

And in an explosion of bright lights and wild colors, I come loud and hard. Pussy juice gushing out, like a roaring sea. Celeste keeps working my pussy with her fingers while sucking on my clit. I am still coming. Wild and nasty, soaking her fingers and hand. Winding my hips, pinching my nipples, popping my clit, I urge her to keep it going. Keep stoking the fire burning deep inside of me. Keep skimming over my clit with her thumb. Keep stroking that highly sensitive spongy area nestled in the pit of my pussy.

"Oh, yesssssss...oooooooooh..."

I climax and shudder and cry out. My body jerks. My breath catches in the back of my throat. My eyes roll in the back of my head. I am feeling possessed. I chant and hiss and purr.

My body tenses, toes curling and fingers clenching in sync with the clutching walls of my pussy as I come so hard I think I'm going to pass out.

It takes me several minutes to regain my senses. I inhale. Exhale. Steady my breathing.

Long after the waves of my orgasm have subsided, my juices continue to drip to her fingers. Finally, as Celeste pulls her fingers out of me, my lashes lift to look at her. She sees need and want in my eyes. Her own desires mirrored in the reflection of my own lust.

I lick my lips, standing up. Warm juices still flowing between my thighs, Celeste grabs me by the hips and parts my legs. She cups my ass as her tongue slithers along the inside of my right thigh, then my left. A soft moan escapes me. Her tongue travels along my skin, lapping away.

"Come," I say, pulling her up from her knees. She looks at me. Her eyes dance wickedly behind her smile.

"What?"

She shakes her head. "I enjoy your company. And I love eating your pussy. It's so wet and juicy."

"And I enjoy yours," I reassure her, then smile. She offers me her mouth and her tongue, and I eagerly accept it, kissing her long and hard. "It's my turn."

I tell her I want her to lean over the damask sofa in my sitting room, walking over to my walk-in closet and stepping in. I flip on the light to retrieve one of my many toys. I open one of the bottom drawers of my mahogany wood aisle dresser, pulling out a black leather case. I have an assortment of colorful dildos of all shapes, colors, and sizes neatly tucked inside.

I grab the pretty pink one, then walk back out into my sitting area. As asked, Celeste is already bent over the sofa, waiting. She cranes her neck, glancing over her shoulder at me. Her eyes catch the dildo in my hand, gleaming with excitement.

She wants her hole fucked. She wants to be taken from the back. Wants her juicy slit stretched and filled. "Open your legs wider. I want to see all of you."

I lick my lips in anticipation.

Her pussy glistening and open, I reach for her swollen lips and pinch them, then nuzzle my face between her heart-shaped ass, pulling open her cheeks. The dizzying smell of her cunt makes my mouth water. My tongue trails her crack. Her wet pussy calls out to me. It winks at me. Puckers its lips. I blow into it, press my own soft lips to it, then flick my tongue across it. A sweet dew trickles out and clings to the swollen petals of her cunt. It cries out to me. Tells me how hungry it is. How deeply it wants to be fed. I smack it.

Celeste moans.

I tightly grip the base of the dildo in my hand—my own pussy wet with need—and push it into the back of her cunt, stroking her silky walls. The pink dick sinks in, deep.

"Oh, God, yesss…deeper," Celeste gasps softly. I oblige, giving it to her however she wants it. I push in deeper and the pussy swallows the dildo, squeezing it, milking it, begging for it. She reaches behind her and holds open her ass. She wants me to see her take it all. Her juices swish and splash up against the dildo as I lean forward, my tongue darting fiercely into her asshole. The smell of her ass and pussy hot and intoxicating.

Soft "ooohs" and "aaaahs" slip from Celeste's lips with each thrust.

Her ass shakes and bounces. "Oh, yes! Oh, yes! Fuck me! Harder! Give it to me, baby…"

I slip my right hand between my own thighs, massage my clit… inch two fingers into my slickness while fucking her with the dildo in my other hand. Celeste groans, pushing back and meeting my hand stroke for stroke, gulping in all ten-inches.

"Yes! Oh, yesssss! Fuuuuuuuuck meeeeee!"

Sweat coats Celeste's face, trickles along the back of her neck, then slides down her arched back. Still fucking her with the dildo, I remove my fingers from my own steamy cunt, then feed them to her. She opens her mouth, hungrily sucking them in until she has sucked away the wet stickiness.

Celeste pulls at her nipples. Her head tossed back, she calls out to me. "Miasha!"

I plunge deeper, the pink silicone slipping and sliding and disappearing into her pussy hole. I am pounding away, hard and purposeful. My only response to her cries of ecstasy—more pounding, more thrusting, more bumping her G-spot.

"Miasha!"

"Yes," I finally say against the swish-swish sounds and swelling of her cunt, relentlessly clutching the dildo. She is panting. Her nails dig into the fabric of the sofa.

"My pussy's on fire!"

Her skin is hot. She is overheating with passion. Her cunt is churning slick like melting butter. "Yes, I know. You want me to stop?" I ask, already knowing the answer. She wants it just as much as I want to keep giving it to her.

"Oh, God, no! Fuck me! Feed my pussy…mmmph…oooooooh… yes, yes, yes…I'm coming…"

Hot juices drizzle out.

I rapidly stroke my clit, bringing my own pussy release, wetness pouring over my own hand.

We are both gasping and moaning, heartbeats pounding in our chests. I pull the cum-soaked dildo out of her fuck hole, her body jerking and shaking, then press it to her lips, smearing her cream all over her lips before sliding the dildo into my own mouth and sucking it clean. We share another long passionate kiss, then curl up on the sofa—the heat from her pulsing pussy pressed up against my ass—and slowly drift into a deep slumber.

Five

Eight a.m., I awaken beneath rumpled sheets—naked, breathing in remnants of last night. Shadowy hints of perfume and pussy float throughout the room. I climb out of the warmth of my bed, my feet sinking into plush carpet as I walk into the master bathroom to wash my face and brush my teeth. I catch my reflection in the mirror, taking in the matted hair all over my head and decide to take a quick shower.

Ten minutes later, I'm back in the bedroom, standing in the middle of my walk-in closet trying to decide what to slip on. After several minutes of contemplating, I settle on a lace kimono slip dress—nothing on underneath, then make my way downstairs, using the spiral staircase that leads directly down into the kitchen.

Celeste greets me with a smile on her face, and a huge coffee mug in her hand. "Good morning," she says, offering me the steamy cup. "I made you some tea. Decaf, right?"

I nod, blowing into the cup. "Yes, thank you." I take a sip.

She wasn't supposed to still be here. Definitely wasn't supposed to stay the night. But here she is. Flitting around in my kitchen, wearing a flowing white, ankle-length dress. Her shoulder-length hair is hidden under a white head wrap. "I snuck out early this morning to go home and freshen up, then stopped by the store to pick up a few things for breakfast. I hope you're hungry. I picked up some fruit, and made vegetable omelets, turkey bacon, and my grandmother's 'make-you-wanna-slap-somebody's-momma' cheese grits—I promise, you'll love them."

I smile. My gaze falls to her ample backside as she moves about the kitchen, remembering how almost eight hours ago it had been bounced up over my face. My mouth waters at the thought of having my tongue buried in it again. "Sounds delicious. I'm famished. Do you want any help?"

"No. I got it," she says, pulling two plates down from the cabinet, then opening another door and grabbing two crystal flutes. "I've made us peach Bellinis."

I nod my approval, surprised at how at ease she is. Aside from my mother-in-law, I try to recall if any other woman had ever been so comfortable in my space, cooking in my kitchen as if this were their home, too. I sip my tea when I come up short, eyeing her over the rim of my cup as she prepares our plates. My stomach growls as she sets a plate in front of me.

"It looks and smells delicious."

"And it'll taste even better," she says, lifting the blender out of its stand and pouring peach puree into each champagne glass, then topping them off with champagne. She waits for the bubbles to settle, stirs the drink, then adds another splash of champagne to each flute before setting a flute on the table next to my plate.

I wait for her to take a seat. She has chosen to sit next to me opposed to across from me. I smile at the gesture. She reaches for her flute, hoisting her glass.

"To special friends, delicious meals, and hot, steamy, decadent sex."

"Amen to that."

Our glasses clink.

Two hours and four flutes of Bellinis later, Celeste and I are sitting out on the back deck, feeling lighthearted and giddy. There's a warm, scented breeze that drifts over us as we sit at the patio table, eating fresh fruit salads.

Celeste slides to her knees in front of me, pushing my already opened thighs further apart. Her hands slip up my skirt. I feel the first touch of her lips on the inside of my thighs and I am already shivering with arousal. I hear her soft groan as her warm tongue slithers up one side of my thigh, then back down the other thigh. I stare out into my expansive manicured yard, then lean my head back, closing my eyes. Luckily, the well-heeled, well-educated neighbors in our gated community aren't privy to the show, thanks to the evergreen cedar trees that line the edges of my backyard and the six-foot, wooden privacy fence with its French gothic posts.

The afternoon sun beams down on my face, adding more heat to my already heated skin. I hear myself moan as Celeste massages the tip of my clit with lips that send ripples through my entire body. Oh, God, yes...I'm caught up in the rapture of lust.

"Oh, yess...mmm..." My hands find their way at the base of her neck, then running through her silky hair before wrapping strands of it around each hand. I grind into her mouth, feeling a euphoria that intensifies the minute her tongue slides across the slit of my pussy, then dips inside.

"I'm going to swallow your whole pussy," she murmurs between my legs. "Then suck the cream out of you." Her hot breath, heating my lower lips, causes billows of staggering pleasure to sweep through my loins.

I moan, enjoying the cadence of Celeste's talented tongue, flicking and darting all over and around the plump folds of my sex. The hot wetness of her mouth envelopes every part of my clenching cunt, causing me to buck in my seat. I slide down in the chair, Celeste's hands cupping and squeezing my ass as I lift my hips, rolling them slightly.

"Oooh, yes…eat my pussy…mmmm…get all in that sweet hole…aaah, yessss…"

"That's right, boo, cum for me," she whispers against my skin. Then slides her tongue over my asshole, followed by a finger. "Give me that sweet cream." She sucks me until my cunt melts in her mouth. Heart beating wildly, I ride the wave of pleasure.

Hours later, the candles are lit and I am luxuriating in my over-sized Jacuzzi, sipping an apple martini while Estelle's album, *All Of Me*, plays in the background. I hum along to "Thank You" as it floats through the surround sound. I slip further down into the bubbles reminiscing, replaying the day out in my head. Reliving Celeste's heat engulfing my fingers, my tongue. The delicious sixty-nine position, face-to-pussy, we were in. Recounting her tongue strokes, and mine, each of our licks making the other wetter, and hornier. I reach for my glass, guzzle back the remainder of my martini, then reach for the pitcher and refill my glass before setting it up on the ledge.

She was on fire. Celeste met my gaze with want, and longing. Smoldering heat that singed the senses burst through her pores as she climaxed, triggering my own need for an orgasm.

I melted inside.

I close my eyes, replaying the sex tape. Her hand slides up my spine, her tongue into my mouth. In my fantasy, she's wearing a flowing yellow chiffon sundress; it's gauzy material barely hiding her nakedness. I lift her dress up over her head, and her breasts bounce free. Without thought, instinctively, I lick my lips. Reach out touch, to roll her nipples between my fingers and squeeze.

She moans.

I inhale, rewinding the tape in my mind. I can smell her arousal as my fingers press the wet silk covering her crotch, rubbing harder as I lean forward and let my tongue flicker across her left nipple, then her right.

Her flesh moves under my hand, and I feel an awakening quake between my own legs. This time I kiss her, my hand still trapped between her thighs, still playing with her, sliding now beneath her panties to touch her hot, wet cunt.

"Take my pussy, Miasha…" she breathes. I can still feel her lips at my earlobe, my neck, the swell of my breasts; her hot kisses setting my skin ablaze.

I feel myself shuddering as we lay, her head position toward my feet, the mouth of her pussy positioned over my face.

"I love sucking your clit. Eating your pussy."

"Ooh, your pussy's so sweet and sticky…"

My hand slips between my legs as I envision Celeste moaning above me, her hips rolling, thrusting deep into my mouth. Her warm, wet mouth clamped around my pussy; her tongue swirling over and around my clit.

I am having an out-of-body experience. Floating. Drifting along the edges of delirium and hysteria. "Fuck me, you pretty bitch… oooh, get all up in this wet pussy…aaah…mmmm…"

I spread my legs wider. Swivel my hips. Allow the sudsy bubbles to slosh up into my cunt as I hover on the brink of coming. "Aaaah… mmmmm…"

My cell rings, stealing my orgasm. I blink. It keeps ringing. I blink, again. I want to ignore it. Want to keep stroking my clit, want to cum. But its ringtone tells me that it's Aaron. I smile, quickly reaching over to answer. "Hello," I say breathlessly, wet fingers gripping the edges of the cell.

"Miss me, baby?" His voice is like hot chocolate, smooth and delicious. My body tingles. He is the only man who can turn me on by the mere sound of his voice.

"You know I do."

"Where are you?"

I bring my fingers, the ones buried deep inside of me moments ago, to my lips.

"In the Jacuzzi."

"Oh, I called the house line, but you didn't pick up." I tell him I didn't hear it. That I have the stereo playing. "Damn. Wish I were there with you. I want some pussy."

"Me too."

Ooops.

"I wish you were here, too," I quickly say. "My pussy misses you."

"Is that so?" In my mind's eye, I see my husband's handsome face, grinning. He loves this pussy. He loves the way I use it to fuck his dick.

"How was your day? Do anything exciting?"

"No, nothing more than my usual pampering when you're not here."

He laughs. "How much is this costing me this time?"

"It's on the house, baby."

"Sounds nice. You keeping that pussy wet for me?"

"Yes."

"Good. I'll be home tomorrow night, ready to fuck."

I smile. "I can't wait. I'll be waiting. Wet and ready."

"Just how I like it."

The call ends. I set my cell down on the ledge and reach for my drink, taking a slow, deliberate sip before closing my eyes and imagining Aaron watching me fucking another woman. Pressing my eyes shut tighter, I inch my hand back between my thighs, eager to pick up where I left off. I imagine him standing in front of me, shaking and stroking his hard dick backward and forward in deep slow movements as Celeste and I spread open our legs. Her right leg thrown over my left leg as I lean in and slip my hand between her thighs and begin massaging her pussy. Celeste does the same. Her fingers pressed against my clit. We both moan, trying to make the other climax as Aaron strokes his dick deeper, harder and faster.

He tells us to kiss. And we do as we cream on each other's fingers. Aaron watches us feed on each other's cum. Then tells us to get on all fours. He takes turns smacking our asses, eating our pussies from the back, then fucking us both doggie-style, his dick stretching the folds of our cunts.

"Oooooh, yesssss…fuck her pussy, baby…mmmm…let me suck her cream off your dick, baby…" I can hear the swishing of her juices as Aaron's dick slides in and out of her. "Oooh, yes…fuck her…" I reach over and stroke Celeste's clit as I stroke my own. Her pussy is deep and wide, and pulls Aaron's thickness into her with ease.

Celeste moans.

I moan.

Aaron grunts and groans, his dick slamming into Celeste. All three of us start moaning and groaning and panting. "Oh, God, yes!" I scream out as my orgasm peaks. "Yes, yes, yesssss!"

I come. Surprised at myself for fantasizing about Aaron fucking another woman, my secret lover. Something I've never done before. There's no way in hell I'd ever share his dick with another woman. Still, the fantasy of it all entices me. I reach for my glass, swallowing down my lascivious thoughts. Three martinis and two orgasms later, I climb out of the water, wrinkled and spent.

Six

I awaken to a ringing cell with my cunt moist and one thing on my mind: To satisfy my lesbian desires before my darling husband, Aaron, returns home this evening. I glance over at the crystal clock on the nightstand. 9:30 A.M. I reach for my cell, glancing at the caller ID. It's Celeste. *She either smells my lust way across town, or she's telepathic.* "Hey."

"I'm horny," she says in almost a husky whisper. "Can I come over?"

I sit up in bed, rubbing my eyes. "Sure. What time should I expect you?"

"I'm on my way."

A smile stretches across my face. Celeste's sexual appetite is as insatiable as my own, which is one of the reasons why we get along so well. Aside from being beautiful, she knows what she wants and needs, and isn't afraid to go after it. And, most importantly, she understands the rules. And she plays by them. She and I will satisfy our yearnings, feast on our desires, while continuing to love our husbands, unconditionally. Should that ever change on her part, she'll be replaced.

I call Aaron's cell in hopes of hearing his voice. I am surprised when my call goes directly to his voicemail. I call again, this time leaving him a message. "Hi, honey. It's about six-forty in the morning there. Was hoping to hear your voice. Give me a call when you can. Love you." I end the call, climbing out of bed. I slip out of my negligee, then head for the bathroom. In less than thirty minutes, I am showered, refreshed, and standing at the front door in a red silk robe when the doorbell rings.

"Good morning, beautiful," Celeste says, walking in. Her eyes wander over my body, approvingly. Her gaze sweeps across my plunging cleavage, then onto my hardened nipples. She licks her lips. "You look delish."

I shut the door behind her. "And I taste even better."

"Mmmm. I'll be the judge of that." She pulls me into her by the neck and kisses me briefly. She tastes like cherry lip gloss.

"I'm surprised to see you so early," I say coyly.

"I woke up thinking about you." Her eyes twinkle as she opens her trench and allows it to drop to the floor. She's standing naked, save a pair of red panties trimmed in lace, and a pair of red Christian Louboutins on her feet. She lightly touches herself with her long fingers over her panties, then slip them inside of her. Her golden skin shimmers from body glitter. "I hope you don't mind."

I lick my lips. My skin tingles, begging to be caressed. My eyes flicker to where her fingers play. "No, not at all."

"What time is Aaron expected in?"

I watch her body shiver as I stalk over to her. "Not until this evening." My fingers brush the lace edges of her panties. "We have the whole day to romp in the sheets."

"Perfect. I can't get enough of you."

An impish smile eases over my lips. "I smell your cunt."

"It's wet for you."

I pull her hand from between her legs, then suck on her fingers. "Mmmmm." When I am done savoring her pungent juices, I take her by the hand. "Come. Let's play." She follows me through the living room, then up the winding staircase to the master suite. I can feel her eyes on the sway of my hips. She's peeking under the hem of my robe, taking in my bare ass cheeks, as we climb the stairs. "I have a surprise for you," I say the minute we walk into the bedroom.

"Ooh, I love surprises."

"Then you're going to love this." My slick mouth moves over hers, my tongue slipping through her parted lips as my hands roam over her nakedness. I pull her into me, grinding my own wet pussy into hers. "This'll be our last day together, like this, until Aaron's next business trip. And there's no telling when that'll be."

She sighs. "I know. So let's not waste a moment of it dilly-dallying." Her gaze lingers on my face as she snakes her hand beneath my robe, probing fingers rubbing through slick lips. They find their way inside of me. My pussy's been simmering in its juices since early this morning. Now it's ripe and ready. I love the feeling of fingers stretching my pussy. Love the sound of my wet cunt being fucked by fingers. My eyes flutter. I can already feel an orgasm swelling up inside of me as she works her fingers in and out of me. "Come for me," Celeste says, her voice wet with lust. "Come all over my fingers."

I moan low, my pussy contracting around her searching fingers. I flush hot. Eager to feel, to taste, to drink in, Celeste's own wetness. As torturous as it is, I deny myself an orgasm—for now, stepping out of her grasp.

"You sneaky little tease," she says, feigning insult. "You deny me your cream. You know I'm hungry for it." She runs her tongue over burgundy-painted lips, then licks her fingers.

"As I am for yours," I assure her, walking into my closet.

"Then don't keep me waiting."

"I promise not to." I disappear into the closet. A few minutes later, I step back out into the room to find Celeste already sprawled out in the middle of the bed. Her legs spread, knees bent. One hand fondles her breasts, the other diddles her clit.

She eyes the items in my hand, then drops her gaze to the dildo jutting out from its harness, smiling. "Ooh, you have treats for me. And a nice big dick."

"Come to the edge of the bed and bend over." She sits up and scoots down, then gets on her hands and knees—ass up, facedown. "Your bare pussy is so sexy," I tell her, stroking her hips and ass. I dip two fingers into her cunt. Then thrust inside of her until her orgasm crashes over her, snatching her breath away.

She winds her hips. "Fuck me."

"Not yet. I need to fill your ass, first." I squirt a glob of lube onto her asshole, sliding a finger over her puckering ass lips. She arches her back and gasps. "You ready?"

"Yes."

I reach for the strand of purple beads. She watches over her shoulder as I press the first bead in, then the second and the third. Her asshole glistens as it sucks them in.

"You like how that feels?"

"Mmmm…yes…it feels sooo good going in my ass…" I push the fourth bead in. "Uhhh…ooooh…"

Her eyes glaze as I push the fifth bead in, stretching her hole. I tell her to breathe through her nose. Encourage her to relax, reaching beneath her and seeking out her clit, rubbing it with two fingertips.

She moans.

I work another bead in. "I'm going to stuff your ass, then stuff your pussy with a dildo. You want your pussy fucked?"

"Yesssss…" She pumps her hips. "Ooooh, yes!"

She gasps as the seventh bead slips in.

"One more bead." I slide a finger into her gushy cunt.

"Mmmm…"

The last bead is the largest. It's almost the size of a golf ball and takes a bit more coaxing and prodding before it pops in. She groans. I lick and massage her puffy asshole. It is stretched tight. I press her ass cheeks together and jiggle them.

She moans. "Oooh, I feel the beads moving around inside of me."

I grin, slapping her ass. "Now it's time to stuff your wet cunt."

She whimpers in response.

The base and the vibrator are centered right over my clit. I flick on the vibrator, then place the tip of the dark-chocolate cock at her opening and slowly slide in, inch by inch. I slide into her slow. Teasing her walls, tip to base. "Is this what you want?"

"Oh, yes…give me more…"

Celeste wants it fast and hard, but I purposefully take my time, wanting to slice into her cunt, making her beg for every delicious inch. She breathes in when we are finally skin-to-skin—my hips pressed up against her plump ass, the base of my cock pressing up against her wet opening.

"Ohhhhh shiiiit…mmmm…"

I pull almost all the way out, then plunge back in. She gasps. I repeat it, then pull out completely, replacing the cock with two fingers. "Oh, noooo…don't tease me…fuck my pussy, please…" She looks at me, her eyes covered in desperation, in longing, in aching desire.

I give in, mounting her from behind, driving the silicone cock deep into the slushy hole she has wet and waiting for me. She thrusts a hand between her legs and grabs onto her clit. I hear myself moaning as I ride her pussy. My own pussy tingly and excited, my hips surge forward, and I lose every inch of myself, my dildo, in her, fucking her, slowly then faster, and faster, and deeper until her pussy is around the base of the strap-on, then pulling out until I am almost slipping out. I repeat. In deep, out to the tip, then back in.

In deep, out to the tip, then back in, again.

I fuck her the way she would want her husband Daniel to fuck her. Fuck her the way Aaron fucks me. Filled with passion and intent. Celeste cries out, opening her body to me as I thrust into her, deep and domineering. She throws her head back.

With each stroke, I am owning her cunt, owning her orgasms. I block out her cries of passion and focus on the sweet throb building in my pussy.

I know I am hitting up into her cervix. Know I am rapidly stroking her spot. She is writhing, bucking, trying to ride the cock faster, harder. She starts moaning and gasping and shivering.

"Oh, god, yes, yes, yes…mmmm…yessssss!"

I can feel her cunt gripping the length of the silicone as her orgasm builds. She grunts. I reach for the ring hanging out of her asshole and quickly yank it, pulling out the string of beads. She moves on the cock. The sound of wet pussy swallowing dick followed by more grunts and growls intensify my desires to please Celeste, to bring her to orgasm over and over. I grip her hips and pull her firmly back onto the dildo. Her sweat-slick hips slide under my hands. But I manage to hold on.

"Uhhh…mmmm…ooooooh…" My eyes shut tight as our groans bounce off the walls.

"Is this how your husband fucks you?"

"Yesssss! Harder!"

Squishy, slippery noises sputter throughout the room as I continue pounding into Celeste, my melon-sized breasts swinging against her sweaty back.

I am slamming into her hips, pushing and stretching and sawing into her. I fuck her, feed her starving pussy, as if this is the last time we'll fuck.

Moaning, drawing in great gasps of air, she clutches the sheets. "Uhhh…mmmmm…uh, uh, uh…fuck me…mmmmm…give me more…deeper…oooooh…"

Her engorged pussy flows like warm honey. Wet and sticky. We're climaxing together. We are both drowning in a sea of our own juices. My heart pounds, my breath comes short. My eyes flutter open. And then…my mouth drops open.

Standing in the doorway is Aaron. His designer trousers unzipped. All eight inches of his manhood protruding out of the slit of his boxers, his fist sliding languorously over the slippery mushroom-sized head of his cock. *Ohmygod!* He is here! He's taken an earlier flight. Or maybe he never really left. I wonder how long he's been standing there, watching me, us—hot and sweaty, in the throes of passion.

A sly grin spreads over his lips.

And, in that moment, I know. This act of catching me in our bed fucking another woman is of no surprise to him. The glint in his eyes says it all. He's known.

I pull out of Celeste, leaving her pussy empty and throbbing. Cum-coated silicone stretched out in front of me, breasts swaying, the scent of my own wetness wafting from the base of the harness, I walk over to my husband as Celeste scrambles to cover her nakedness. I pull Aaron into me, slip my tongue into his mouth, then drop down to my knees and welcome him home.

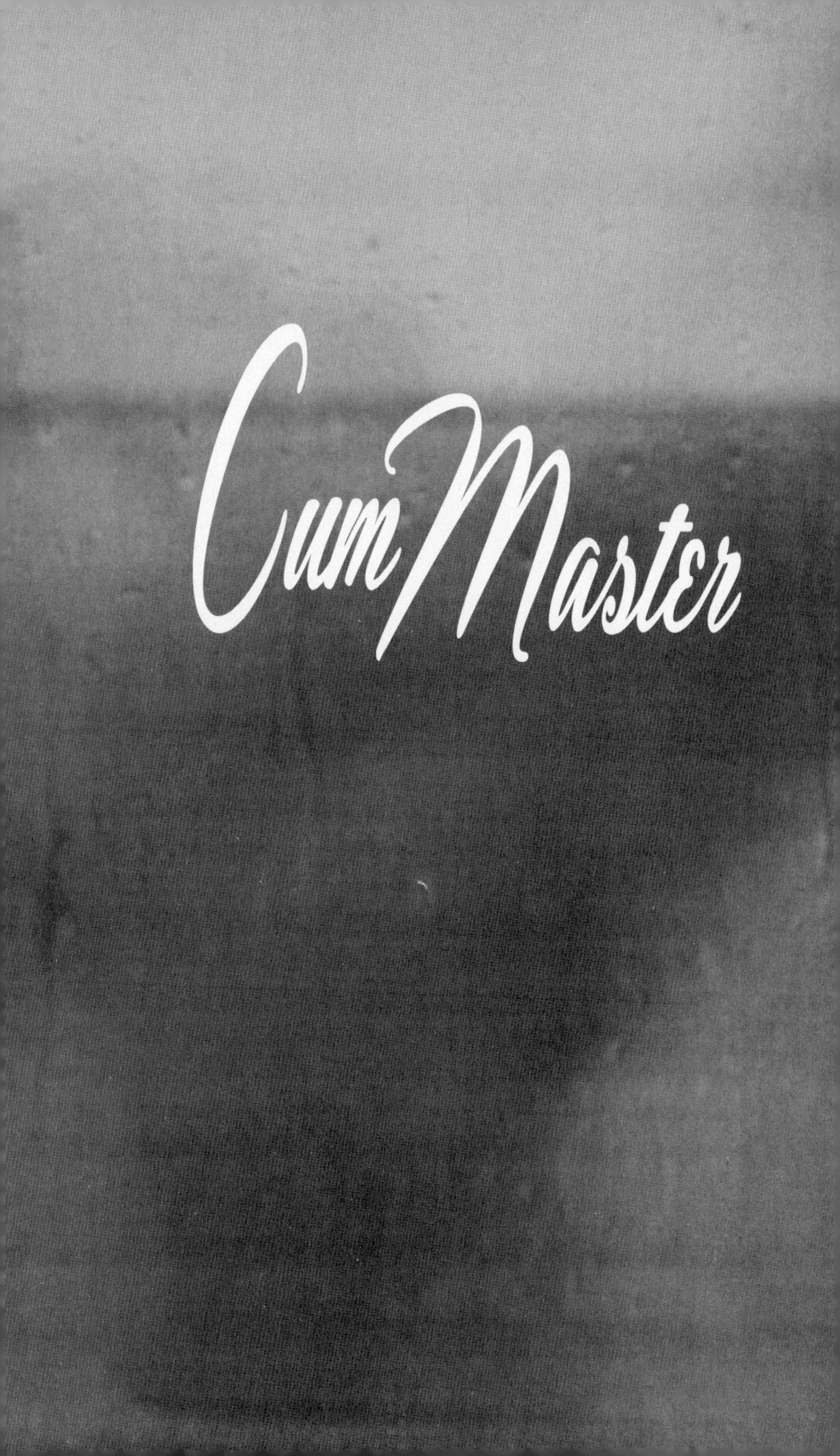
Cum Master

One

My pussy is swollen and on fire. The flames shoot through my asshole. Swirl up to my clit. Cause me to break out into a chilled sweat. It's a deliciously, sweet, stinging burn that has my clit engorged and my gooey nectar oozing out of my slit, clinging to my enflamed lips. The searing heat that screams through my cunt heightens the arousal of my senses, and my libido.

Legs spread, knees bent. I am hoisted up in my sex sling, blindfolded and donned in a pair of crotch-less black skintight leather pants, six-inch spiked books, and a black corset.

Usually, with the crack of a whip, then the flick of the tongue, I bring pleasure to women who desire, want, need…seek to release their inhibitions, to indulge their secret cravings, to feed their hunger for submission and control.

But then there are times, like now, when I want to be the one on the receiving end of a flogger, or a belt. Sometimes I want the *sting* that comes from the thinner width and length of the falls—the number of attached thongs. Sometimes I crave the *thuddy* feeling caused by a flogger no longer than the length of my forearm with wider, thicker falls made from heavier grades of leather.

Oh, yes, the flogger—my favorite whip.

My mind travels back to my first time bringing another woman this kind of deliciously painful pleasure. I was twenty-three. My new lover, at the time, Nicole, was twenty-eight. And less experienced in matters of kink, and sexual freedom. We had been dating for almost six months before I broached the topic with her. We were lying in bed, spooning, after an afternoon of lovemaking.

"You ever had your pussy whipped?" I asked, my hand sliding over the curve of her naked hip.

She craned her neck over her shoulder and shot me an alarmed look, then scowled. "No. Why the hell would you ask me some crazy shit like that?"

I shrugged. "It's not crazy. It's a question."

"Well, the answer is *no*. Ain't no one smacking up, punching up, or whipping up *my* pussy."

"It's erotic," I whispered.

She sucked her teeth. "It's nasty."

I kissed her bare shoulder. "You know I love you, right?"

"Of course I do. And I love you, too."

I leaned over and kissed her on the lips. "I know you do."

"But…?"

"Do you love me enough to be open to exploring new things, sexually?" She said she was open to some things. And asked her if she trusted me. She said she did. She wanted to know where this idea to flog her pussy came from. I told her how I had been fantasizing about it for over a year. That I had accidentally walked in on a friend and her lover in the throes of something sexual, and kinky. And it wasn't the gleam of their nakedness that had turned me on that day. It was seeing her lover holding a flogger in her hand, wielding it with precision and skill, its leather straps popping against her flesh. It was the vision of seeing her inflict pain on her lover that had aroused me. The moaning that followed each time the whip crackled into her skin excited me. I could smell her pussy from where I stood.

I felt like I was prying into a secret world of debauchery as I inched a hand up my blouse, pinched my nipples, then slid my other hand down into the elastic band of my cut-off sweatpants and eased my way into my panties. I inhaled, my breath catching in the back of my throat as I pressed on my clit. My panties were already soaked long before my hand or fingers even touched my insides. They didn't see me standing there watching them. Or maybe they knew I was there all along. But it hadn't mattered. Unbeknownst to them, standing there watching them—with my fingers slick in my own cum, they had ignited my curiosity.

I told Nicole how, a few weeks later, I had approached my friend about what I had seen between her and her lover. And how, the next day, she arranged for her lover to give me my first taste of being flogged. My breasts were first to experience it, then my cunt.

"It really turned me on," I explained, taking in her. I gave pause to see if she had anything to say, if she wanted to ask anything. She didn't. I continued, "I never knew experiencing pain could be so damn pleasurable. It's like being on a rush. Once my endorphins kicked in, it still hurt like hell, but I didn't want the feeling to stop. That night I had one of my greatest, most intense orgasms."

She turned over to face me. "So you have some kinky fetish for me to whip your pussy?"

I shook my head. "No. I want—"

She shot up in the bed. Her eyes widened slightly with realization. "Ohmygod…you really…want to…whip…*my* pussy…?"

A lecherous grin spread across my lips. "Yes. I want to whip you. I want to lie you on your back, yank off your panties, spread open them sexy thighs and whip your beautiful pussy until it spurts wet heat."

She blinked. Blinked again. Then swallowed. "Hard?"

"No," I whispered, stroking her right nipple. "Gently, lovingly, at first…until your pussy glows red. Then harder as your cunt heats up. I want it to hurt so good that you beg for it." I reached between her legs, cupped her pussy. "I will stroke your pussy with each lash and make you wet, like now, so wet your juices are pooling into your asshole." She gasped as I slid two fingers into her dampness. "Can I spank your pussy, baby?" She grunted as I strummed on her clit. "Look at you, all slippery. Just the thought has your pussy heated, doesn't it?"

She gasped again. "Oh, god. You're into some real kinky shit."

I pulled her nipple into my mouth, nipped it, sucked it, then pulled back. "No, I'm into being sexually liberated. There's something very freeing about embracing pain, giving and receiving it. I wanna be free with you, Nicky." I slid another finger into her pussy. "Mmm. Your pussy's so wet. I know you wanna try it. Say it." She bent her knees, spread her legs wider, meeting my fingers and hand with hungry thrusts.

"Uhhh…mmmm…so…if…aaah…I let you…"

"Let me what, baby…? Go 'head, say it."

"W-w-whip my pussy," she stammered breathlessly. "W-w-will you fuck me with a strap-on afterward?"

"Maybe." I plunged my fingers into her deeper, worked them faster. She bucked and thrashed as I hit her G-spot. I kept talking in her ear, kept planting the seed, while I finger-fucked her. Then I removed my fingers from her gushy snatch and popped her clit, then smacked the front of her pussy. She let out a loud moan. I did it again. "We can come up with a safe word that you can use whenever it becomes too much for you." I slapped her pussy again. And that time…she came, hard.

After two weeks of coaxing and smacking her pussy with my hand, she'd allowed me to paddle her pussy. I'd paddled her sex until it was clenching and creaming. And then I would nestle between her thighs and cool her torrid cunt with slow, wet strokes of my tongue, slowly dipping it into her drenched slit. It took me another two weeks before I had her comfortable enough to accept her first flogging. But not without, first, explaining to her the different types of floggers there were. She needed, wanted, to understand their purpose. Wanted to wrap her mind around the sweet torture I had finally convinced her—after weeks and weeks of prodding and preparing—to endure.

And that first time…the night I delivered swift, yet gentle, lashes to her waiting pussy, she screamed out and cried, giving in to the sensation and the waves caused by each lick. Eyes wide, pussy puckered, her vibrating groin and buzzing clit built the pressure within her to dizzying heights. She barely had time to gather her senses before her orgasm slammed through her, cracking open her insides, and spilling out in rushed spurts.

She gasped and wriggled and thrashed as she came, her back arching, her breasts swinging. Her opened eyes brimmed with tears as the thumping in her clit slowly subsided. The pain had made her feel helpless and powerful at the same time. Made her feel alive, every nerve ending tingling through her entire body—sensitive and on high alert—had her body overheating.

"Do you still trust me?" I asked, dropping the soft suede mini-mop with its burgundy tails as I knelt between her legs, my own pussy aching and drenched in its juices.

She nodded. Then tossed her head back and loudly moaned as I flicked her clit, then slurped the front of her pussy into my mouth. Another climax built, and she came over and over and over—welcoming its freedom.

"Are you ready?" the silky voice asks, lightly sweeping the flogger's tails over my sex, cutting through my reverie. I blink behind the blindfold, swallow back drool while adjusting my thoughts back to the present. The feeling of the flogger's tails brings out a Pavlovian response: my pussy juices, excitement rushes to my clit, and my long, thick nipples swell. A thick sexual energy surges from my breasts to my nipples, causing them to become erect.

I can't take it anymore. The need is excruciating. The want is unbearable. I ache for the stinging burn. I arch my back. "Yes. Give it to me. Make my naughty pussy weep."

The beautiful woman with the rich, deep Hershey chocolate skin standing before me—my lover, Sasha, holds a suede flogger with pink suede tails and angled tips in her slender, manicured hand. My pussy clenches, watching her grip its wooden handle. Oh, how I love the feel of suede. The way it snaps into the skin with just the right amount of thud and sting.

That's the beauty of floggers. Used properly, they can create many delicious sensations that bring about a steamy session of scintillating discovery.

Swoosh!

I gasp. The sting is followed by an exquisite burn that singes into my sex, its heat dancing over my skin. My clit starts to throb.

"Whip my pussy, again," I whimper.

In my mind's eye, behind the blackness of the silk, I see her raising the flogger up over her head, bringing it down over and around. Its fluid movement etched in my memory. Its lashes embedded into my skin.

Swoosh!

Another wave of heat vibrates through me and my pussy goes up in flames. It's so fucking hot. So hot, it feels like melted wax is being poured over my clit.

"Oh, yesssss! Again! Give my pussy more!"

Swoosh!

The flogger bites into my clit. Gnaws at the lips of my cunt. I ride the pleasurable pain, screaming myself hoarse as I cum, each spasm harder and sweeter than the one before.

The stinging lashes, my cunt's burning need, my wetness all amplified by the intoxicating sensations floating around me. I breathe it all in.

The scent of my lover's excited pussy and my own.

The sound of my moans and whimpers echoing throughout the loft.

The sizzle of the lashes.

My senses are ablaze. I am melting in hot fire.

"Again," I demand in almost a whisper.

Swoosh!

Her strikes caress my naked cunt. The suede ribbons slapping into my sex, causing the stinging fingers to pinch at my skin. I arch my back into the flicks, loving the sweet agony of pleasure and pain. My hands are not tied, or cuffed. They never are. I have mastered holding on to the reins or the ropes or the chains without removing my hands.

Swoosh!

Passion boils up into the pit of my pussy, then bursts out the tip of my clit. A huge tsunami of erotic heat crashes through me. My breath hitches. I am being swept up in another orgasm, my cunt spasming as I tremble and shake. When my climax finally subsides to gentle throbs, I reach in back of my head and untie the blindfold.

Our eyes meet.

I motion Sasha toward me with a finger.

"Now come lick my pussy."

She slowly licks her lips, dropping to her knees. She eases herself between my opened legs, her breasts brushing against my inner thigh as she settles herself in position, then slowly laps over my juicy, cum-drenched sex.

A wave of white heat smashes against the walls of my cunt as her lips circle my burning clit and she suckles on it. I bite my lip as she kisses the mouth of my pussy, then laves it. Her cat-like tongue strokes become an extinguisher, and a soothing balm all in one. I give into the sensation, eagerly letting her tongue caress my pussy, my clit, and asshole. I come in her mouth.

When the flames subside and finally flicker into a smoldering heat, tender pussy exposed and still soaked from the lashings and her spit, I reach for the flogger in her hand, ease myself onto my heeled feet, then wait for her to take her place in the sling until her thighs spread and her bare pussy opens. I cuff her hands. Then grip the smooth, wooden handle. I twirl it over my head. Sasha will now become the floggee; the one being flogged. And I will now become the wielder, the one doing the flogging.

She has a very low pain tolerance, so it is important for me to warm her up, first. The more I warm her, the easier it is for her body to turn the feel of the flogger from a painful sensation to one that is pleasurable. The more physically aroused she is, the higher her pain tolerance. The endorphins pumping through her body will keep her from feeling a lot of pain.

Her safe word—a simple word that alerts me that our play exceeds her tolerance for pain signaling me to stop—is *Pink Panther*. We've been together for close to three years and, so far, she's never had to use it. The hope is, she never will. The objective for me, for us, is always mutual gratification. Not to whip the dog shit out of anyone. Flogging isn't meant to cripple or maim. And it should never be done in anger. It should be approached with empathy, understanding, patience, and compassion.

Mmmm. Done right, flogging can be one of the most pleasurable forms of S & M, sadomasochism. I know it is for me. It is sensual and hardcore. And after a good flogging session, I haven't met many who don't fall in love with these tails.

I walk over to the table and reach for another flogger; one with buttery soft, suede tassels that fall in a gentle sweep from the base to deliver the most intoxicating sexual experience. Lighter-weight floggers, like the one in my hand, are used for the tender parts of the body, such as the breasts, inner thighs, and genitalia. Sasha enjoys when I deliver light, wispy strokes, like that of slender fingers lightly caressing and arousing her sex. Its wide falls are almost impossible to inflict trauma, and leave little to no marks or bruising. And they are scrumptious warm-up whips for either a long session, or as a variation to foreplay.

Swoosh!

She lets out a low moan at the first stinging swat. A stinging kiss. It is a soft blow delivered to desensitize the skin, and to trigger her body's endorphin response to the pain. Slowly, I increase the tempo of the swats causing her to cry out. She begs and pleads and screams. Her head snaps back.

Pain gives way to pleasure.

Swoosh!

The leather tongues slice into her clit, then gently over her breasts. "Oh, yesssss…uh…uh…uh…"

I can smell her, her thick lush scent clinging in the air.

Swoosh!

Before every smack of the flogger, her hips shift, then lift to meet the fall of the flogger's suede tongues. She pants and tenses.

"Oh, my sweet, sweet, beautiful Sasha. Look how your clit flares. You like your pussy whipped?"

"Yes…oh, god, yes…I love it."

Swoosh!

She yells out. Her juices splash out of her slit. Her body shakes. I can almost taste the tangy sauce that seeps out of her cunt.

"Mmm, look at that wet pussy," I say, gliding my tongue over my lips as I wield the flogger up and over.

Swoosh!

Skin crackles. Her pussy hisses. She groans.

Swoosh!

I pause in between sets—the number of seconds, minutes, between lashings. I tell her how beautiful she is. Let her know how much I adore her, how much I love seeing her splayed pussy open and wet, red and on fire. When I am done flogging her, I uncuff her. Her right hand slides between her legs. She starts to strum. I watch her. Then close my eyes. Breathe in the slick clickety-click sound her finger makes in her wet folds. I hear and smell her arousal.

She moans.

I open my eyes. My mouth waters at the sight before me. Her turgid sex—wet and swollen and welted, is a vision of ecstasy. It causes my own desires to lick her cunt to churn beneath my skin, hot.

My own pussy starts to drip.

She begs for it again—the dueling sensation of pain and pleasure lapping at her soaking wet sex. She shakes with need, tightly wrapping her hands around the chains, hanging overhead.

I give her what she wants.

Then, with her eyes glazed, I abruptly pull back the flogger, then stalk over to her and lean in between her legs. Her slick clit thickens against my tongue. I flick it. Flick it, again. Then capture it in my mouth, lightly between my teeth. The smell of her arousal fills my nose. I take my time. Tasting her. Tracing the tip of my tongue over her labia and clit in long, slow, swirls.

Who am I, you ask?

I am Laila Reynolds.

A lesbian.

A lover of pussy.

I am the Cum Master.

Two

"My pussy aches for your touch," the female voice on the other end of the phone says, breathing heavily. Her tone is lusty and thick with urgency. I'd know her warm, honey-coated voice anywhere. It's Samantha Willis or, in this case, Invoice 21348 aka Miss Creamy. "Can I see you today?"

"And what would you like, my darling?" My tone is sultry and hot. The caller starts panting. She has called into the 800 number located on the CONTACT page of my website, *Cum Master*. A website I created over two years ago after sifting through hundreds of sex sites that catered to lesbian and bi-curious women and realizing that there were a countless number of strong, confident, beautiful women, like myself, who secretly craved surrendering control, who wickedly fantasized about being submissive and unyielding in their quests for unadulterated and blissful pain. The kind of pain that makes them scream out and flinch and thrash about, clutching sheets and gnashing teeth, begging and pleading as they orgasm.

And through my website, *Cum Master*, I cater to those same women who love the sweet sting of a whip licking their clits and slits, or the thud-thud of a paddle paddling their pussies, then having a warm tongue lapping up the sweet juices that have gathered around their swollen pussy lips.

Women who spend their days and nights daydreaming and

fantasizing, careening between salacious thoughts and forbidden desires, pleasure and pain, their trust, their orgasms, their throbbing bliss...all at the mercy of me.

And—with an assortment of floggers, paddles, leather belts, vibrators, dildos, and my long, warm tongue, I deliver—um, after I've collected their payment for my services—the best fucking orgasms these women will ever experience, one lick at a time.

I cross my legs. "Are your panties wet?"

"Yes. Soaked."

I smile. I imagine her cum-stained panties sticking to her lust-drenched hole. The scent of her cunt, warm and wet, wafting through the air, slowly drifting through the vents at her office building where she is calling me from. "I want to stuff them in your mouth, then..." I pause, snatching back her moment of fantasy.

"Then what?"

"Tell me how you want me to touch your pussy?"

Her breath catches. "Surprise me."

"Take 'em off. Your panties."

"I can't. Not right now."

"Yes, you can."

"I'm at..." Her voice trails off. "Hold on. Let me go into another room."

I smile, envisioning as she struts off, her damp scent trailing behind her. I consider having her—with her porn-star body—beg me to give her the spanking she craves. Miss Creamy loves her lush pussy spanked. She loves punishment fantasies. Loves to let go of her real life lawyer self to indulge in her fetish. All of my clients are beautiful, well-educated, upper-six-figure-making women who use fake names, and have fetishes for pain. It allows, helps, them to detach their real worlds where they tend to be in power and yield control from their fantasy worlds. Allows them to be carefree and uninhibited. It allows them to explore their submissive limits, to uncover that very thin line between pain and pleasure. Being handcuffed, and oftentimes blindfolded, allows them to give in to being powerless, yet liberated. Unshackled from fears, they become slaves to their secret desires. And I possess the key to unlock all of their secret thrills.

Yes, I give it to them good. Bewildered and painfully aroused, I help my clients explore their deepest, darkest sexual cravings. Then when it's all said and done, when they've been pushed and manipulated sexually, and they've climaxed and their roaring cunts have finally quieted, they walk out feeling liberated as they go back to their happily-ever-after lives where much of who they are has become scripted and predictable.

"Okay, I'm back," she says, breathing life back into the other end of the phone. "I've found someplace a little more…private."

"Slap your pussy for me," I tell her low into the phone, my voice barely above a whisper. "Heat your cunt up. Get it ready for me." She lets out a soft moan. I hear the faint thud of a hand. "Harder. I want to hear it." *Whap!* I close my eyes and envision her raising her hand high and bringing it down against her bald pussy. "Again." *Whap!*

"Uhhh…can you fit me in today?"

"Why should I? What dirty little things has that greedy little cunt of yours done?"

"She's been begging for release."

"Does that little pussy throb? Does it ache between your thighs?"

"Oh, yes. She's been wet and horny for days, needing you. It's been excruciating. She's been a whiny, miserable, horny slut. She needs to be punished, real good."

"Has she been fucked?"

"No."

"Why not?"

"She wants to be spread open and spanked."

My moist tongue glides over my lips in anticipation. She loves talking about her pussy as if it's a human being. As if it has a mind of its own and freedom of free will. "Does that horny pussy hole want to be fucked after I've spanked it raw?"

She groans. "Oh, yes…"

"How many inches do you want me to fuck you with? Seven? Eight? Nine? Oh, no. I know what that filthy little whore of a cunt wants. She wants to be fucked deep, and stretched wide, doesn't she?"

"Yes."

"She wants to scream out as she's being fucked, doesn't she?"

"Yes, yes…oh, god, yes…"

I tell her how I'm going to paddle her pussy until it is saturated with her juices, then fuck her with an eleven-inch purple dildo.

My legs are spread. My fingers are playing with my clit. My own pussy throbbing as my fingers skim over my clit, then plunge into my wetness. I am surprised at how swollen my lips are. "Smack your pussy again."

She does, letting out a soft moan. The sound of her hand going down on her sex is like music to my ears. Instantly, it flames my own excitement, causing the swishing sounds my fingers are making to become louder than my own breathing. My hips pump onto my hand, two fingers lodged deep inside my cunt. I am so wet. Each time I push in or out of my juicy slit, it makes a slurping sound. My knuckles make a slapping noise against the wetness as I finger-fuck myself listening to Miss Creamy play in her own damp sex. Drops of nectar kiss their way down my smooth, toned thighs.

She takes a deep breath. "I need to see you. You have my pussy so wet. Don't make me beg for it, please."

I grin as salacious thoughts swirl through my head. There's no other way for me to say this. Miss Creamy is a freak for the paddle. Her pussy, her ass, she loves it smacked and paddled until blood rushes to the surface of her skin and her flesh swells, until she is tender and sore as if she were being rammed mercilessly by a huge cock. That's the kind of searing pain she enjoys. A few times she's begged for bruises over her cunt, saying she wanted the sting to last well into the night, or through the week. She wanted to feel the burn as her panties brushed against her sex, a sweet reminder of what she's endured, of what she's surrendered to. And, today, at this very moment, there's no telling how far she will want to go until she steps through these doors.

"What time can you get here?"

"I'll be there in an hour." She tells me that she needs to change first, then will head over. She disconnects. And then, suddenly, I am coming, loud and hard and strong, my cunt pulsating as I ride the tide, and hot, wet juices flow over my hand.

Three

Beneath her long black coat, Miss Creamy is wearing a school-girl's uniform. Her high, C-cup breasts spill out of her white, low-buttoned blouse. Cinched around her tiny waist is a wide, black belt. Her pleated, plaid skirt rides up over her round, voluptuous ass. Her ass cheeks peek from under the hem. She's either wearing a thong, or nothing at all. Knowing her, it's the latter.

I am donned in all black leather—corset, hip-hugging pants and seven-inch platform stilettos. My long ponytail is pulled up over my head, stuffed under a black leather cap. I am sitting in a red leather chair centered in the middle of my sparsely furnished loft with its vaulted-ceilings and floor-to-ceiling windows. In my hand is Miss Creamy's coveted prize—the paddle. I have chosen a black leather paddle for the occasion. Leather paddles feel like a warm burn at contact and do not cause a lot of pain to the skin, in this case her hungry cunt.

Leather is sexy. The way it feels. The way it smells. The way it snaps into the skin, and kisses into the flesh. The way it streaks when wet. Oh, yes…there's nothing more tantalizing than leather, especially when it's wrapped around a paddle.

I eye Miss Creamy as she closes the distance between us, her heels clicking against the polished wood floor. In the far left corner of the massive space, there's a portable leather sling with stirrups. On top of a glass table cart situated next to the sling are wrist restraints, a suede flogger, a black leather strap with a walnut handle used to deliver punishment—or encouragement, depending on the situation, a three-inch and four-inch butt plug, a bottle of Elbow Grease Fusion Silicone Body Glide lube for ass play, and nipple clamps.

Depeche Mode's "A Question of Time" plays low in the background.

"Stop right there," I say, crossing and uncrossing my legs. A sly grin eases across my lips as the thought of her being completely helpless...and at my mercy comes to life in my mind. I can see it in her eyes, her own excitement at this knowing. I can almost smell the sticky wetness seeping out of her, sliding between her thighs. "Turn around and bend over."

She turns around, slow and seductively, then bends over. Her plump ass cheeks peek out from under the hem of her skirt. She wiggles her ass, then makes it clap. I take in the view, licking my lips.

"Get over here."

She turns back around. My clit pulses as she makes her way toward me.

"You naughty little slut. Is your pussy already creaming for it?"

She casts her mink-lashed eyes downward, then sheepishly looks up as she murmurs, "Yes."

"I can smell you. Your cunt makes my mouth water." Hands on hips, she stands a few feet away from me, her wet crotch wafting in the air, her pungent scent staining my senses. "You nasty little whore! I see you need a good spanking."

I pat my legs.

Without a word, she knows. I grin to myself as she slowly walks toward me—one heeled foot in front of the other as if she's walking a tightrope. When she reaches me, she bends over my lap. I flip up her skirt, and catch another whiff of her clean, musky scent. I run my hand over her smooth, round caramel ass, caressing her skin. My mouth waters, staring at her mesmerizing ass. She grinds herself against me.

I slap her ass. "Don't you grind that nasty, little pussy on me, you naughty slut!"

She groans.

I slap her ass again. My palm slapping against her beautiful ass sends jolts of electricity through me, and a pulsing need pounds between my legs. I feel a warmth flooding through her heating her skin, her ass.

Whap!

She moans, lifting and wiggling her hips, then spreading her legs. She wants me to touch her. Wants me to see, feel, how wet she is. She purrs as she lies over my lap and I smack her ass and thighs, soft and sensual at first, then gradually building up to fast, hard strikes, causing her ass cheeks to heat.

"Oooooh, yes…mmmm…yes, spank it…"

She raises her ass higher. Begs for more. And I give it to her, faster and harder.

Pop!

Pop!

Whap!

Her ass cheeks bounce as I alternately smack each cheek, building a rhythm that mimics the sounds of a drum. She screams out. Tells me how hot and tender and huge her ass feels.

I plant a hand on the back of her head to hold her in place. She moves a hand in attempt to slip it between her legs.

Whap!

"Bad little whore!"

Whap!

"You don't move unless I tell you to, understand?"

Whap!

"Yes…ohhhh, yesssss…"

"Your horny cunt doesn't deserve to be touched. Leave it empty and starved…for now."

"Oh, god, please," she begs and whimpers. "Let me touch my pussy."

I smack her ass, again.

"No."

"Mmmmm…my pussy's throbbing…*please*…"

Whap!

"Please, what?"

"Let me touch…" *Whap!* "…uh, my pussy…"

"What about that bad, nasty pussy? You want it paddled?"

"Yes! Mmmm…paddle my clit…paddle my pussy…"

I forcefully bring my hand down across her ass in rapid succession. "Beg for it, Miss Creamy! Tell me what a whore you are for the paddle."

Whap!

Whap!

"Oh, god, yes! I'm such a dirty, fucking whore for it, baby. My pussy loves the paddle. It gets so wet for it. I want you to fuck me with the handle, then paddle me good."

I spank her ass harder, feeling my own body heat and my juices flow through me. My anxious pussy feels closed in and bound by panties that have already seeped up between my puckered, wet pussy lips, and the constraints of my leather pants. My whole body tingles excitedly and comes alive by the vibrations caused each time my hand comes down on her now red and bruised ass. Every time my hand smacks down, Miss Creamy rises up to meet it, eagerly. She grinds her hips against my leather-covered thigh.

I can tell she's on the edge. Each slap, each grind, bringing her closer to climax. She is moaning and groaning and begging, winding her hips. "Please," she whimpers desperately. "My pussy needs it…I need it… Oh, god, I'm coming…"

Her hips crash against my thigh as my hand comes down on her ass. She screams. Her body shudders. She is panting. Her breathing becomes erratic. I smile, plunging two fingers into her cunt. She gasps. She's sopping wet. Her slick lips suck in my fingers. Finger-fuck her spot until her body is convulsing again. I take her to the edge, then swiftly pull out, leaving her drenched cunt vacant.

"Now you're ready for the paddle," I whisper, offering her my cum-slick fingers. She feasts on them, then slowly lifts up from my lap. Her pussy has left a pool of juices over my legs, leaving the leather shiny and wet.

Without prompting, Miss Creamy leans into my lap, extends her tongue, and laps at the wet leather, cleaning up her cum, then struts over toward the red leather chaise across the other end of the room. I smile lovingly at the emblazoned handprints on her ass; her caramel-colored skin now crimson.

I eye her as she lies back, spreads her thighs, then bends her knees back. I lick my already wet lips. My excitement, the heated scent of her lust, and the feel of the paddle in my hand, pushes my own libido into overdrive.

I stand up. My cunt is still pounding from this morning's sex-athon with Sasha. We had started our passionate lovemaking session around three A.M., in the sixty-nine position with Sasha beneath me, licking around my plump, thick lips, then using her fingers to pull me open and dart her tongue in and out of my slit as I covered the mouth of her pussy with my own hot mouth. I used my jaw muscles, feverishly sucking and pulling, trying to suck the cream out of her. I wanted her to shoot into my mouth, the way I was shooting into hers. A rushing gush of wetness flooding her mouth, coating her lips and chin as her tongue unerringly found my clit, and began lapping and nibbling it, her hands stroking between my legs, spreading my wetness over my lips, a thumb pressing into my ass. I shuddered, coming again.

Mmmm…

An early morning romp of pussy eating, followed by intense fucking is how Sasha and I usually start our day, with either me dominating and her being the submissive or vice versa. Our hungry need to please shows in the way we stroke and ride and grind each other.

This morning, after almost two hours of oral pleasure, we ended our last round with my legs up over her shoulders and her pushing nine thick inches of a golden brown cock into my over-flowing sea of juices. I offered up my beautiful fat pussy for her pleasure, and she reveled in the sight of it before plunging in. I gasped and dug my nails into her back as she pounded my insides. Her breasts pressed against mine, she grinded her hips into my bucking pelvis, my tight cunt gripping the dildo as it pistoned in and out, my pussy lips sucking along its length. Her dick plunged in deep and fast.

"Oh, god, yes! Fuck me! Fuck me!"

I was so turned on—as I always am—by the slick sound and smell of my deliciously fucked cunt caused by Sasha's dick hitting my spot just so.

She cupped the underside of my ass and rammed in and out of me, fucking me faster and deeper with each thrust, the slap of skin, the squishy-sounds of juices coupled with grunts of lust egged her on until her lusciously thick strap-on inched out of my cum-wetted cunt and finally found its way into my ass, stretching it open.

I gasped. Sasha fucked me. Slowly at first, pushing deeper with each thrust. When she cupped my left breast, then bit down on my nipple, a piercing heat shot through me, causing my asshole to open wider and wetter. I was burning with desire, welcoming Sasha's thrusts into my ass as I breathed in shallow gasps.

And as quickly as she had invaded my ass, she swiftly attacked my pussy with a thick, veiny, ten-inch flesh-colored dildo, ramming it into my soppy hole. "Oh, god, yes! Mmmph...oooh, oooh, ooooh...uh...yes, yes, yes..."

"You love it in your ass?"

"Yes!"

"You love both of your holes fucked?"

I grunted. I was being fucked speechless. Sasha knows my body well. Knows how to deliver the right amount of pain to take me over the edge. She rhythmically worked the dildo and strap-on in me, causing me to grab at her breasts, pull them into my mouth and ravish them, licking and sucking and biting down on her nipples.

Both holes stuffed and overheated, my clit burned and sent sparks shooting through my asshole. I came again and again and again. Screaming out Sasha's name, my nails raking along her back. She groaned and grunted, rolling off of me, leaving my asshole gaping. I pushed the dildo out of my pussy, then impulsively ran my tongue up and down the big realistic-looking phallus, savoring my tangy flavor.

She smiled at my dazed look, then inched up on her forearms. "Well, I guess I better get ready to catch my flight." She was heading back to her home in Santa Monica for three weeks.

As an executive of a major print ad firm with offices in both New York City and Los Angeles, her job affords her the luxury of being bi-coastal. This arrangement, our long distance relationship, is perfect. I have a lover who satisfies every ounce of my being and I am able to cater to the needs of my clients without her ever knowing.

"Oh no, you don't," I said, reaching for her and pulling her back onto the bed. "We're not done, yet."

Our eyes locked. "Oh, you want more?"

I grinned, twisting her left nipple and pinching her clit simultaneously. She gasped. "I always want more."

Four

I bat my lashes. Blink away the sweet memory of this morning and take in the view before me. In anticipation, I lick my lips at the image of Miss Creamy's thighs spread open and wide. My pussy growing wetter at the sight of her, I sweep my eyes over her shivering body. She lets out a low moan as her gaze locks on the paddle in my hand as I reach her.

"Look at that horny cunt all ready for the paddle." I twist her clit.

"Uhhh."

I lean in, lick the nectar that begins to trickle out from her slit, savoring her tasty juices. I lick her again, then gently pat her clit with the paddle. Another moan escapes her mouth. My pointed tongue swipes her slit. Flicks her clit. She whimpers as I pat her clit with the paddle again. "Look at your dripping pussy." She arches her hips to meet the paddle as I slide it over her puckering lips. She groans. "Is this what you want?"

"Yes."

I push the edge of the paddle into her wet hole, teasing it with the tip, pulling out, then pressing it up to her mouth. I rub the paddle over her pouty lips. She opens her mouth, and sucks. "Yeah, that's right. Suck it like it's a dick coated in your cum."

She sucks and moans and licks all around the edges of the paddle, her hand inching its way down into her slick valley. I give her a few minutes to stir the heat in her cunt, fingers disappearing deep, then reappearing wet and sticky.

I imagine the inner lining of her soft and tender pussy milking her fingers, her swollen inner lips hungrily sucking and pulling them inward as if it were a drooling, toothless mouth sucking a dick.

I reach for her wrist, pulling her hand away from her sex, then wrapping my own salivating mouth around her fingers.

Whap!

A moan bursts from Miss Creamy's throat, the stinging pain catching her off-guard as the paddle comes down over her cunt. "Ooooohhhhh! Ooooohhhhh!"

I can smell it. There's a huge ball of intense fire, seemingly, burning somewhere deep inside her. The opening of her cunt seems to glow in its heat. *Whap!* The paddle delivers a burst of pain and pleasure. "Uhhhhh...oooohhhhh..."

Whap!

She gasps. Then yelps out. But she doesn't try to get up or tell me to stop.

Whap!

I paddle her again, and again, heating her hole real good. She stuffs her fist in her mouth to keep from screaming. Tears spring from her eyes. Her pussy grows wetter with every blow. Each time the paddle strikes her naked cunt I'm closer to coming in my damp panties.

She grunts and growls. A gush of sweet, steamy juice shoots out of her. Her tight, hard-cumming cunt contracting, pushing out in rhythmic spurts a steady flow of liquid pleasure. She's gasping and clutching her chest, gulping in air as her orgasms possess her body.

"Ohgodohgod...ooh, ooh, ooh...uhh, uhh, uhh...I can't...stop... cum...ming...aaahh, aaahh, aaahh...mmmmmmm..."

"Yeah, that's it, Miss Creamy...let it all go... Let your pussy flow."

She cries out. Her body starts convulsing as my tongue disappears abruptly into her erupting inferno, zigzagging over her clit, then back into her burning sex. I flick my tongue rapidly over her clit. Plant my mouth over her sex and capture her essence as her arousal coats my tongue and seeps into my mouth. I lick and suck her well-paddled, cum-filled cunt until I've slurped out every delicious, naughty ounce of her hot cream.

Another twenty minutes, Miss Creamy saunters out the door basking in the afterglow of a good lashing and a deep, probing tongue-sweep.

Five

"You've reached the Cum Master. How can I help you cum today?" I say into the phone, glancing at the caller ID. I recognize the telephone number and to whom it belongs to without hearing her raspy voice. It's Invoice #3323, Kenyatta Lambers aka Slick Heat.

She's a photographer's dream—smooth, ebony skin wrapped around a sleek body, tall and thin with delicate, peach-sized breasts, a tight waist, and a high, round ass. Her angular face, narrow cheekbones, slanted green eyes, slender nose, and perfectly white, straight teeth add to her exotic look.

"By whipping my pussy," she coos into the phone. Kenyatta, I mean, Slick Heat, enjoys the feel of a leather belt stinging her bare sex. Each time the belt kisses her clit prickly heat sprouts out through her pores and causes her cunt to hiss. The cutting sensation and torturous mixture of pain and pleasure bring her the sweetest agony. One she continues to chase. The euphoria, it's become her drug, her addiction.

I think back to the first time she hired my services, over a year ago. She had waltzed into my loft with a fiery gleam in her eyes, wearing a simple, yet elegant, black tunic dress and a pair of orange six-inch platform stilettos. And tangerine lipstick coated over her luscious lips. She wore her black hair bone-straight with blunt-cut bangs and it fell past her slender shoulders. She was breathtakingly beautiful.

Seeing this gorgeous, runway-ready creature one would be none the wiser to ever suspect that beneath all the glamour this nearly six-foot-three (when in six-inch heels) bombshell loves the heated magic of a leather belt welting her bald cunt, searing her clit, and twisting out painfully scrumptious orgasms.

During her initial session, I had her sit—as I do all my first-time clients—in one of my sex slings, the one with the stirrups. I buckled her ankles, forcing her shapely legs wide open. The smoothly waxed lips of her cunt were already shiny from the juices seeping out of her. She was anxious and wantonly ready.

"Are you always so wet?" I asked, brushing my knuckles up against her clit, then across the seam of her lips. Her heart-shaped pussy was one of the prettiest I'd ever whipped.

She licked her painted lips and squirmed in her seat. "Yes. My pussy stays wet."

"And what would you like me to do to it, huh?"

"Whip my wet pussy until it burns." I slid the belt over her clit, teasing her. She groaned, aching for the sweet stinging kiss of leather. She arched her back and thrust upward; eager to greet the swift blows I was about to deliver. She gripped the chains above her head, twisting them around her wrists as I slowly began to heat her cunt. Blow after blow, she let out a garbled cry, her breath strangled in the back of her throat. Each strike of the leather bit into her pussy, her pinkish clit stubbornly erect, causing it to clench.

"Oh, yes! Whip it! Uh!"

I lifted the belt over my head and brought it down against her flesh, how she liked it—hard, swift, and calculated.

Whap!

Whap!

Whap!

Lash after lash, her puffy cunt wept, bringing forth more wetness, more jolts of electricity; more surges of heat; each strike reverberating in her cunt, ricocheting off the lining of her walls.

"Yes! Yes! Yesssssssss!" she cried out as I swatted her breasts, her swollen nipples sensitive and erect, with the belt. She arched into the lashes, offering up more of her pussy. She strained to keep from screaming out her safe word. She gave into the pain. Gave into the pleasure. And came.

Slick Heat moans into the phone, snapping me from my reverie. "Oooh, I'm so horny. It's been weeks since my last session. And I'm long overdue."

I smile. "Yes, you are. And you know I aim to deliver you your greatest pleasures one lick at a time."

"Oooh, yes. I know. I have the rest of the day free. When can you fit me in? The sooner the better."

I glance through my appointment book, the one I keep hidden and locked. "I'll see you at four."

"See you then," she says excitedly.

My clit tingles at the thought of beautiful strong women with secret punishment fantasies. The lascivious sound of leather and suede lashes stroking, cutting deep into their pussies. The animalistic growls and grunts and groans of horny, needy, powerful women who—with the strike of a paddle, or hairbrush, or flogger—submit to pain, give in to pleasure.

Six

Four P.M., Slick Heat saunters through the sliding doors, stylishly dressed in a pair of faded low rider jeans and a white gauzy blouse that reveals her flat stomach and hangs over her smooth shoulders. The diamond stud in her navel sparkles beneath the edge of her shirt. As always, she's in a pair of gorgeous strappy heels. Six-inch, I'm sure. Her towering presence, the light scent of her perfume, commands attention. My attention. And I eagerly wait to give it all to her.

I smile, standing up to greet her. Today I am wearing a chain halter-top and matching thong with a pair of wet-look latex leggings, latex gloves, and seven-inch platform heels. She eyes the sway of my breasts and chains as I reach for her hand.

"Come. Let's get started."

"I can't wait," she says seductively, allowing me to lead her by the hand. Today, I will take her into The Chamber. I have converted one of my three bedrooms into my personal dungeon, complete with faux rock panels covering the walls, recessed lighting, soft gray carpet, and thick window treatments to shut out light. Hanging from the walls are a pair of stainless steel daggers, several whips, and two pairs of handcuffs. Several pieces of erotic bondage artwork are situated on each wall to add to the sexy, sensual, yet sinister, aura of the room.

Over in the left corner is a multi-position Saint Andrews Cross—

an X-shaped support with restraints for the wrists and ankles—
that can, in a matter of seconds, change from a cross to an inversion
table to a spanking stand. It is for my more daring clients who
crave being strapped to the cross, then whipped and strapped
unforgivingly.

A portable stockade, spanking stand with red leather padding,
a bondage box, as well as a black leather bondage chair—with its
fully adjustable back, removable arm boards, and multiple bondage
points—are situated about the room to add to the theme.

And for the final touch, a four-thousand-dollar steel bondage
bed, with an adjustable sling support system, is centered in the
middle of the room. Oh, how I love this room.

I unlock the door, then step in with Slick Heat on my heels.
She takes in the décor. Her eyes gleaming with excitement as she
walks deeper into the room. "I love being in this room." Her hand
glides over the St. Andrew's Cross, then touches the manacles
that hang from the arms.

"Remove your clothes," I instruct, shutting the door behind us
and turning on the recessed lights.

I eye her as she kicks off her heels, pulls her blouse off over her
head, then shimmies out of her jeans. She peels off her silk panties,
unveiling her slick petals. I lick my lips, eager to inhale her scent.

"Toss me your panties."

She grins, tossing them in the air. I step in and catch the delicate
fabric with one hand, pulling them up to my nose. The crotch area,
damp and scented in her warm musk, causes my own cunt to pucker.

Her aroused pussy, excited by her sinful desires, always smells
so sweet.

"Are you ready for your lashings?"

"Mmmhmm. I've been ready all day."

I smile.

For today's session I have decided to use the Saint Andrew's Cross. And she is pleased, so very pleased. I can tell she is already on the edge of a climax as I take each of her wrists and place them in the padded restraints. Then I bend down and do the same for her ankles. After I have her strapped in, I slowly flip the cross up. She's now upside down, her ankles and wrists bound; her legs spread apart. Her cunt and clit are wide open and ready. She is already soaked. Her shaved cunt dripping like a faucet.

I look down into her wanting, powerless eyes. Ease two fingers inside her pussy.

She moans.

She is hot. She wants to be touched. Wants the thudding ache in the center of her cunt to be caressed away. Not by fingers, not by tongue. But by lashes of a belt.

I pull my fingers out of her. Kneel down and force my wet fingers into her mouth. She licks them without direction. Her tongue thrusts out. She greedily sucks my fingers in.

"Yeah, that's it, greedy little spoiled bitch. Suck my fingers clean." I reach up with my other hand and reach between her thighs. She is wetter than ever.

I grin, pulling my fingers from her mouth, standing up.

She whimpers.

Anticipation is a powerful aphrodisiac.

She knows how magical the belt is. How it hangs limp, then comes alive. Lash, by lash, the heat of the leather, the thrash. The end of the thick buckle wrapped around my hand. The sound it makes as it's whirled into the air, then brought down, slashing into her aroused sex. The jolt of electricity that shoots through her after her cunt has been set afire over and over.

I tease her with the leather. Lay it over her sex, lightly tap it, then slide the length of the belt over it. She moans.

I taunt her with it. Popping her clit with it in rapid succession, stopping, then starting back again.

Pop!

Pop!

Pop!

"Ohhhh, yess!"

Her moans rise in pitch with each smack of the leather against her sex, gasping with each strike.

Seven whacks in a row, that's what I deliver. Seven sharp lashes of leather against her clit cause her head to thrash and her eyes to snap shut. She bites down on her bottom lip.

I watch as she breathes through her nose. As her breasts rises and falls, her heart practically thumping out of her chest.

Her pussy still throbs. And, before she can collect her thoughts, before she can prepare for the next blow, the belt is slicing back between her thighs, crashing into her cunt again and again. Wetness splashing out against the leather.

She gasps.

She whimpers.

Slick Heat wants more.

She begs for it. "Oh please. Mmmm."

The belt strikes again, sweet pain coursing through every nerve ending. She thrust her hips upward, welcoming its stinging contact. This time, she screams out.

This time, tears well up in her eyes.

This time, she is lust-crazed.

She's moaning and groaning and grunting. Her hips winding, her pelvis thrusting, her orgasm rampages through her.

I walk over to the closet, sliding back its door. Inside is a six-drawer dresser. The first drawer is where I keep lubes, creams, scented oils, condoms, and other essentials. The remaining five drawers house an assortment of wooden hairbrushes, paddles, vibrators and dildos. Along the wall hangs an array of floggers, ball gags, and harnesses. Everything neatly lined in order.

I pull open the first drawer and open a tin, popping three Altoids mints into my mouth, then shut the door, walking back over to Slick Heat. She is still whimpering and winding her hips from the lashings to her sex. She looks up at me with pleading, teary eyes.

I marvel at the beautiful welts that have puckered up beneath her smooth skin. Her skin the canvas, the belt the paintbrush. Her whipped pussy is a masterful work of art. I lick the drool that has gathered in the corners of my lips. Her tender clit swollen and throbbing, her wet cunt crying out for me to fuck her, fill her, stretch her.

"I'm going to soothe your pussy now." I rub a finger over her slit. She moans. Thrusts her hips upward. "You want me to make sweet love to your stinging cunt?"

"Yes! Mmmm…"

Pushing forward, I kiss the tip of Slick Heat's clit, then kiss around it before placing my mouth over her juicy sex. She moans loudly from the added heat in my mouth and the tingly sensation it causes. Her clit is rigid against my tongue. I massage it with my lips, then suck it deep into my mouth, slicking it with spittle.

"Oh, yes…oh, yes…uhhhh…uhhh…"

"You like that, huh?"

Her hips thrust upward. "Yes."

I fuck her with my tongue. She moans and cries out, pleasure rising from within. Her engorged cunt, slick and on fire, is beating as I lap her clit, then suck on it harder and faster.

Finally I give her what she's aching for, what her cunt thirsts for. A ten-inch black dildo. I grip it by its smooth, faux balls and carve it deep into her pussy, probing her, stroking her, fucking all the way into her while swirling my tongue over her clit. She bucks and whimpers, then lets out a loud groan. I fuck her harder, faster. Her pussy swallows in every inch, tip to base buried deep into her. I slowly pull out, then slam back in. Pull out, slam back in. The slit of her pussy stretches open wide. I can almost feel it pulling and gripping and sucking the dildo as I fuck her with it.

It doesn't take long before Slick Heat comes and cries out, her head thrashing to and fro. Five minutes later, she leaves the confines of her padded restraints, liberated and carefree. Her secret cravings fed, her thirst for the forbidden quenched…until the next time.

Seven

Three weeks later, I awaken to the sound of Art of Noise. "Moments in Love." And to the smell of bacon and fresh roasted hazelnut coffee. I breathe in the aroma and sound, stretching and yawning. Then shut my eyes closed again, lying still in bed, inhaling. Exhaling. Inhaling, again. I take in the music, the smells. And a smile sweeps across my lips. My beautiful Sasha's back in town. I live for the sight of her, for the feel of her touch.

Instantly my pussy tingles and I am compelled to touch it, to tease it, to bring it to the edge of pleasure, then dangle an orgasm over the cliff, denying it release. I let out a moan as a soft tremble washes over me as my hands glide over my breasts, fingertips lightly brushing over my nipples.

My hand dips between my legs as salacious memories and pure lust flower in loins, forbidden urges satisfied with fierce love-making. My fingers settle over my pussy lips, then between the wet folds. With my other hand, I pinch my swollen, sensitive nub between my forefinger and thumb, gasping, massaging and kneading it, running my fingers in tiny circles over it.

In my mind, I imagine it is Sasha's hand over my mound, her fingers teasing and playing in my overheated pussy. I spread my quivering legs wider and arch my back as I thrust my middle finger deep. I open, then close my eyes, blinking images of Sasha slipping a single wet finger in and out of my slick opening. I use my thumb and flick my clit.

A cry catches in my throat.

I thrust two fingers deep.

Then a third.

I take in a deep breath.

Everything about Sasha makes me ache with hunger and need. She allows me to give into my primal cravings. And I allow her the same. She fuels my rampant need, feeds my every desire. I lick my lips, fondling and toying with my clit. I am swollen and throbbing and sopping wet.

I breathe in another deep breath.

I can almost smell Sasha's warm, spicy pussy. Can almost taste its sweet pungency. I imagine her hips hovered over my face, the bud of her flower poking out from its hood, erect and ready. She lowers her cunt to my mouth, my probing tongue pushing into her slickness as her muscles are pulling me in, welcoming me into her warmth.

I let out a soft moan at the thought, spreading open my labia and plunging two fingers into the heat and wetness. I push them in and out of me until I can hear the slick sound and smell my own arousal. Heated by slippery fingers that have found my spot, steam curls out of my cunt, swirling around my clit. And when I can no longer take it, I reach under my pillow and pull out my Wonderland vibrator, turning it on low speed and gasping the minute the vibrating tip touches my clit.

I close my eyes, whimpering softly, as I massage my clit. I stroke my clit over and over, bringing myself close to orgasm. "Oh, god, yes…" I spread my legs wider and slide the tip of the vibrator into my wet pussy. Its vibrations ricochet against my inner walls. "Ohhhh, yessss…" I slide the vibrator into my smooth pussy, slowly at first, then with more urgency, pushing it up into me as far as it will go. "Oh, yes…mmmm…ooooh…" The vibrations pulse through my body. "Oh, god, yes…"

My orgasm crashes over me. Endless waves of intense pleasure soak the sheets beneath me. Several minutes later, when my breathing and heartbeat steady, I blink my bleary eyes a few times, focusing on the digital clock. 8:47 A.M.

Enigma plays. "Principles of Lust" pours out through the surround sound. I hum its tune in my head, climbing out of bed and heading for the bathroom to freshen up.

Ten minutes later, barefoot and naked, I descend the winding staircase, making my way into the kitchen. Sasha's hot gaze roves over my body as I enter the kitchen. "My, don't you look scrumptious." She's wearing a red Essence Festival apron over a white mini-skirt and form-fitting blouse.

I greet her with a kiss. "Good morning."

"I hope you're hungry," she says, wrapping an arm around my waist, then cupping my ass. "I know I am." She wiggles her eyebrows up and down.

I smile. "I'm famished."

My hand slides between her legs. And then my lips are on hers. Her tongue explores my mouth, with urgency, with a longing need, that matches my own. She tastes like Wrigley's Cobalt chewing gum. I press my pussy into her. She squeezes a chunk of my ass, biting my bottom lip, and then her mouth moves from mine down the side of my neck, along my collarbone, leaving a trail of warm kisses before moving to my breasts. Her mouth travels over my left nipple, sucking it harder than it already is before traveling over to the other one. Her right hand releases my ass cheek and slides between my legs. She cups my pussy, then allows her wandering fingers to discover what I already know. I am soaking wet.

She grins. "Looks like someone's excited to see me. Or did you start the party without me?" She lowers her voice to a hushed whisper, the heat of her gaze scorching over my body and turning up the heat in my already heated cunt.

"Both."

And now she is kissing me again. Her tongue is hot and lush, swirling around my own. I grind into her. And she grinds back. Then after a few more minutes of deep, tongue-probing kisses, she pulls away and holds my gaze as she removes her hand from between my legs and places her two fingers into her mouth. There is a feral look in her eyes as she watches me watch her suck away my juices from her fingers.

"Let's eat," she says, stepping back.

"I'd rather eat you."

"And you shall. But first I want you to eat what I've—" She goes to walk away and I reach for her. Gather her hands behind her back and hold her wrists together with one hand. My warm breath is on her ear.

"So glad you're home." I nip her ear. One of her weak spots. "I've missed you."

"Me, too," she manages to say, wriggling.

I breathe her in. "Mmm. You smell so sweet." I kiss the back of her neck, nuzzle her earlobes, then slide my hand up her skirt. She shivers, her cantaloupe-sized breasts rising and falling with each anticipated breath she takes. I slowly inch my hand up her thigh, teasing her with whisper-soft-kisses along the side of her neck.

"God, you're so beautiful," I murmur against her skin. "My pussy missed you."

"And mine missed you. But we need to…" My fingers reach the edge of her panties. The French-cut cotton panties that hug her beautiful, smooth ass like a second skin.

"I wanna bury my fingers, my tongue, into your soft, wet pussy. You want that, baby? You want me to pull your panties to the side and fuck your hungry hole with my fingers?"

She grinds her ass into me. "Mmm. Stop teasing me."

"I'm not teasing you."

She spins out of my grasp, slapping my hands away. "Yes, you are. Now let's eat. We'll have all day for play."

I roll my eyes, sucking my teeth, then groan, begrudgingly pulling out a chair. I pause from taking a seat, thinking about the wet stain that's sure to soak into the cushion if I do not place something over it. "You have my pussy so wet." I smack her on the ass as I brush past her, walking out into the pantry.

She laughs. "Don't blame that on me."

"Oh, and you're not wet?" I ask, walking back out into the kitchen holding a thick white towel in my hand.

She glances away from the stove, gazing at me over her shoulder. "I'm always wet for you, boo. Thought you knew."

I wink at her, smiling. "I love me some you." I lay the towel across the cushion of the chair, then sit down. "Now what you got to eat that's better than eating you?"

"Girl, hush. Aside from this breakfast I made for you, there's nothing better than you eating me, than *me* eating *you*. But that's beside the point."

"Pussy's the breakfast of champions, sweetie," I tease. "Thought you knew."

She laughs, walking over to the counter for two plates. "I know you better eat before this food gets cold." She returns placing one plate in front of me, then sits the other on the placemat next to me, pulling out her chair and sitting. She's prepared vegetable omelets, turkey bacon, and potatoes with green peppers and onions. My stomach growls.

"How you spoil me. I don't know what I've done to deserve you."

"Well, maybe I should help you figure it out." She leans over and kisses me lightly on the lips. "Eat."

I smile at her. "I'd rather eat you."

"And so you shall. But not until after you've eaten all of your breakfast."

I laugh, lifting a forkful of potatoes to my mouth. We steal sly, flirty glances at one another, alternatively feeding each other from our plates until we've pretty much cleaned our plates. I'm ready to make love and cuddle, but Sasha's obsessive need to have the kitchen clean before doing anything else will prevent her from letting go, from spontaneously fucking me. So I get up and help her with the task at hand so we can move onto more exciting things, like me having my way with her.

"Laila…" she breathes.

"Sssh." I press my lips to hers, gaze into her eyes, then take a step back. "Take your clothes off."

"Right here in the kitchen?"

"Yes, right here." She suggests we take our play into the shower so that she can shower off the grime from the red-eye flight she was on. "That won't be necessary," I say, walking over to the island counter and pulling open the middle drawer, removing a wooden spoon. From another drawer I pull out a thick brown silicone dildo I keep hidden there in case I am in the mood for a quick fuck in the kitchen, like now. Dildos and butt plugs and other sex toys are tucked in miscellaneous drawers and closets throughout my loft.

Sasha's eyes twinkle with anticipation as she eyes the wooden utensil and dildo in my hand. A sly grin spreads across my lips. "I want to fuck you right here. I've missed you, Sasha."

"I've missed you, too." She watches me watch her as she slowly removes her apron, then her blouse and bra. Next, she steps out of her skirt. She leaves on her purple panties and her heels. "My pussy has missed you, as well."

"Then you won't deny me."

I watch her lick her lips. Her eyes darken with arousal. "No. Never." She slips a hand between her legs.

I take a step toward her. Then another. Then another until I have her back pressed against the kitchen's cool tile wall. My mouth brushes her ear and she shivers, turning her face until her lips meet mine. She opens her mouth to me. She wraps her arms around my waist. My tongue slips in as I draw her in closer, one hand closing on her hip, the other around the back of her neck. The urgent press of her pussy against my pelvis tells me she is as hot and wet and needy as I am.

I bite her neck lightly. She moans. My hands smooth over her ass, touch over the curve of her hips, then cup her breasts. Her nipples go hard as I alternately lick around each one, grazing them with my teeth. I pinch them between forefinger and thumb, then lick them, all over again, before sucking each one into my mouth.

Sasha's moans as her hand eases its way down my body. I gasp when she finds her way to my treasure. She feels the wetness that has gathered between my thighs. I gently bite her bottom lip, and then move mouth from hers down the side of her neck, licking and kissing until I find her spot slightly above her collarbone. Sasha's fingers moving steadily over my protruding, erect clit, then to my slit. My breath catches.

"Oh, yes. Mmm…"

I let one hand snake down into her damp panties, while the other teases her nipple. We are both moaning now as we purposefully run our fingers up and down the slick folds of each other's cunts.

I dip a finger into hers.

She dips a finger into mine.

Then two, then three. Buried to the knuckles.

Our lips lock, our tongues dance around the others. We groan softly and begin pumping our fingers in and out of each other's pussy, grazing each other's clit just enough to bring the other to the edge of a climax. We have become seduced to rhythm and the sound of our hands and fingers.

Sasha is so hot and wet and slippery.

So am I.

We stop kissing and hold each other's gaze while our fingers continue to explore our cunts. There are no words needed. She sees it my eyes. And I see it in hers. The feral look of want and need and heated passion.

I slip my hand out of her panties and put my cum-soaked fingers to her pouty lips. She licks around them, her luscious tongue cleaning each finger clean as she continues stirring in my dripping cunt. My husky groans turn sharp with lust and desire as she pulls her own fingers out of my soppy wet heat, spreads my spicy juices over my lips, then licks them, slowly trailing her tongue over my bottom lip. My fingers sink back into her sticky center. Then hers back into mine. Our thumbs flick back and forth over each other's clit. I fling my head back and explode. My juices soak her fingers and my pussy clenches and unclenches.

A few seconds later, Sasha is climaxing as well. Her sweet moans boomerang around the kitchen.

"Y-you like that?" I whisper in her ear, on the verge of climaxing myself.

She shudders beneath my hand, clutching my fingers. "Y-yes."

I gasp, biting down on my bottom lip as another wave of heat erupts throughout my body.

Another second, and Sasha is pulling her fingers out of me, placing them back up to my mouth. I part my lips and she slips them in. She moans as I suck her fingers. I remove my fingers from her pulsing warmth. And now she is sucking on my fingers.

When she has finished cleaning my fingers with her mouth and tongue, I kiss her long and deep, then tell her I want her on the granite counter. Tell her I'm ready to serve her, to feast on her. I slap her on the ass with the wooden spoon as she cups my pussy, then walks over to the counter. She lifts herself up on to it, then leans back and parts her legs. This is how she will give herself to me. Her pussy naked and exposed for my greedy pleasure. She knows better than anyone that I can spend hours suckling and nibbling her, luxuriating her soft moans and gasps.

As I saunter over to her, my lips curled seductively, I can feel my own juicy pussy pulsing—nectar slowly trickling out, then sliding down the insides of my thighs. "You ready for your tongue-fuck, baby?"

"You know I am." Her hand slips over her smooth mound, she rubs over it slowly, taunting her clit. My lust-filled gaze connects with the burning fire in her brown eyes. "I can't wait to feel your hot, wet tongue all over my pussy; all over my clit."

"Be careful what you ask for, my sweet love," I tease, placing the dildo beside her, lifting her right foot and licking the ball of her foot before sucking in her big toe. I then slowly make my way over to her pinky toe. She gasps. I do the same to her left foot. She grabs the edges of the counter as I lick up the back of her calves, then kiss the inside of her thighs.

"Mmm…"

I nudge her legs wide, grasp her hips, then pull her to the edge of the counter. I dip my head between her legs and lap up her tangy juice. Sasha moans as my tongue and lips move over her.

"Oooh, baby, your sweet pussy tastes so good," I murmur against her sticky wetness.

I look up at her. Her lids are half-closed, her eyes glazed over in a fiery haze of lust. "You want more?"

"Y-yes," she rasps, her voice thick with passion. "Give it to me, baby."

I resume lapping her juicy pussy, then sink my tongue into her drenched slit. Her inner heat burns my tongue as I suck her clit voraciously. I tease her toward an orgasm, then pull away, leaning up and pressing my mouth to hers. We kiss, our tongues parting starving lips, the passion between us surging like a swelling sea. And I know—without a doubt, with every aching fiber in my entire body, that I love her. That Sasha is my life partner. What had started out as simply mutual desire has blossomed into a relationship of burning need, of unadulterated longing, and never-ending want.

"I love you," Sasha pushes out almost breathlessly as if she's read my thoughts.

I reach for her face, cup her cheek, a smile spreading over my cum-coated lips. "I knew I loved you from the moment you whipped my pussy."

"And I loved you more." She pulls me into her, sucking on my lips, tasting herself on me, then slipping her tongue into my mouth. Her body bows as she grabs my shoulders and slowly pushes me downward. "Finish eating my pussy. I wanna come all over your tongue."

She does not need to say more. Her command is my wish. I part her swollen pussy lips. Inhale deeply. Her sweet musky scent engulfs me. I breathe it in like one of my favorite perfumes before licking the tip of her crowning jewel. Her moans embolden me to pull it deeper into my mouth. My mouth latches onto her clit, sucking it lovingly—in long, lascivious pulls—as her hand cradles the back of my head.

She moans again as I swirl my thumb into her wetness. I keep sucking her, bringing her close to orgasm, then pulling back only to have her grind her pussy harder into my mouth.

"Oooh, Laila..." she gasps and starts to come. If her clit were a cock she'd be ramming it down into my neck, coating my throat with her orgasm.

My gaze meets hers with a sly grin as I breathe in the wetness of her pussy. It's smell reminding me of heated rain during a summer storm. "Mmm. I love the way your pussy smells."

She giggles. "Oh, yeah? And what does it smell like?"

"The scent of want, of hungry need." I lean in closer, the tip of my nose practically pressed into her slit, and breathe her in again. Then within seconds, I am pushing the tip of the wooden spoon's handle between her pussy lips, circling her entrance, teasing her, and making her whimper and clench.

I flick my tongue over her clit, looking up at her. "You like that, baby?"

"Yes. Mmmhmm. Give me more." I slide more of the handle into her slit, pulling it all the way out slowly, then pushing it back into the folds of her velvety softness. Sasha throws her head back and moans loudly. I continue spoon-fucking her until her cunt soaks the wooden utensil with its juices. I pull it out, then lift it to my lips and slide it into my mouth. I hold her gaze as I suck the handle clean. Her eyes twinkle in anticipation. She knows what's to come. Her pussy starts to drip.

And then she feels it.

Whap!

The back of the spoon snaps against her wet sex.

Whap!

She yelps.

Whap!

The fire's lit. A sizzling ball of heat rolls around her clit; presses into her pussy as I deliver one blow after the other. I watch as her toes curl, as she arches her back into the sensual flames. "Oh, god, yes…"

I tease her. Taunt her. Torment her. Give her everything she knows I'm good at. Spanking and fucking and licking her pussy. She purrs and begs and gasps as her orgasm ripples through her body and heats her inner walls.

Whap!

Whap!

Whap!

I land three more smacks of the spoon to her reddened, dewy cunt. I lean in and lick her drenched labia, slipping my fingers into her slit. I pull out. Then push my fingertip back in, repeatedly teasing her pussy. Sasha's head whips from side to side and hands open and close. This teasing, this taunting, is sending her over the edge.

"Stop fucking teasing me," she demands, breathlessly. "Give my pussy what it needs."

"Do you surrender to me?" I ask the question, knowingly. Sasha turned over her sexuality to me, surrendered what little inhibitions she may have ever had, the moment she laid eyes on me.

"Yes," she says, rolling her hips. "Now lean in and kiss my pussy, *please*, goddammit. You've teased me long enough." I lean in and close my mouth over her wetness, lapping every so often. "That's it, go slow. Ooooh, yes… Tongue my pussy. Mmmm, yes…like that, yeah. Kiss it. Mmmm. Give it to me good, baby. Oooh, yes… That's right…"

I take her clit in my mouth and lick the tip, then around the edges. Her fingers slid into my hair, fisting, as she grinds deeper into my mouth. Her pussy becomes hotter and wetter to my touch. The more I lick, the hotter it gets. The hotter it gets, the wetter she becomes.

A river of juices flow out of her.

I slip a finger into her hot wetness, curling it to an arch until I find her spot.

"Mmmm…yes, that's it."

I take her pussy deeper into my mouth, wriggling my fingers inside of her, hitting her walls before replacing my fingers with the tip of the wooden spoon. I dip it in and out of her as if I'm preparing to taste a special sauce. Her delightful, creamy cunt sauce.

I slide the spoon down through her crack, over her tight asshole. Then smear my wet fingers over it. I push a finger into her damp tightness. Her anal climax is what will send her over the edge.

She chants, "Yesyesyesyesyes… Mmmmmmmmm…"

She is coming again.

As her clit fattens, the lips of her pussy swell, I slide my tongue into her slit while pushing the dildo into her ass. She gasps. Her chest heaves, her nipples tighten. I push the dildo in and out of her ass. Plunge my mouth over her clit, licking and laving, teasing and taunting. My fingers dig into her hips, plowing my tongue into her thudding cunt.

"Oh, yes…mmmm, fuck…ooooh, yes…my pussy, my ass… uhhh…it feels…so good…"

I pull back, peel open her sticky lips with my wet fingers. "Look at this naughty cunt, all wet and juicy." I smack it with my hand. Then reach for the wooden spoon, again.

Whap!

Whap!
Whap!

She flinches and whimpers flexing her calves as she spreads her legs wider. I smack her cunt, again and again and again. She grits her teeth. Lets out a low growl. Another intense wave of heat shoots through her, I'm sure, as she bites her lip. I give her two more whacks of sweet torture, then bury my face back between her legs. Glide my tongue over and around her clit, then wet lips. I suckle and lick and nibble. Then dive my tongue inside her drenched heat. She grinds her hips and moans, coating my tongue in her sweet, slippery juices as she shudders out a moan of ecstasy.

I lick deeper.

"Ohhhh, " she whispers. "Don't stop. Please. You make my pussy feel so good."

My eyes flicker upward. A fire dances through me, causing my cunt to clench, my juices trickling out of me. Sweet surrender, I think, cupping Sasha's pussy and pushing a finger back into her and curving it upward. My fingertip presses against her spot. And in rushing waves, Sasha comes fast and hard, her body shuddering as her pelvis crashes into the pleasure I have given her.

Who am I?

I am Laila Reynolds.

I am the Cum Master.

Liquid Heat

My pussy juice covers my fingers like a thick heated blanket as I ease them in and out of me; slow and purposefully, at first, then faster, rhythmically, smoothly. The heat of my pussy pulses around my fingers. I can feel my slick, silky walls clenching around my knuckles. I can't believe how wet I am. How hot I am. Then again, that's a lie. I am always wet. Always hot. Wet with want. Hot with need. Wet and hot with hidden desires. Unspeakable desires. Dirty wants. Filthy needs.

Rough and degrading.

Name-calling.

Hair-pulling.

Neck-biting.

Fucking.

Fucking.

And more fucking.

Deep and fast.

Hot and nasty.

Shamelessly misogynist.

Fucking me raw.

In my pussy.

In my ass.

In my throat.

Oh, yes! I love to fuck. Or should I say, be fucked. Love to be dominated—even smacked and choked to get my juices flowing. There's no other way to say it. Fucking, being fucked, is heaven. It's blissful. It's oh, so, delicious! And there is nothing reprehensible about being fucked.

Give it to me filthy!

The dirtier it is, the nastier it is, the better. Period.

And there's nothing more tantalizing than a hot, sweaty, cunt-throbbing, ass-pounding fuck. And, no, not the kind of fuck that involves having my pussy gutted or my asshole stretched by some big, ol' black dingaling attached to some tall, dark, scrumptious thick-bodied man. Oh, no. I'm talking about dirty, sinful fucking.

The kind of fucking that's laden with the smell of sweaty bodies—curvy and firm with beautiful breasts and wet, horny cunts; blanketed in soft moans, feminine wiles, and lascivious growls. The kind of fucking that is filled with reckless abandon and cum-slick fingers.

And that's what I'm masturbating to right now—the thought of being fucked mercilessly, all three holes filled and stretched beyond their limits, by an array of beautiful women of all shapes and sizes—at my desk in my office, behind a locked door.

It's my ritual. Masturbation. Playing in my pussy. Bringing myself to orgasm. Fantasizing about being gang-banged in an abandoned building. Being fucked like a slut. Being tossed around like a two-bit, cum-loving whore. Naked women wearing harnesses and strap-ons with soft skin, full breasts, long tongues, and wet, horny pussies fucking me, choking me, stroking multiple orgasms out of me.

Oh yes…

Tongue hot. Pussy churning. Hard nipples rasping against the fabric of my lace bra, my print jersey shift dress is hiked up over my smooth, round hips as I play out my fantasy in my head.

As an educated, professional woman—who sits on the board of

directors for numerous organizations and has spent practically her entire life fighting for women's rights and speaking out against injustices against women, the fact that I have this desire to be gang-banged rolling around in my head is almost ludicrous. No, it *is* ludicrous.

It's crazy.

But I can't shake it.

The images.

Being dragged behind a dumpster or the back of a dilapidated building or forced into an abandoned car on the side of railroad tracks and fucked mercilessly. The urgency that comes with being fucked multiple times over and over and over by random participants, cunts exploding in my mouth, cocks fucking into my holes. My pussy wet with spit and cum, my throat raw.

In my personal and professional life, I'd never allow myself to be disrespected. Calling me anything other than my name, Ebony Jaleesa Rice—or maybe a pet name if we're intimate—is a no-no. To do so is grounds for getting cursed out from A-Z. Or worse... getting slapped.

But behind closed doors, in the throes of hot, sweaty, shameless sex, I welcome it. Calling me whore, and bitch, and slut. It heats my pussy.

I am a walking contradiction. I should not have these kinds of twisted thoughts. Should not have these kinds of desires. But I do. And the hushed conversations, the whispered giggles, the sideway glances, the accusatory fingers that would sure follow if any part of my secret fantasy came to light all fuel my sick want.

"There she is. Nasty bitch."

"Someone said she was found naked, gagged and bound."

"I heard they fucked her in all three holes."

"I heard she liked it rough."

"I knew that bitch was a whore."

Oooh, yes…mmm…

Yes, I'm a whore! A dirty, filthy, fuck-box!

Oh, fuck me! Fuck my slutty pussy!

I lean back in my leather, high-back chair and spread my legs wider. My ass sinks deeper into the memory foam cushion of the seat as my fingers press against my clit, just so. Then slip into the softness, the slickness between my legs, into the hot slit where warm juices lubricate my pussy and coat its swollen lips.

I feel myself about to be swept up in a thrashing wave of carnal need. The need to feel a tongue in my pussy, a finger in my ass, a cock in my throat; the need to be fucked from the back, fucked sideways, fucked upside down. The burning need to smell pussy, to taste it, juicy and wet; to feel it, hot and horny and pulsing. To have my face pressed into its musky, sweet feminine odor.

To be forced to eat it. To have my face smeared in it. To have my head yanked back and my face slapped. To be thrown to the ground, hands held down, legs snatched open, and one cock-wielding woman after another, fucking me over and over.

Dirty whore!

Slut!

I close my eyes.

I am on the verge of climax, my sex spasming as I delve my fingers deeper into my slippery slit. My mouth is full of saliva, drooling at the thought of my wet tongue laving a clit, feeling it swell against my licking tongue as I slowly suck it between my lips, then use my mouth so that it almost feels as if it's fucking a wet juicy cunt.

In my mind's eyes, my fingers become replaced with the cocks of three women. One woman is beneath me. I am straddling her. The second is in back of me. They are double-penetrating me.

Both of their cocks stretching open my cunt. I am screaming and gaging as the third woman shoves her dick into my mouth, fucking my throat. Woman number three's cock is neither as long as woman number one's nor as huge as woman number two's. But it's thick, and it's one of the prettiest shades of purple I've ever seen. She pulls it from out of my throat, slaps my face and lips with it.

In my head, I grip it with my hand. Take control of it as I take it back into my mouth and massage the tip with my lips as if it were a real dickhead. I imagine it being her clit. Imagine my lips squeezing hard around it, sucking her creamy juices out.

Oooh yessss…

In my mind, I hear myself screaming out in ecstasy, coming in the hungry heat that deluges the inner space between my thighs as my fingers fuck into me, caressing my cunt walls with each stroke.

Mmmm…

My eyes float behind my lids as my free hand slides into the opening of my dress and caresses my right breast. My nipples are so hard, begging to be touched. I pinch it, then roll it between my fingers, finding the exact rhythm that intensifies the sensation.

The air from the vent in the ceiling brushes against my pussy, cooling my slit and causing my clit to stiffen. Even with the chill in the air from the air conditioner, the softly oozing slickness and warmth of my pussy has my body overheating, melting.

I gasp, pumping my hips onto my hand. The more I pump, the more I want, need. I need more than fingers stroking and stretching me. Removing my fingers from my sex, I lick my fingers clean, then reach over into my oversized purse and fumble inside, pulling out a bottle of Pink, one of my favorite lubes, and a thick dark-colored, three-inch silicone butt plug, its bottom flaring out into a curved base.

My pussy floods with liquid heat and my nipples tighten at the thought of the plug being pushed into my ass, greedily and hungrily—my empty, aching holes being filled.

Oooh, yes…

One hand slipping back between my thighs, I rub my clit between my pointer and middle fingers, then dip them back into my wet pussy while using my other hand to slide the butt plug in and out of my mouth, wetting it with spit. I suck it as if it were an enlarged clit, suck it as if it were covered in sweet, decadent chocolate.

Oooh, yes…

I lift my legs. Plant my heeled feet up on the edge of the desk, spreading my thighs wider. I let my hand go from the base of the butt plug, sucking it as if it were a pacifier, while reaching for the lube. I pull my fingers out of my pussy, smearing my juices over my asshole, then remove my butt plug from mouth and squirt a globe of lube over it. I smear some into my hole, the cool lubricant causing my hole to pucker. I poke the spit-lubed plug into my tight ass.

And gasp.

"Oh, yes," I whisper, pushing the plug deeper into me until the base presses up against the rim of my hole. Vivid images of a room full of naked women come into view. Colorful wet panties are tossed up on my desk. And the women are sprawled out around my office, fucking and sucking one another while I look on. I am a voyeur.

My fingers sink into my cunt, getting entranced in wetness and heat and imagination, as thick brown nipples are licked and nipped and sucked into greedy mouths; as soft hands spread open ass cheeks and fingers dig into dark heat; as hairy and shaved and bald mounds are being stroked by wet tongues, the sweet sensual sound of pussy being licked and eaten; as cunt walls are caressed by thick, gliding cocks, being fucked into deep, delicious orgasms.

The explicit visions cause my breath to quicken.

"Oooh, yes...mmmm...fuck them sweet pussies..." I softly murmur, pulling in my bottom lip and using my free hand to pinch my nipples.

I shut my eyes tighter and, surprisingly—well, okay...it's not a surprise since I've had these images of the stuffy bitch two office doors down from me pop in my head twice before. Ellen James—with her smooth, milk chocolate skin, full hips, small waist, and big beautiful ass, clutching her black Mikimoto pearls—comes to view. She's peeking through the slits of the blinds covering the long glass window that looks into my office, watching my fingers click in and out of my wet folds with prying eyes—judgment and curiosity coursing through her body.

I imagine the prudish bitch dropping to her knees in her Joan & David pumps and knit pantsuit, crawling over to me, wildly flapping and flicking her tongue out as she makes her way over to me. She purrs, soft and kittenish. A possessed need in her eyes as she slithers in between my legs.

"Yeah, bitch, eat my pussy," I hear myself sneering, snatching her by the back of her shoulder-length, Brazilian weave and thrusting my pelvis into her face with its high cheekbones and narrow chin.

Snotty bitch!

I smear my pussy all over her lips. Bang my hips into her mouth.

I should fuck your teeth loose, bitch...

Ellen moans and licks my pussy in hungry, wet sounds.

Oooh, yes, lick my pussy...

Frigid bitch!

I giggle at the image of Ellen's full lips being glazed with my cunt oil as I am wiggling another finger, my third, inside of me, lifting my legs and pushing the butt plug in and out of my ass, stretching heat into its tightness.

A gasp catches in the back of my throat.

Ellen and I were both hired on at our firm around the same time. And were in the same training program. From day one of meeting her, I disliked her. She seemed to turn her nose up at everyone, like she was better than everyone else. My first impression of her: She's a phony bitch! And ten years later, nothing's changed. She's still phonier than ever. Still stuck up. And—from what I've overheard around the gossip mill—a bore in bed. An Ice Queen.

Hence her miserably single, lonely, sexless existence.

I imagine yanking her prudish ass up on her feet, spinning her around, bending her over my desk, hiking up her skirt and tugging her underwear down to her ankles. I envision her wearing some basic cotton panties—white, maybe or some other boring color, her cunt hairs neatly clipped.

I visualize myself pulling open her ass, pressing my clit into the center of her crack, my breasts rasping against her back as I lean forward and reach between her legs, playing with her slick cunt as I ride into her ass, my clit swelling with each thrust.

I groan, arching into the pleasure and pressure that shoots through me, flooding my beautiful pussy with liquid heat, pumping hard and fast.

I blink my eyes open, steadying my breathing. My face and body feels flush from the fire still burning inside my pussy. I shut my eyes, lean my head back, and finish riding out the flames.

"Miss Rice, there's a Miss Swan on line one for you," my assistant announces over the intercom, startling me. I quickly compose myself, reluctantly pulling my fingers out of my warm wetness.

A smile eases over my wet lips.

Tamara Swan, with her tall, voluptuous body and large breasts, is my fantasy fuck. Even though we flirt unabashedly with one another, we've not once slept together, yet, in the two years that I've known her. But there have been plenty of nights where I've fucked myself to sleep imagining her thick body pressed against mine and my legs wrapped around her waist as she fucks—what I imagine to be—her large cock, into me.

I take a calming breath. "Thanks, Kristina," I say, clicking over. "This is Ebony Rice speaking." I slide my fingers into my mouth, licking them clean, then reach into my bottom drawer for my box of Wet Ones, tear open two packets, then wipe my hands.

"My, my, aren't we the formal one today." The minute I hear her rich, sultry voice on the other of the line, my pulse quickens. And I feel myself on the edge of another climax. "Did I catch you at a bad time?"

Oh sure. I'm sitting here with a wet pussy and sticky fingers.

I lick my lips. "No, not at all. I was just finishing up lunch."

"Mmmm, yum. What did you have?"

Pussy.

"Wouldn't you like to know," I tease, shifting the phone to my other ear. She lets out a soft chuckle, then tells me she tried reaching me on my cell before calling the office. I reach for my iPhone and see that I have four missed calls, and six text messages. "Well, I'm glad you called. I'm wet with desire hearing your voice."

"Such the flirt."

"I'm serious, Tamara. As much as I enjoy our cat-and-mouse play, why don't we stop toying with one another and go right for the kill. I wish you'd just take me and have your way with me already."

She laughs. "Some things are best left untouched. For now, anyway."

I grin. "So there's still hope."

"Maybe."

"Ugh, you're such the dream-killer."

She chuckles. "Umm. Sweetie, I make dreams come true. So I would wait to hear my reason for calling you before you go labeling me."

"Oooh, do tell, my love." I swivel around in my seat. "You have me tingling with anticipation." I glance out the forty-first floor window of my office, taking in the skyline.

"Oh, my darling Ebony. That's not the only thing that'll be tingling when I finish sharing what I have planned for you. Do you remember the night you shared your fantasy with me?"

My cheeks flush. How could I forget?

I replay the conversation in my head. It was several months ago after a night of drinking Apple Martinis when I blurted it out to her. We'd been out having drinks, sitting at the bar talking about sex and sexuality and the power of fantasies when I admitted to her about my own fantasy.

At first she looked at me like I was half-crazy. "Girl, are you fucking serious?" she had asked, sitting her glass down on the bar. "How could anyone in their right mind fantasize about being gang-raped?"

It was clear then that she had misunderstood me.

"*Gang-raped?* Girl, no. You got it confused. I *said*"—I glanced around the bar, making sure no would overhear me, then lowered my voice—"I want to be gang-*banged*. Big difference."

I explained the differences to her. That the act of wanting to be fucked, consensually, by multiple women is nothing like being forced into having sex, like in a rape-type scenario. I told her how I would never subject myself to something like that.

"But, I definitely would like to experience the act of being degraded. I want to be called whores and sluts and a bunch of bitches. Be told to suck dicks, and to bend over and take it in the ass."

"Whew." She shook her head. "Girl, you're a mess. I can see having a threesome, or even a foursome, but a *gang-bang*...?"

"We all have our secret fantasies. And that's mine. I don't want everyone else fucking each other. I mean, it would be cool if they were sexing each other prior to me getting there. But once I stepped into the room, I'd want all eyes and cocks on me. I want to be the center of attention. The only one getting fucked while everyone else is standing around watching and masturbating, waiting for their turns to gut all three of my holes."

Tamara gulped down the rest of her martini. "Girl, I can't with you tonight. I have heard it all." She flagged over the bartender. "I need me another round." We both stopped talking when the bartender came over to us, then eyed her when she walked off. "She's cute," she said almost as an afterthought.

"She is, but her hands are a bit mannish and she seems a little too masculine for me. I like my women with soft hands and feminine."

She grinned. "With big dicks, huh?"

"No, with *good* dick, and excellent pussy eating skills. She needs to know how to work it."

"Girl, yes. I'm with you on that. She has to know how to work a tongue over a clit and slit." She licked her lips in thought, shaking her head. "Mmmph."

The bartender returned with two more martinis, setting one in front of her and the other in front of me. She walked off as Tamara lifted her glass and took a long sip of her drink, then set it back on the bar. "Okay, enough about pussy eating and women with good dick. Let's get back to you and this fantasy *gang-bang* of yours. Would you want to be fucked by women you know?"

I shook my head. "Oh, no. I don't want to know them. I want the spontaneity and anonymity of it all. I'd rather not know their names or anything about them. All I want is for them to be different shades of beautiful and have varying dick sizes. I want small dicks, medium-size dicks and, definitely some big dicked women to pound this pussy out."

I couldn't believe how freely I had shared this fantasy of mine with her. It was actually liberating. And I could tell by the way she was licking her lips and shifting in her seat that the more I talked about it, the more turned on she was getting. I would have bet my four-hundred-dollar heels that if I would have reached over and slid my hands between her legs I would have found her panties were soaked.

"Girl, you have me beat. I can't say that I'd ever want to be gang-banged, but I have fantasized about being in a threesome and even a foursome, but nothing more than that."

"Been there, done that. I've already had several threesomes, and a foursome once."

She blinked, shifting her weight on the barstool. She licked the sugared rim of her glass, then lifted it, eyeing me over the rim. "Girl, you're freakier than I thought."

I shrugged, lifting my glass to her. "We all have a freaky side."

"I'll drink to that." We clinked our glasses. "So do you think you'd ever want to live that fantasy out?"

I shrugged. "I don't know. I mean. I get so turned on fantasizing about it. But the likelihood of it coming to reality"—I shook my head—"I don't see that happening anytime soon; if at all."

A sly grin eased over her lips. "You never know. Some fantasies do come true."

I lifted my glass to her. "Then let the fantasy begin."

"Well, my beautiful friend, what if," Tamara says, bringing me back to our conversation, "I told you I know how to make that freaky little fantasy of yours come true."

I swivel my chair back around. "Girl, don't play with my emotions. If this is your way of playing some sick April Fools' prank on me, you're two weeks too late. And so not right."

She laughs. "No, hon. No April Fools' prank. This is me wanting to do something special for you."

"Get out. You're kidding me, right?"

"No, I'm very serious. I—"

"Wait a minute," I say, leaning up in my chair. "Why exactly would you want to do this? I thought you were repulsed by it."

"Ohmygod, that's a bit harsh. I wouldn't say repulsed. More like shamefully turned on. After we left the bar that night, I couldn't wait to get home to masturbate."

"Ooh, I would have loved to have been a fly on the wall for that. Now who exactly is the real freak in the room? Do tell."

She laughs again. "Okay, okay. I confess. Guilty as charged. That night you piqued my curiosity. And aroused a whole lot more than my senses. So I decided why not live vicariously through you by helping you live out your fantasy."

It isn't until my pussy starts throbbing that I realize I have the butt plug still lodged in my ass. I lift up and pull it out of me, licking it clean before wrapping it inside a few sheets of tissue, then slipping it, along with the lube, back into my bag.

I can feel excitement coursing through my blood, my heartbeat pounding in my ears. "I'm listening. Tell me more."

"Well, without going into great detail, I'll say this: I was out having drinks with a few colleagues and I shared with them what you told me…"

I gasp. "Girl, no. I told you that in confidence. How could you?"

"Now don't go getting your panties all twisted in a knot. I never mentioned your name. They don't know anything about you. I simply told them that I had a friend who wanted to be gang-banged. And they *all* seemed quite intrigued and turned on by the whole possibility. And they were wondering…" She pauses, leaving me hanging on the edge.

"They were *wondering* what?"

"Oh never mind. I don't even know why I called you with this."

"Ohmygod, Tamara. If you don't stop tormenting me I swear I'm gonna claw out your eyes the next time I see you."

"Oh, alright, party pooper. Geesh. They were wondering if you were interested in living out this fantasy."

My heart leaps in my chest. "And what did you tell them?"

"I told them exactly what you told me. Now the question is, were you serious? Is this something you really want to experience? Because if so it'll go down this Saturday."

I almost choke on my tongue. "This Saturday, like in two days away?"

"Yes. This Saturday."

"Ohmygod. I-I…don't believe this. This sounds all too good to be true."

"Well, believe it, boo. And it will be good. So are you in or not?"

I pull in a deep breath, trying to calm the pounding in my chest, and my pussy. If what she's telling me is true, I am in for one hell of an experience. She tells me she has secured a secret location far out in the woods of nowhere. That she's rallied up a number of women who are ready to fuck me into a daze. The way she says it, it sounds deliciously dirty and dangerously sexy.

To be fucked, anonymously!

I press my damp thighs together, then cross my legs to pinch back the budding throb in my clit. "If I agree to this, it will be kept in the strictest of confidence?" I trusted Tamara, but I'm not so sure about these so-called colleagues of hers.

"Of course. These are all professional, highly educated women who simply enjoy living on the edge and pushing the sexual envelope—so to speak, in secret of course. So discretion is assured as well as required."

"And they're all lesbians?" I ask, practically whispering into the phone.

"Yes, every last one of them. And beautiful I might add."

"And feminine I hope."

"Trust me. They are everything you could ever imagine."

"Mmmm. And why are they willing to go along with this?"

She sighs. "Because they are women who enjoy helping other women enhance their sexualities. It's a sisterhood of sorts. Now enough of all these endless questions, are you in or out?" I can hear her tapping something, impatiently. "Look, I have to get ready to go into a meeting so speak now or forever hold your piece."

"Well, geesh. Can I at least have a few hours to think on it? I mean, you've kind of caught me off-guard with this."

"Sweetie, from what you've told me about this fantasy of yours, you've spent more than enough time thinking about it. Now it's time to let that little freak flag of yours fly and just do it. The time clock's ticking: five, four, three…"

A wave of intense heat rolls over me. A ton of questions race through my head. How does she know these women? Where are they from? What do they look like? Where will she be taking me? Will she be one of the women fucking me?

I stand. The seat of my chair soaked in cunt juice.

Dammit!

"I'm in."

"Good. I'll let the others know. I'll pick you up Saturday at eight-thirty. Be ready. I'll fill you in with more of the details when I have them."

"Okay."

"Oh, and one more thing."

"What's that?"

"No panties."

Saturday, at the exact time, Tamara said she'd be picking me up, she pulls up in my driveway and blows her horn. I give myself one last look in the mirror, then head for the door.

Before I can get into her Benz good and buckle my seatbelt, she hands me a beautiful silk rainbow scarf and tells me to blind-fold myself.

I stare at her as if she's lost her mind. "Blindfold? Are you serious? You expect me to sit in the front seat of your car wearing this bright thing over my eyes? Don't you think that it might raise suspicions or cause alarm for those who might see us driving by?"

"No. I don't. It's dark out. So who cares who sees or thinks what. The blindfold is to ensure you don't know where we're going. And it is non-negotiable."

I roll my eyes, reluctantly doing as I am told. Everything around me becomes a shadow of darkness. I have no idea where we're going, or what to expect. And now not being able to see only heightens my anxiety. But it also adds to the allure. So far, the whole night is being kept a mystery. All I know is what she's already told me, which has been much of nothing. Other than she's taking me to a secret location where I will get the fucking of my life.

I decide to sit back and stay in the moment instead of letting my nervousness get the best of me and spoil my evening. Like I said, I trust Tamara. And I trust that she will make sure that whatever she has in store for me tonight will be everything I have asked for.

I lay my head against the headrest and settle into the butter soft leather seat, allowing my mind to drift off, imagining all the dirty, nasty things that will happen tonight. My pussy heats as I close my eyes and give into the images.

"We're here," Tamara finally says, waking me from a deep sleep. I yawn and stretch, surprised at myself for falling asleep. I apologize to Tamara for falling asleep on her.

"Girl, no worries. Considering the night you're about to have, sleep is exactly what you needed. I trust you are rested and ready for what's ahead."

"As ready as I can be."

"Good." She tells me to remove my blindfold. I blink, shifting my eyes to the clock in the console. It's exactly 10:15 P.M. It has taken us an hour-and-forty-five minutes to finally arrive to our destination. I watch as she opens her door and gets out to open an ornate rusted gate. It is overgrown with vines. I can hear it creak as Tamara pushes it open. She hops back in the car, drives through the gates, then gets back out and closes it.

I start to wonder what I've gotten myself into as I stare out of the passenger window. No one in my professional circle would ever believe that I'd be into acting out a gang-bang scenario with a group of strangers in some dirty old building. I press my thighs together as filthy thoughts race through my mind.

Save from the car's headlights, it's pitch black out, and rather frightening. "Umm, where exactly are we?" I ask, turning to look over at her.

She takes her eyes off the winding road for a brief moment and glances at me. Her lips curl into a smirk. "We're someplace where everything you hoped for is about to come true. I didn't have access to an abandoned warehouse, but this is the next best thing. Please tell me you're not getting cold feet?"

"No, not at all."

"Good. I've gone to a lot of trouble to set this up. And I promise you, it will be a night you will soon never forget."

A mixture of fear and excitement churns inside my pussy.

I shift in my seat. "I'm looking forward to it."

She pulls around a huge circular driveway and parks in back of several other luxury cars. We are at what appears to be—from the outside—an abandoned mansion. "The others are already inside," she says, shutting the engine and pulling her key out of the ignition. She checks herself in the rearview mirror, then opens her door. "Are you ready?"

I glance around—what I assume was once a sprawling lawn— and spot several large, beautiful white sculptures of naked woman made out of some sort of stone. Alabaster, I guess. They look well cared for in spite of their surroundings, and seem out of place here. Although the lawn and hedges are unkempt, I can tell this place was once a beautiful estate. I wonder whose property it is, but dare not ask. Not now, anyway. Real estate is not what I'm looking for tonight. Being fucked is the only thing I am interested in.

I swallow, taking in the house. "Yes."

This place is huge.

"Then let the fucking begin."

Where the hell am I? I wonder, stepping out of the car, the heels of my stilettos sinking into the gravel. "I can't wait."

Although I am someplace out in the middle of nowhere and Tamara still hasn't given me much details as to what I can expect tonight, I keep reminding myself how much I trust her. I have no reason not to. Still, my stomach is doing flips as we make our way up to the huge wraparound porch with its huge columns. Two large torches are lit on either side of a huge red double door. Vines and moss creep their way up over and around it.

The place looks haunted.

Over the door there's a sign that reads: WET PUSSY WANTED in big red-painted letters. I lick the drool that gathers at the corners of my lips, swallowing back nervous excitement. Images of swaying breasts, flicking tongues, wet pussies stretching over silicone churn around in my head, causing my skin to tingle and a pulsing throb to ache between my legs.

Last night while we were on the phone, Tamara had suggested I wear very little clothing, or to wear nothing I may not want torn/ripped off of me. The thought of having my clothes torn off, then being tossed to the ground and having my pussy fucked to shreds excites me. However, I have chosen to wear a simple red wrapdress with red six-inch fuck-me heels. Beneath my dress, I am only wearing red lace panties. No bra so my breasts can bounce freely.

I am covered in red.

Red like a hot, blazing fire.

Red like a well-fucked whore.

Red like the cum-loving slut I want to be, split open and raw. Fierce and on fire and fucked by a group of strangers.

My cunt dripping wet hotness.

I am red with passion.

Red with desire.

Red with lust.

I am full of fiery heat.

"So, are you nervous?" Tamara asks as we walk up the steps.

I shake my head. "Not really? I mean. Yes, kind of. I'm excited. But I'd be remiss if I said that I didn't have a few nervous butter-flies beating in my stomach. But that's to be expected."

She holds my gaze. "Yes, it is. Truthfully, I'd think there was something wrong with you if you *weren't* feeling some level of anxiety about tonight. Although this is your fantasy, one I have helped you bring to reality, you are still about to walk into the den of the unknown. And that in itself can be a bit nerve-racking."

I nod knowingly as I take a deep breath, shaking my hands out. Now that this, my fantasy of being gang-banged, is finally about to become a real experience for me, my anxiety-level is starting to kick up a notch.

What the fuck am I doing? Some fantasies aren't meant to be fulfilled, right? Maybe this is one of them.

But why live with regret?

Life is about exploring and experimenting. It's about being daring and living on the edge. There is nothing wrong with role-playing and indulging in our secret fantasies.

Tamara must sense my budding apprehension. She touches my arm. "Even though it took a great deal of coordinating to pull this scenario off for you, I want you to know you can change your mind, right here, right now. No worries, no hard feelings. But, if you chose to go through with it, be clear. Once you walk through those doors, there'll be no turning back. You will be fucked, and you will be tossed around. You *might* even be spit on, if that's what you desire."

I cringe at the thought of that. I said I wanted it rough and dirty. And I know being spit on can be a form of that. But that level of degradation I think I'd rather do without. I tell her this.

"Okay, understood. There'll be no spitting. I'll be sure to let that be known."

"I know I said I wanted to be treated like a whore, but there are some things I draw the line at. Spitting is one of them."

She may have set the stage for what's to come. But it is my fantasy. And I want it to be lived out exactly—or as close as possible—the way I've envisioned it. So the only bodily fluids I want to taste, or be drenched in, is that of sweet, sticky cum.

"And I don't want," I add, "anyone squatting over me and taking a shit or pissing in my face or anywhere else on my body."

She frowns. "Now you're taking it to a whole other level of kink. There will definitely be none of that. Unless of course…"

"No, thank you. Not interested."

She smiles. "But you're okay with everything else. And you are absolutely sure this is what you want…?"

You have no idea. I've never been more ready.

My eyes drop to her red-painted lips.

They are wet and succulent. Their lusciousness causes an irresistible desire to kiss them, lick them and…ride them, to sweep over me. My eyes flutter shut for a brief second, and I imagine sinking my teeth into the plump skin of her bottom lip. They look deliciously sweet.

I swallow.

"Yes."

She offers a sly grin, a carnal hunger twinkling in her eyes as she palms my cheek and grazes my lower lip with her thumb. "Behind this door there are ten, horny, beautiful women waiting for you…"

Ten women alternately fucking me? *My god!* This knowing is thrilling and intoxicating.

"…Two of them will greet us once the door opens. They will be nameless. Each woman will be wearing colored masks covering their eyes. These masks represent the colors of our flag, like the scarf I had you tie over your eyes. Speaking of which, where is it?"

"I left it in the car." She disarms her car's alarm and tells me she needs me to go get it and bring it to her. I do as I am told, feeling her burning gaze on my ass and hips. I return a few seconds later, handing it to her.

"Thanks. Now as I was saying. Some will want to finger-fuck you, maybe in your pussy, maybe in your ass. Others will want to tongue you. And, some—if not all—may want to fuck you…"

My breath quickens. My pussy clenches. Her words, the promise of being fucked dirty and raw, have become a powerful aphrodisiac.

"…with dildos or strap-ons, or both," she pauses, letting her gaze drop slowly to my swelling breasts. My nipples have become hard with want. She reaches out and cups one of my breasts, bouncing it gently before grasping a nipple with her fingers. She pinches it over the fabric of my dress, and I gasp. My clit swells in my panties. "At some point you will be blindfolded, again, and your hands will be tied. You will be fucked and sucked and stretched beyond your slutty imagination. Everything you've said you wanted is behind that door waiting for you."

Thoughts of fingers fucking my ass, my pussy, while a cock is fucking my throat, pushing past my tonsils and stretching my neck, has me practically drunk with want.

"Are you wearing underwear?"

Oh, shit. I forgot. She said no underwear. And my panties are sodden with heated lust. I nod. She steps into me, hiking my dress up over my hips and skating her hand over my pussy. Her sudden aggressiveness takes me by surprise as she goes into script. It is brazen and sensual. "You sweet, messy slut. Can't follow simple instructions, I see." She plays with my clit over the fabric. A soft moan bubbles out from the back of my throat as her hand slips into the waistband of my panties. "Take these off. You won't be needing them. Or would you like them ripped off of you?" My underwear sticks to the folds of my horny pussy as she inches them down over my hips. They drop around my ankles and I slowly step out of them.

Tamara breathes in the air around her. "Mmmm. I smell your arousal. I can't wait to see you getting fucked." I blush, attempting to squat down to pick up my underwear. "No," she says, grabbing my wrist. "Leave them."

I blink. She leans in and licks my bottom lip, her hand slowly sliding down my body. "Sweet messy slut, pretending to be little Miss Innocent. Miss Money Maker. You're nothing but a horny bitch." Her mouth covers my taut nipple, clamping it between her teeth over the fabric of my dress.

My pussy is dripping, liquid heat dampening my inner thighs.

She pulls back, her gaze burning through me. "You want it rough? You want it dirty? You wanna be fucked senseless, filthy bitch? You want to feel the ram of a thick cock deep in you, don't you? Well, tonight you will get exactly that."

I groan.

Oh, god, yes!

I ache for Tamara to fuck me—right here on this filthy porch with its chipped paint and ivy-covered walls. Ache to have my orgasm mercilessly fucked out of me. To have my face pressed up against one of these dirty windows and be fucked from the back, deep and fast and hard.

Dammit, let's fuck and get it over with! I know she feels what I feel.

Tamara peers into my eyes. She sees it. She hears what's in my head. My hungry want. "You want me to fuck you, don't you?"

"Yes. But you already know this."

She pulls me into her. Gives me a long, slow, juicy kiss that lingers long after she pulls back. Her hand continues downward, up my dress, her fingers searching through the neatly trimmed triangular patch of hair.

I part my legs, slightly, welcoming her in. She cups my pussy, then smacks it. "You're going to be fucked like the slut you are," she sneers, narrowing her eyes. "Is that what you want, whore?"

I wanna be your whore! I want you to fuck my slutty pussy!

"Yes."

"Are you wet, yet?"

She doesn't wait for my answer. She plunges two fingers into me, pushing through more wetness than I could ever imagine possible. She moves her fingers deliberately until she hits my G-spot and swishing sounds overwhelm me.

Oh, god, yes!

I swallow a scream.

She adds a third finger, and my knees almost buckle. With her free hand she pulls me in by the back of my neck and flicks her tongue over my lips, then into my mouth, savoring the lingering taste of cinnamon.

I climax instantly.

She kisses me deeply one last time, the intensity and passion behind it leaving me almost breathless, before pulling back and sharing one last-minute detail. "You're a whore, so don't expect any passion tonight. There will be no kissing. There will be no lovemaking. Whores don't kiss. Whores aren't made love to..." The more she talks, the more overcome I am with desire. This prolonged waiting is sweet agony. She knows exactly what she's doing. Making me wait. Keeping me standing on the opposite side of a door that holds my fantasy.

"...Whores are fucked. They are disrespected." She glances at her timepiece. "Your fantasy starts...now." Her face hardens, her tone becomes harsh. She hikes her pencil skirt up over her hips, revealing her bare cunt. "On your knees and eat my pussy, bitch!"

I sink to my knees, not bothered by the splintering wood planks that cut into my skin, and bury my head between her legs. She braces herself up against the doorframe and wraps a leg up and around my shoulder. Her pussy opens to my touch. I alternate between flicking her clit with my tongue and thumb while moving my fingers deep inside her.

She moans as her juices ooze out of her. I squeeze her ass, my fingernails sinking into her skin as I nibble her clit. Her body jerks. She pumps her pussy into my mouth in a delicious rhythm. She grabs my head as I smear my face all in her dripping cunt, my nose furrowing into her slit to smell her, my tongue lapping around her thick, dewy lips to savor her.

"Finger-fuck me, bitch," Tamara hisses. "Put a finger in my hot cunt and fuck me good."

My burning pussy tightens as I slip my index finger, then middle finger, into her juicy center—the heat from her cunt sending electric waves through my fingertips as I pump my hand in and out.

I lick up and down over her clit.

When my lips circle her clit and start suckling, she groans. "Oooh, yes, eat that pussy."

I smother her sweet wet pearl with soft kisses, and feel an upsurge of heat crashing through her as she grabs my head and fucks into my mouth. "Ooooh, yes, you freak-nasty bitch. Get all in that pussy, slut."

This experience, eating cunt…*her cunt*, outside in the night air, is exhilarating.

I circle my tongue over her clit, then dip into her wet slit as she gives into the decadent pleasure of an orgasm. I get lost in her moaning and the rushing liquid that bubbles and boils out of my own cunt as she coats my tongue. I swallow in her juicy pussy, savoring every drop of her. Her sweet, tasty nectar is everything I imagined it would be.

Delicious.

"Get up," she commands, yanking me by the arm. I jump to my feet and in one swift motion she is spinning me around, pressing her pelvis into my ass, entering my pussy from the back with two fingers. She growls in my ear. "I'm going to play in my wet cunt and watch you get fucked raw, you slutty bitch. Would you like that?"

"Yes," I murmur, my voice cracking. "Oh, god, yes…" Her fingers continue plunging in and out, her fingernails scraping my inner walls and sending delightful waves of heat through my pussy.

And then…she withdraws her fingers, leaving my pussy vacant and needy.

"Now you're ready."

She knocks on the door three times. A few seconds later, it swings open and she nudges me forward. The place is cold and damp and dark. Lit torches and white candles of varying sizes are positioned about the area. Portable fog machines situated throughout the large space fill the room with a thick white cloud of fog, making it difficult to see. There are no introductions. Tamara air kisses the two women standing on either side of the door, then hands the one wearing a red mask the silk scarf. She whispers something into her ear, then walks off. I eye the sway of her hips as she walks in the opposite direction, the floorboards creaking beneath her clicking heels as she disappears into the fog. Not once does she look back.

I bring my attention to the two naked, masked women standing in front of me, waiting. "Welcome," the one wearing the red mask says. I quickly take her all in. Blue rhinestones adorn the edges of her mask. There's a rainbow scarf tied around her slender neck. She has honey-blonde hair, and skin the color of maple syrup. Her shimmering skin is flawless. My gaze drinks in the deep chocolate areolas that encircle plump mouthwatering nipples.

I swallow back my nerves, then say, "Hello." My eyes trail downward. She's wearing a corset harness with a purple Double Delight strap-on. I'd know that dildo from anywhere. I have one of my own. My inner walls tighten knowing she has six-inches of thick pleasure already inserted into her pussy while another six inches curve upward in front of her, waiting to please. Me.

Neither smiles. Red Mask's lips curl into a sneer. "We're here to fuck you raw, you worthless *bitch*."

I gasp, slightly taken aback by the callousness in her voice. Although I know this is what I have asked for, I am still stunned.

Be careful what you ask for…

Erotic need.

Wild, dirty sex.

Snaking hands through my hair, head yanked back, thighs forced open, pussy lips pulled apart, teeth sinking into my velvety skin. Multiple cocks filling my holes. No-strings anonymous fucking. I know this is my fantasy. A mixture of conscious and subconscious desires colliding into reality. One I've yearned, waited for, for what seems like forever. And now…here I am.

"That *is* what you want, isn't it, *whore*? To be fucked inside out? To be treated like a slut?" the one wearing an orange mask with beautiful green feathers asks. She is tall, slender, and dangerously feminine. Behind her half-mask her green eyes shimmer like precious emeralds. Around her waist and hips is an elastic harness. There's a red eight-and-a-half-inch dildo attached.

My pussy tingles.

Without thought, I lick my lips. "Yes."

In one swift motion, she rips open my dress. "Take this off. You're here to fuck, bitch. Not look pretty. You want to be dominated, huh, you dirty slut?"

Let the games begin!

My pussy clenches. "Yes. Give it to me dirty, boo."

In one swift motion, her hand is around my throat and I have to quickly remind myself that this is all an act. That it's all part of the script. "I'm not your *boo*, slut!"

Orange Mask snatches my dress down off my shoulders, then looks inside at the designer name. "Oh, this stuck-up bitch is a label whore."

Red Mask lets go of my throat. "Mmmph. We'll have to make sure she's fucked even harder then."

Orange Mask balls up the four-hundred-dollar garment, then tosses it in my face. She yanks me by the arm. My heartbeat quickens as she slaps my right breast nipple, the sudden sting shooting straight to my clit. She slaps my left nipple.

I bite down on my bottom lip, and moan. She cups my left breast, then my right, gripping my nipples with her fingers. She pulls my left nipple, twists it, stretches it while pinching my right one.

My body shivers.

"Mmmm."

Red Mask catches me off-guard, grabbing me by the throat again. This time her nails sink into my skin. "You like it rough, huh, slut?"

She is not hurting me, but she is choking me hard enough so that I am starting to get lightheaded. Unable to speak I nod my head. She loosens her grip, but keeps her eyes locked on mine. She leans in and bites down on my top lip.

My cunt vibrates.

"Being treated like a whore makes your pussy wet, doesn't it? I hear you want to be gang-banged, is that right?"

"Y-yes," I push out as she rams a finger into my still wet cunt. She stirs my pussy. A moan escapes me.

Red Mask withdraws her finger, shoving it up to my lips. "Suck it like it's a dick, bitch." My lips part and she rams her finger in. My mouth closes around it, then sucks. Her finger pushes in and out of my mouth as if it's a dick fucking a wet pussy. My mouth waters and drools as my tongue laps around her knuckles.

Oh how I love the taste of my pussy.

"Spread your legs, bitch," Orange Mask says in back of me, pressing a thigh between my legs and nudging them apart. She places her dick between my legs and tells me to close my thighs. She pumps her hips. Her smooth, red cock glides over my pussy lips. She reaches around and cups my breasts. "I wanna coat my dick with your juices before I fuck you."

I blink, trying to adjust my eyes to the fog-filled room.

The rest of the house is in half darkness. I don't see anyone else. But coming from another room the space is filled with what sounds to be the lascivious sounds of women sucking and licking on pussies—wet and hungry. In my mind's eye, cum-coated fingers are flicking over slippery clits. I think I hear low moans of pleasure. But can't be for sure. Maybe it's all in my head. My mind is racing a mile a minute with all sorts of salacious thoughts. Still, so far, it is everything I imagine it would be—and I'm hoping even more. At least that is what my imagination leads me to believe.

Red Mask steps in closer. "Don't worry. The others are warming up for you. Right now we are simply preparing you for what's to come." I can feel the sexual heat of the two women pressing against me. They have me sandwiched in between them. Orange Mask's dick continues teasing my pussy lips, taunting my cunt as she slowly slides back and forth on it. I wish she'd ram it in me already. But she doesn't. I don't know how much of this sweet torture I can take before I explode.

Red Mask's delicate hand slinks between my legs and she rubs my throbbing clit. My legs part slightly to her touch. She toys in my cunt, then pulls back.

Orange Mask steps back, her dick leaving the warm, wet space between my legs.

"Suck my dick," she demands in a husky voice, snatching me by the arm and spinning me around to face her. She whirls me around so fast I almost get whiplash. "I want your cum-hungry lips on my dick. You like sucking dick?"

"Yes," I whisper. "Love it."

"Then suck my shit like you love it, you dirty little cock whore."

I reach for her dick. My fist slides up and down her shaft, pressing the base into her clit with every stroke. I bend over. Lick the head and run my tongue around it, tasting myself all over it. I work the length of her into my mouth, down into my throat, rubbing my pussy as my jaws clench around her shaft. Her cock slides smoothly, wetly, in and out, in and out.

I slip a finger into my pussy. Orange Mask bends her knees, her hands sliding through my hair, gripping my head.

"Yeah, suck that dick, you slutty bitch," Red Mask urges, slapping me on the ass. "You want your pussy fucked hard, don't you?" I grunt, bobbing my head back and forth over Orange Mask's cock, sucking and slurping and gulping her in.

Red Mask presses the head of her dick into the back of my pussy, then slams it in. I gasp, almost choking on the dick that's being shoved into my throat. A flash of searing pleasure blazes through me as Red Mask's and Orange Mask's thrusts become rougher.

They switch positions. Red Mask's cock, slick with my pussy, enters my mouth. Orange Mask sticks her fingers into my pussy. "Your tight pussy's real wet for this dick, huh?"

I groan as the crown of her dick brushes my pussy, then plunges inside of me, every inch of her dick disappearing in and out of my wetness.

I scream out when Red Mask pulls her cock out of my mouth. "Oh, yes! Fuck me! Ooooh, yes…your dick is so big. Uhh…uhh…"

Orange Mask grabs me by the hips and bangs her pelvis into me. "Is this how you want it, hard and fast? You want your cunt stretched?"

I am so overwhelmed with pleasure and heat that I am only able to grunt as she fucks me hard. I grow wetter than I already am around her, making her able to slip and slide into me, and fuck even deeper.

My gaze stays locked on Red Mask as she strokes herself, fucking into her pussy with the other end of her cock. She lifts her right breast with her free hand and slides her tongue over and around her nipple.

Everything is happening so fast. Orange Mask pulls out of my pussy and now Red Mask is backing me up against the wall and bending her head to my breasts, sucking them into her warm, wet mouth. I moan as she sucks my hard nipples into her mouth and slides her thigh between my legs. I ride her thigh, until my slick cunt clenches, and I am coming all over again.

"Come," Orange Mask says, slapping me on the ass. "It is time. We've kept the others waiting long enough." She hands me the scarf Tamara had given her. Tells me to put it back on. And once again, I am shut in darkness. And then…

Someone whips me around and presses me against the dirty, paint-chipped wall. I am breathless. My heart jumps.

My pussy tingles.

My clit pulses.

"Is this how you want it, whore?" I recognize the voice. It belongs to Orange Mask. She rams what feels like two fingers into the back of my pussy.

"Oh, god, yes! This is how I want—" I let out a gasp when someone twists my nipple.

"You want what, dirty bitch? Greedy little whore!" This voice belongs to Red Mask.

"This. Mmm." My voice, tiny and faltering, gets lost somewhere in the back of my throat between a gasp and a scream.

Orange Mask presses into me, her erect nipples grazing my back. I force myself still to keep from grinding into her. I feel the firmness of her cock pressing against my ass, the steam from her pussy wafting around the base.

"What is it that you want?" she growls into my ear.

"For you to fuuuuck me," I whisper.

"Pull open your ass," she demands. I reach in back of me, grab each ass cheek and pull them open. She thrusts her hips forward and slams into me, her thick curved dick carving into my cunt. She fucks me deliciously rough, yanking my head back and grunting and groaning in my ear.

"Greedy whore! You love getting fucked, don't you?"

"Yessssss! Mmmm…ooooh, yessss! Give it to me good…"

She fucks into me for what seems like forever before pulling out, then Red Mask is behind me, fucking me. They take turns fucking an orgasm out of me before taking me by the hand and leading me into another room.

I am tempted to yank this scarf off from my eyes, but something stops me. Maybe it's my freaky desire to be in this situation, maybe it's the fact that my cunt is incessantly clenching and unclenching that keeps me from pulling it off.

Someone leans into me. And I can smell her perfume. Heat by Beyoncé, I think. Her soft fingers graze my nipples, then pinches them. I hiss.

"You like that, huh, bitch? Dirty whore!"

She twists my nipples, and I scream out. "Yesssss!" My pussy explodes.

"Get on your knees," another voice says.

"Yeah, whore, crawl," someone else says.

As I get on my knees, there's someone else on the other side of me. The light scent of her perfuvme reminds me of one of my favorite scents. Signorina by Ferragamo. I breathe in her calming scent, steadying myself for what's to come next. She drags what feels like a finger down my slit. Then back over my ass. Her hand comes down on my ass, sending shockwaves through my pussy.

"Open your legs. You want your pussy fucked doggie-style, slut?"

I answer with a grunt as someone gets in back of me and rams their dick into my waiting cunt. I count in my head.

One, two, three, four different women with different sized dicks take turns fucking me from the back. "Oooh, yessssss! Give it to me! Fuck this pussy!"

"Yeah, take this dick, bitch," the fifth woman grunts. She feels much heavier than the other four who've finished fucking me. Her breasts are much larger. I guesstimate she's at least a double-E the way they bounce against my back, like overstuffed beanbags, as she fucks her hips into me.

I grunt and groan, enjoying the varying sensations each woman delivers as she fucks me. I don't know how long I am fucked on my knees before I am finally allowed to remove my mask.

I blink, adjusting my eyes to the candlelit room. Standing before me, I count eleven colorful-masked women—all wearing the same silk scarves either around their necks or tied around their wrists, stroking their dicks watching me.

"The party is just beginning," a mocha-colored woman says wearing a multi-colored mask of all the colors in the rainbow. I recognize the voice, and the body—although it's my first time seeing her naked. It's Tamara's. She's wearing a leather harness with a huge pink dick jutting out of it. It looks to be about eleven inches. She's smirking as she strokes it. "You wanted some big dick, didn't you, whore?"

I lick my lips. Finally, I am going to have her between my legs. My insides catch fire at the thought of it. "Yes," I push out in almost a groan.

"And big dick is what you shall get. But first we have some other holes to fill."

I let out a moan, anticipation throbbing through every inch of my body. "Yes. Oooh, yes. Fuck all of my holes."

Another yellow masked woman steps forward. Her dick is also pink but with ridges. It's about six inches long and not very thick. She tells me to stay on my knees. Tells me she wants my head down and ass up. I arch my back, watching her over my shoulder as she reaches for a bottle of oil and slathers some around her cock and then onto her fingers. Then positions herself in back of me, pouring warm oil all over the smooth globes of my ass, her hand sliding with ease over my skin, along the seam of my ass, before plunging her oiled finger deep into my ass. She quickly adds a second finger, then a third, stretching the passageway for her jutting cock.

"Nice tight little asshole. I'm about to fuck you real good in it."

I moan.

And then she is easing her cock deep inside of me, groaning with each thrust until she is base deep. She pumps inside of me, causing my breasts to bounce and jiggle as her flesh smacks against mine. She fucks me hard in my ass. And a wave of ecstasy rolls over me. I squirm and gasp and groan as my ass spasms around her dick. It's shoved deep…ooh so very deep…inside of me. She reaches under me and cups my pussy, pressing wet, oily fingertips against my clit, each delicious stroke sending surfs of heated ripples through me, the sweet burn shooting sparks of fiery need all over me. My pussy, my ass, my clit become a ball of fire.

I shake and shiver.

"You like that pretty pink cock fucking your ass?"

"Yesssssss. Oh, god, yes…"

She emits a low growl, nipping my ear as she fucks deeper into my tightness. My asshole expands and burns and aches sweetly with each thrust. It hurts, but it feels so good. I reach under me and toy with my clit as I groan and ride another wave of an orgasm, the smooth walls of my pussy contracting as Yellow Mask pinches my nipples and rapidly pounds her dick in me. Her breasts sweep across my back.

I tremble and gasp and moan. I crave more. I ache for more. I scream out, my pussy clenching to be filled, my asshole stretching and straining for more cock as I writhe and beg and plead.

The ten other masked women stand around us, holding their cocks in their hands, stroking them while watching. Exactly the way I envisioned it. "You want more dick in you?" Yellow Mask yanks my head back. "Is that what you want, slutty whore?"

"Yes!"

"Beg for more dick, bitch!" she growls, biting into my shoulder. I shriek, a mixture of pleasure and pain coursing through my shuddering body.

"Give me more! Give me more! Oh, god, yesssssss! Give me more! Fuck my holes deep!" She shoves her hips forward and a piercing heat shoots up through my spine. I hear the rest of them whispering sweet, dirty words as Yellow Mask slams her pink dick in and out, in and out.

I'm being called a whore. A slut. A filthy cum-loving cunt. They call me every kind of bitch known to man loaded with threats to fuck me into a coma. I am loving every moment of it.

"Fuck that bitch good," someone wearing a violet mask says to her as she inches her nine-inch, chocolate dick between my drooling, spit-slick lips. I open my mouth and she shoves it in, hitting the back of my throat. "Gag on this dick, whore."

I close my eyes. Behind my lids colors of red, orange, yellow, blue, green, and violet swirl through a kaleidoscope of sensations, a rainbow of cocks fucking me. Taking my pussy, my ass, my throat with force and fiery need.

"I think this horny bitch is ready for some more dick," Yellow Mask says, slapping my ass. "You ready, bitch?"

Her fingers slide into the back of my pussy.

"Ooooh, yessss."

She grunts in my ear. "Yeah, that's it, bitch. Come all over my fingers. Wet pussy. Mmmm. You like that cock shoved deep in in your ass, don't you? I'm going to fuck your ass raw."

Yellow Mask pumps and pounds, relentlessly, pinching my clit as the other women look on, stroking their colorful cocks. Their moans mixing in along with mine.

Violet Mask fucks my throat shut with her dick, every so often pulling it out and telling me to spit on it. She likes her dick sucked messy, sloppy. Droplets of pussy juice glisten around the edges of her cock's base. I lick around it, inhaling her scent.

Her pungent heat inebriating, I slide the tip of my tongue under the edge of the base, and attempt to lick one of her thick pussy lips. I want to taste her pussy. Want to feel her heated wetness on my tongue. She yanks my head back.

"Open your mouth back up. And suck on this dick."

She is back in, pushing past my tonsils.

Yellow Mask pulls out of me. Blue Mask is now in me. Her

fleshy eight-and-a-half-inch blue Jel-Lee cock slides deep...so very deep...into my ass.

"Ohh, yes..."

"You like that, huh, cum whore?"

"Yes...mmmm...ooooooh..."

She pulls back to my asshole, tip-fucks my entrance, then plunges back in. I gasp. I can feel her dick vibrating inside of me. She is coaxing another orgasm out of me.

"Mmmm...oooh, yesssss..."

"It feels good in that stretched ass, slut?" She pulls my ass cheeks open. "Look at that big hole taking all this dick. Nasty whore-ass bitch." She alternately slaps each ass cheek.

I moan.

Violet Mask pulls her dick out of my mouth, slaps me across the face and mouth with it, then steps back. Another orange-masked woman is now shoving her dick in. Hers is blue and looks close to nine inches. I close my eyes and suck her cock deeper into my mouth. As her thick curved cock fills my mouth, I fuck the length of her with my tongue. Softly, caressing the head of her dick with my lips. She grinds her hips, grunting.

Blue Mask pulls out of my hole.

Green Mask gets in back of me.

One finger...two, three, four...move in and out of me, pushing through a river of desire, my juicy cunt opening wide and eager. I gasp as fingers fold inside of me, then knuckles press into the mouth of my cunt.

"Oooooh, yes...uhhh...mmmm..."

Green Mask is twisting and pushing. I hiss and push back harder. Juices splash against her hand as my pussy clenches and un-clenches, sucking in her fist, swallowing her hand, whole. My pussy feels fuller than it's ever felt in my entire life.

Ohmgod! I can't believe I am being fist-fucked!

"Oh, god, yes!"

She moves her fist faster, harder, pulling and pushing. Stretching out my orgasm. My heart nearly stops beating as my pussy floods and I cum all over her fist—fire sweeping through the balls of my feet, up my thighs, inside my cunt, settling into the pit of my belly.

I cum.

And I cum.

And I cum.

The walls of my pussy constrict against the pound of her fist, against the warmth of my juices as she fist-fucks the cream out of me. "Yes! Oh, yes! Fuck, yesssss!" I buck my hips, my ass jiggling around her wrist.

She slowly pulls her fist out of me, grazing my thick pussy lips. And I am immediately weak with dizzying want. I want more and more. I beg for it.

And one by one, they give it to me. Six-inch, seven-inch, eight-inch, nine-inch cocks take turns fucking my mouth. Nine-inch, ten-inch, eleven-inch dicks alternately fucking my pussy. My stretched, burning asshole becomes a playground for vibrating plugs and anal beads. I am being pounded and pushed, stretched and twisted. One after the other, they fuck into my holes. Slice into my smoldering heat.

Now I am on my back. My legs spread, my arms hooked in back of my knees pulling them up to my chest. And one by one, they all fuck me. I am being fucked and yanked and tossed around in a sea of wet passion.

Fucked until I am raw and burning.

The intensity shooting sparks through me. I am being fucked so deep and so good that I am sweating and shaking as if I am about to go into convulsions.

Finally the moment I have been longing for. Tamara. She inches between my legs, then leans into my ear as she pushes her huge dick in me. "I saved the best for last."

I gasp as she stretches all the way into me. "Oh, yes. Fuck me. Mmm."

"Suck my titties," she says, lifting up on her arms and grinding her hips. I wrap my legs around her waist, reaching for her breasts. I suckle them. Nip them. Lick them. Pull them into my mouth and milk them. She moans. And I moan. The ten other women have now encircled us. Their cocks slick with spit and cum and lube, slide in and out of their pumping hands as they watch Tamara fucking me.

Oh, God, there's nothing more delicious than this. Being alternately fucked by ten beautiful, harness-strapped women in some rundown, dilapidated house.

Gang-banged relentlessly.

Fucked and stretched to the limit.

My holes are burning.

My throat is raw.

I am on the verge of another climax.

I close my eyes.

Growl and grunt.

Arch into the piercing fire shooting through the walls of my pussy. Scream out in pain-pleasure as flames of passion engulf me then…give into the liquid heat shooting out of me. And, then, without warning, everything around me starts to fade as I get swept into the blaze.

Straight No Chaser

Yo, real shit. The first time I saw her, I wanted to eat her pussy and fuck her. Wanted to get her in the backseat of my black 2013 Durango with the tinted out windows, rip off her panties and fuck her with my tongue and fingers until her pussy juice splashed out all over me, then dig her guts out from the back with my long, black dick. I wanted to fuck her fine ass mercilessly.

And if I couldn't have her in the backseat of my whip, I wanted to be in back of her, pushing her up against a wall, my body ramming into her in time to the music, my mouth at her ear, my dick digging in and out, slamming into her, pounding her into the wall, fucking her on the edge of a thick, sweet nut.

Fuck yeah! I wanted to creep up behind her, kiss her neck and slink my finger underneath her black pencil-skirt, into her panties and into her pussy hole. I wanted to finger her until she cried out in pleasure, begging for me to fuck her with my rock-hard dick.

And tonight is no exception.

I wanna fuck her!

I wanna sink my fat dick into her wetness until I melt inside of her, until I bust this nut up in her. Real shit.

Kendrick Lamar's "Poetic Justice" is blaring throughout the club. I'm surrounded by her perfume. The peach flowery scent makes my dick hard as she spins around on the dance floor. I grab at my dick over my True Religions, sipping my Corona as she gyrates to the beat. Her dress is so fucking short that I can see the edges of her ass cheeks jiggle. Her ass-shaking, sexy moves are heating my loins, causing my dick to get harder and harder with each shake, bounce, dip, and spin she does.

Sexy-ass bitch!

Her eyes shut, then flutter open as she gets lost in the music. I know she sees, feels, me watching her. Shit, *every*one's watching her!

And she's killin' it!

Tonight she's wearing a skimpy red dress that's mad short, and red platform heels. She's smoking hot, like fire. Shit. She's the hottest bitch in the club. And she knows. It. Her cocoa brown skin matches her sensuous brown eyes, which are framed by thick, long lashes. Her full, voluptuous lips are painted red and coated with lip gloss to give them that shiny, wet, ready-to-suck-a-niggah's-dick look.

I lick my lips as her titties bounce up and down and she throws that pussy at me. Shit, a'ight. Maybe she ain't really throwing it at me, *yet*. But she's throwing that shit. And I'm tryna catch it... all of it. Before the rest of these hungry-ass muhfuckas try to get up in it.

My niggahs always tell me chicks like her—straight and strictly dickly—ain't checking for muhfuckas like me. That I need to stay in my lane and stop chasing dreams. They swear that all I'ma ever get from tryna fuck with a straight bitch is heartache. But I ain't tryna hear that shit.

I know what I want.

And I know what I like.

My women straight.

Still, my niggahs stay tryna clown a muhfucka for prowling the *straight* clubs for my next victim, my next conquest. My next good fuck of the night. Shit, I love sex. And I love fucking straight chicks. It's like a hunting game to me. To see how far I can go without being clocked, which is usually hard to do since I look like a straight-up niggah.

Real rap, yo. I'm that pretty boy type with mad swag.

Six-pack on deck. Tight, toned body. Spinning waves. Deep dimples. Smooth baby face.

I'm a chick magnet.

And I stay getting pussy, yo. Stay baggin' them sexy-ass dimes. A'ight, a'ight, real spit. I haven't bagged a bitch in a minute 'cause I ain't out shopping like that. But when I was baggin' 'em they've always been badder than a muhfucka. All tens, hands down! But that was then. And this is now. And right not, the only thing on the menu is me tryna fuck.

Still, my peeps think I need to fall back from chasing these straight broads. They think I'm crazy for not wanting to link up with a broad on my own level for some relationship-type shit, instead of wasting my time tryna bag a chick who's only gonna put the brakes on shit once she finds out who—or should I say, what—I really am. But, for real for real, gay chicks ain't what I'm checkin' for. And I ain't looking to be booed up.

And the truth of the matter is, I ain't looking for love.

I'm looking for one-night stands.

I'm looking for good pussy.

Unsuspecting pussy.

And lots of it. Something I ain't never had a problem getting. Like I said, my dick *and* this long tongue stay wet. And I got the text messages, voice messages, and panties to prove it. Yeah, maybe it's a psychological thing, a mind thing. Shit, a'ight. It is mental for me. But fucking straight pussy is the best kinda pussy there is.

And, hands down, I know this sexy mama right here working

the dance floor got that goodie-goodie. I can tell by the way she seductively moves those round hips, the way she's thrusting her pelvis into the music, that she knows how to ride a dick. And so far I ain't been wrong at spotting that good pussy.

Yo, I'm feeling good as fuck. The four shots and two beers I've already tossed back got me right. Fuck what ya heard. I'm ready to get it in.

The DJ slips on Rihanna's "Pour It Up." I bounce my head as I watch baby girl slowly spin around, raising her hands up over her head, then dropping down low. She bounces and rocks her hips. My dick throbs between my legs. This sexy-dime got my mouth watering, yo. I toss back the rest of my beer, then set the empty bottle up on the ledge. It's time to make my move.

I inch my way over to her and sidle up on her. Her back is turned so she doesn't see me as I place my hands on her hips and press up on her ass. I rock to the beat in sync to her movements. She cranes her neck to see who's up on her, then smiles. That grin on her face and the way she tosses her *phat*-ass up in my crotch tells me all I need. She's with it. Well, me dancing with her, that is. Fucking her might take a little more work. Or maybe not…

She spins around. "You sure you ready for me?" she says over the music, eyeing me up and down, then spinning back around, grinding and bouncing that thing-thing up on my dick.

For the last three Saturday nights, I've hopped in my whip and driven into the city to hit up this spot, Club Sensations—a straight club that plays hip-hop on Thursday, Friday, and Saturday nights, and house and club music on Sunday nights. And each time I've come through, she's been here. On the dance floor, seducing the muhfuckas who've been eye-fucking her. Instead of tryna press up on her, I've stayed in the cut, eyeing her, watching how she moves. Solo, it seems. Mad niggahs stay tryna press up on her, but from what I've peeped, so far, she doesn't seem to give 'em too much airplay. Yeah, she dances with 'em. And I've peeped her at the bar, grinning and smiling while she runs their pockets on drinks. But then she keeps it movin'. And even after the club, when the lights flick open and it's finally "Last Call for Alcohol," she bounces out the door, hops in her black-on-black Range Rover with the Jersey tags and tinted windows and peels off. Yo, I ain't gonna front, I had to really check myself from tailin' her fine ass home. Not that I'm some psycho-type muhfucka who stalks a bitch, but, uh…I was tempted.

But, tonight, temptation has taken over me, and now a muh-fucka's ready to take a bite into that forbidden fruit, yo.

"Yo, I stay ready, ma," I yell over the music.

She spins back around, facing me, slipping a leg between mine. "We'll see." She quickly skips back a few steps, then hops forward when the DJ starts playing a Rick Ross joint. The dance floor is straight up packed with chicks and muhfuckas getting it in, chanting and throwing their hands up. They're all caught up in their own worlds getting their two-step and sweat on. But I ain't really caught up watching them when I got this shorty right here practically letting me do whatever I want to her on the dance floor. Am I surprised? Yeah, sort of. But I ain't really putting too much thought into it 'cause I know I'ma smooth muhfucka.

Right now I got her pulled into me; one arm around the front of her while my other hand is down on her thigh. Her skin is hot and mad soft, yo.

She leans back into me as more heads pack up on the dance floor. Little by little she and I keep getting pushed further and further back into the crowd until we are practically pinned up in our own little corner along a wall of mirrors.

It's mad dark over here. And that's my cue to see just how far this hot tamale is willing to let me go as we seductively sway back and forth to Rihanna's joint, "Diamonds in the Sky." She's bent over, ass bouncing into me as I grind my hips into her. I slide a hand up her dress, and like I thought *and* hoped—she ain't wearing drawers, not even a thong.

Yeah, she's out here tryna get fucked tonight.

I slink my hand further up her dress until I'm touching her pussy lips. She leans forward, grabbing her ankles, giving me easier access. I stroke her wet lips, then push a finger into her. She lets me slide it all the way into her, moving her hips in a slow, seductive grind, then speeding up as I slip another finger in. Her ass clapping around my hand as her cunt pulls in and grips my fingers until I can feel the music start to vibrate through her wetness. Her pussy clamps onto my knuckles. "Blow the Whistle" starts to play and she nuts on my hand. And I feel my own nut building up inside of me.

She spins around to face me, locking her gaze onto mine. She sees what I see. Lust. Hungry need. We both wanna fuck. She grins as I taste her sticky-sweetness, licking my fingers on the sly as we keep our pace to the music. I grin back at her. "You like that?" she asks, slipping a thigh in between mine and grinding on my leg. Her hands go up my muscular arm to my biceps, then back down to my forearms.

I lean into her ear. "What you think?"

"I think you ain't ready for it."

"Yeah, a'ight. Whatever you say."

"It's what I know, baby." She spins outta my arms, then backs her ass back up into my crotch. A Lil' Kim joint starts playing and this sexy thing-thing starts getting all nasty with it. And all this humping and grinding is doing is making me hornier by the minute. So fucking horny that I'm ready to bust in my drawers.

I pull her into me real close, then lean into her ear. She slips a hand in back of her and starts tryna grab at my dick. I almost nut on the spot as the base of my dick presses my clit.

"Ma, real shit. You mad sexy. I wanna fuck you, yo."

"Then fuck me," she demands. Her bluntness shocks me at first, but it doesn't take me long to quickly recover. It's game on, yo. Right here in the dark corner of the club I'ma 'bout to bust her pussy open. I remove my hand from her waist, glancing around the club to see who's peepin' us. No one, so it's all gravy. We 'bout to get our fuck on. I quickly unzip my jeans, then reach inside the opening of my boxers and fish my thick, eight-inch dark brown dick out—it's smaller than the one I usually pack. But it's still thick enough to bust her guts out. It's smooth, not too veiny, and matches the color of my skin almost perfectly.

She tries to reach for it in back of her. She wants to stroke it, but I shove her hand away, dipping at the knees. I brush my thumb over her slit, then dip the tip of it in. She's so wet. I grip my shit and circle her sticky lips and opening with the head. She moans over the music.

And I don't give a fuck who hears her. This pussy is 'bout to be mine for the night. I keep teasing her slit, circling the hole of her pussy with my dick. I bring my thumb up to her mouth, circling and teasing it the same way I'm doing her cunt. She sucks it into her mouth as if she's sucking my dick. Finally, I give in, giving her this dick. I push it into the back of her ready pussy, slowly. Then grab her hips and pull her toward me, forcing my whole dick in. I hear her gasp as Soulja Boy's "Tear It Up" starts playing. I grind into her pussy.

"Mmmmph…fuck me!"

"This what you want?" I growl into her ear over the music. "This hard dick?"

"Yes! Fuck me!"

I grab her by the waist and ram my dick in her. She's handling it like a pro, giving it as good as she's getting it, humping and pumping her hips. I repeatedly bang into her pussy—tip-to-base, tearing it up, nearly lifting her off the floor with each thrust. She bucks her ass, pushes me back up against the mirrors and rodeo rides my dick. To the drunken club-goers we simply look like two drunken heads freakin' each other on the dance floor, not fucking our brains out.

Still, I peep a few heads stealing glances over at us, muhfuckas tapping their boys and nodding over toward us. But I ain't sweating that shit. The only thing I'm tryna do is get this nut. She works my dick as I work her pussy. I can feel sweat on my neck and down the center of my muscled back. Her cunt grips my dick. I can feel her coming over the music. The bass, the rhythm, the lyrics, moving through her as her body shudders. Fast and hard, I cum with her, then hold onto her waist for a few extra minutes, grinding into her gooey center. She keeps dancing on my dick.

We stay in this position for another full song, rocking back and forth, trying to catch our breaths before I finally pull out and stuff my wet, sticky dick back in my boxers, then zip my jeans up. On some real shit, if this was poppin' off under different conditions—with her knowing who and what I really am—I'd have her sucking my dick clean. But since it ain't that kinda party, I gotta stick 'n' move. She pulls down her dress, then turns toward me. She has a fresh-fuck glow on her sweaty face.

She presses her moist lips up to my ear. "That was real good."

"No doubt. You got some good pussy, ma."

She grins. "And you got some real good dick. I'd like to get another round. You got a name?"

"It's Reggie."

"I'm Nicole."

"That's wassup." I grab a chunk of her ass. "Yo, check it. I'ma 'bout to dip. But let me get them digits before I bounce." She hits me with some dumb shit 'bout not giving her number out, but she'll take mine. Yeah, whatever. The bitch let a random muhfucka fuck her on the dance floor, but she doesn't give out her digits. Go figure. It ain't no biggie, though. I already got what I wanted. My dick wet. And there ain't gonna be no second rounds. There never is. "You know what, yo. Don't sweat it."

I lean in and give her a kiss on the cheek. She says some other shit, but I done already started blocking her out. The only thing on my mind now is getting in my whip so I can finish stroking out the rest of this nut.

She blows me a kiss, then dances off as I make my way through the crowd and out the door.

"Yo, muhfucka," my boi Prince says, taking two pulls off the blunt we just rolled, then passing it to me, "you stay stylin', son."

"Nah, my niggah, real shit," I say laughing at her. It's a little after twelve in the afternoon. We're chilling at my crib, smoking a blunt and eating shrimp. And I just finished telling her what popped off down at the club last night. Prince and I been mad cool for like fifteen years, around the same time we both came out to our families. I was fifteen. She was like sixteen going on seventeen.

Anyway, it wasn't really no surprise to my fam when I tol' 'em I was gay since I stayed rockin' baggy jeans, Timbs and wife beaters. And my ponytail stayed stuffed up under a fitted hat. Or I stayed posted up in a pair of baggy sweats and a hoodie and sneakers. I wasn't beat for nothin' girly. Give me a football or a basketball over some Barbie dolls and makeup and I was good.

My moms said she already knew it. Shit. I guess even if she didn't already know, she woulda known for sure after walking in on me and seeing me rocking a pair of men's boxers with a seven-inch dick hanging outta the flap of them.

I had been experimenting for a minute with harnesses and dildos, and had even started wearing them to school, which is what I was preparing to do the morning my moms walked in. For weeks, I'd been alternating from jock-style to thong-style harnesses tryna decide which one was really the most comfortable fit for me. I'd like them both, for different reason. And this particular day, I'd chosen the jock-style harness under my boxers.

I was standing in front of the mirror, my gaze fixed on my reflection, upward curved dick hanging outta the slit of my boxers, my hand gripped around it. I was standing there grinding it into my hand, imagining I was fucking some pussy. I was getting juicier by the minute as I stroked my thick black dick, the harness rubbing up against my clit. My legs were cocked open as I fucked my hand. I let out a deep moan as I bust my nut.

Moms walked in on me jackin' off. Her eyes popped open in shock. She quickly shut the door, leaving me with my silicone dick in my hand. I was mad spooked that she had caught me with my dick hanging out. She ain't say shit 'bout what she saw as I eased outta the crib for school. The only thing she did say—well, actually it was a question—later that night when she got in from work is, "Is there something you wanna tell me?"

I shrugged at first, still embarrassed.

Then she added, "Regina, I'm going to always love you, no matter what."

But she stayed looking at me all crazy-like until I said, "Mom, this is who I am."

"And who are you, Regina?"

"Not Regina," I answered, feeling myself getting choked up. I had tried to pretend, tried to cover up who I was, who I felt I was, behind awkward moments attempting to date boys and hang with giggling, silly-ass girls. But that wasn't me. What she saw was. "Regina's dead to me, Ma."

She narrowed her eyes, absorbing the weight of what I had told her. "Well, if my daughter's dead, then who the hell am I standing here looking at?"

"Reggie."

Moms stood there, staring at me, hard. Then before I knew it, she broke down and cried, walking over and pulling me into her arms. And that night we cried together. In that moment, layers of shame and guilt for hiding who I was were shed. And for the first time in my young life, I felt lighter and free.

I didn't have to hide in secrecy.

Didn't have to live in shame.

My moms loved me. She accepted me.

Prince's mom, on the other hand, wasn't having it. She called her all kinda *bull-dagging, dyke* bitches and told her to get the fuck outta her crib 'cause she wasn't having no *gay bitch* living up under her roof. She told Prince she needed prayer as she literally threw all her shit out the door. Prince ended up sleeping on the streets for almost two weeks until she swallowed her pride and asked if she could crash at my crib. She ain't have nowhere else to turn. And there was no way I could turn my back on her. So I brought her home with me, asked my moms if it was cool if she stayed with us—which it was. And from that moment on, we've been mad tight, like brothers. Real shit, I got mad luv for her. There's nothing I wouldn't do for her. Or her for me.

Shit, we've fucked mad bitches together. Even ran a few trains on a few tricks. Prince is my dawg, for life, yo.

I eye her. "Yo, you know I don't ever front on my dick game."

"True that. I ain't gonna front, son. You be gettin' it in. But, yo, fuckin' a straight bitch in a straight club, in the middle of the dance floor...sounds like a damn dream."

"On e'erything, fam, I fucked that sexy bitch in the club. And, word is bond, yo. She had some juicy-ass pussy, son. I was fingerin' that shit 'n' e'erything, yo."

She grins, rubbing her chin. "Word? It was like that?"

"Hellz yeah. I told you she was sexy as fuck, yo. I was all up in that shit, son. I had her up on that dance floor giving her this dick real good. Afterwards, I ain't even gonna front. I wanted to bend her over 'n' tongue all up in that gushy shit." I take a pull from the blunt. She's looking at me wide-eyed with her jaw dropped. "I tol' you I was gonna hit that shit, yo. Didn't I?" I blow out a cloud of thick smoke, then take another pull.

I had told Prince about her the first night I peeped her, and was dead-ass 'bout getting at her, even though she tried to tell me I should at least let her know that I was a stud and not a real niggah if I was gonna step to her and try to get her to peel them drawers off. I wasn't tryna hear it though. My mind was already made up. I was going back to the club and was gonna holla at her. And telling her who, or what, I was wasn't in the cards. I just didn't think I'd be fucking her in the club, on the dance floor. Yo, that was some wild-ass shit. That broad's a real live freak. I'm still trippin' off that shit.

Prince grins, giving me a pound. "No doubt. You def said you was gonna smash that. Yo, my niggah, you a beast, yo. Word is bond. I can't even style on you, son." She reaches out her balled fist for another pound. "You stay baggin' them straight hoes." She shakes her head. "I don't know how ya ugly ass be doin' it, though."

I give her the finger. "Fuck outta here, muhfucka. I'm fine as fuck, yo. Front if you want. You already know what it is, niggah."

She laughs again. "You know I'm only fuckin' wit' you, yo. I know ya rap game is sick. But, real shit, fam. That shit you be doin' trickin' them straight chicks is…"

"Yo, hol' up, fam, be clear. I don't be trickin' them chicks." She raises a brow, shooting me a "fuck outta here" look. "Aiight, so I don't tell 'em. It's not like they be asking me if I'm a real niggah, or not. So why should I volunteer the info. If I can get away wit' it, why not? It ain't like I'm hurting anyone. Shit, they see what they see, and like what they see. And nine times outta ten they want what they see."

"Correction, fam. They want what they *think* they see. A real muhfucka with a real dick that can spit a real nut, not a stud muhfucka with a strap-on frontin'."

I shrug. "Then maybe they should ask, first."

"Niggah, you crazy. Why the fuck would they think to ask some shit like that when you look like a straight-up muhfucka wit' ya flat-chested ass. I hate yo' ugly ass."

I crack up laughing at that shit. She hates the fact that she has double-D's, and there ain't shit she can do to hide them muhfuckas. They ain't going nowhere. "Yo, fuck outta here, muhfucka. Don't hate"—I run the palm of my hands over the front of my shirt—"'cause my shit's all chiseled up, and you"—I reach over and flick her right breast—"all flab, muhfucka."

She punches my arm. Then flexes her biceps. "But I hit hard, niggah. And, what? Point is, you still shouldn't play games like that, yo. You know I got nothin' but love for you, but"—she shakes her head—"that shit you doin' is fucked up."

I frown. "Yo, how is you gonna fuckin' judge me, fam, when you stay trickin' ya paper up on bitches? You don't see me callin' you out on how you stay tryna wife up them stripper hoes, do you?"

"I ain't judging you, fam. All I'm sayin' is, maybe you should keep it a hunnid wit" them broads and let 'em know from the rip what they 'bout to get into. You know and I know, them broads ain't gonna ask if you swingin' a real dick or not when they be all liquored up."

I tsk. "Suck my dick, muhfuka. Liquored up or not. They still wanna fuck. And I give it to 'em. So how's that trickin' them?"

"Niggah, you know what I'm sayin'."

"Muhfucka, I don't know shit. Hand me that blunt, and let's move on."

She shakes her head, taking two deep pulls, then passing it off. "A'ight, yo, justify it however you want. No matter how you cut it, you still deceivin' them, yo."

I take a long pull from the blunt, then pass it back to her. I blow smoke up, then inhale it back in through my nose. "Nah, like I said. I ain't deceiving anyone. What I'm doin' is keeping my dick wet. And putting some good dick and tongue in their lives…for the night, anyway. Shit, I don't put a gun to none of them broads' heads, forcing them to do nothing they don't already wanna do. So it is what it is."

"Aiight, slick ass, riddle me this: how many of them straight broads that you've already smashed do you think would have still given you the pussy if they woulda known you wasn't no real niggah?"

I shrug. "Fuck if I know. Prolly half of 'em would still let me hit it, if for nothing else, solely on the strength of being curious. You know bitches stay sweatin' us 'cause we look like straight-up, real-ass, sexy muhfuckas."

I'ma keep it a hunnid. If I got down with Studs like that, Prince is def someone I'd holla at. At six feet, she's sexy as fuck. Even wit' them big-ass titties, she's got a mad tight body from playing ball, and stays laced in all the hot shit. And the chicks stay wanting to play all up in her long wavy hair, which she keeps in fresh cornrows.

She nods, rubbing her chin and grinning. "True, true. But the difference is, they know who we are. It ain't no secret. We ain't misleading them. And them broads still wanna get at us, especially the bi-curious ones. But going to a straight club, frontin' like you a straight niggah ain't cool, son."

I frown, narrowing my eyes. "Yo, you already know what it is with me. So ain't no use in you tryna beat me in the head 'bout it. You know ain't shit changing. I'ma still do me. So you might as well save ya breath for that smoke 'cause I ain't tryna hear it. So movin' on, muhfucka."

She laughs. "Yo, whatever. You still my niggah 'n' shit, but you know I still think that shit's fucked up, yo. And I'ma keep sayin' it. Real spit, son, you need to stop misleadin' them straight broads before you end up gettin' caught up in some crazy shit. Niggahs get bodied behind doin' that dumb shit, yo."

"Yo, fam, relax. I got this. Ain't nobody gonna do shit over here, yo. You already know gettin' shot at ain't never pumped no fear in a muhfucka like me. You know I'ma do what I do, regardless."

She shakes her head, reaching for the blunt. "Yeah, I know. But I still love you, wit' ya punk-ass."

I laugh. "Yo, fuck you, muhfucka. I got ya punk, aiight."

She laughs with me. "Yo, you know you my, niggah, fam."

"Yeah, right. I'm only ya niggah, greedy muhfucka, 'cause you stay tryna smoke up my shit. Pass me that blunt wit' ya lil'-ass dick."

She grabs her crotch. "Hahahaha, muhfucka, my shit's bigger than yours." She lifts her hips from her seat, pulls her sweats down over her hips, then reaches inside the opening of her striped boxers and pulls out her long chocolate dick. "Nine-inches niggah, and what?"

"Yo, son, you wildin', yo. I ain't tryna see all that. Put that shit away. You dead wrong, muhfucka. How ya yellow ass gonna have a dick five times darker than you?"

She gives me the finger. "Niggah, I ain't yellow. I'm light-skinned."

I crack up laughing. "And ya light-skinned ass still look like Big Bird, muhfucka. Hand me the blunt with ya tall, yellow ass." She cracks up with me, taking another pull, then handing back what's now practically a roach. We joke 'n' pop shit and smoke two more blunts before she gets a call from one'a her jump-offs and dips off for some pussy.

I light another blunt, smoke half of it, then start feeling kinda horny. I rub my dick over my jeans. I want some pussy, but I ain't beat for none'a these broads around here. I pick up my cell and hit up one'a my out-of-state sidepieces, Kamisha. She's a sexy lil chocolate dime I snatched up after a night of partying at this club in Atlanta a few months ago. She was checkin' for me hard, diggin' my swag and my Northern accent. And, of course, the bulge she peeped in my baggy jeans. And I was diggin' her thick hips, tiny waist, and that big juicy ass she had stuffed inside a pair of faded jeans.

Yo, I saw it in her eyes. She wanted to fuck. And I was more than happy to serve her this dick. I got up in her ear, spit game at her, and bought her a few rounds of drinks. After three drinks in, I got her to come outside with me, where we ended up sitting in my rented SUV, talking. Then kissing. And, eventually…fucking.

Yo, I had this sexy chocolate bitch in the backseat of the truck I rented riding her ass nice and deep, her pussy around my con-dom-wrapped dick. Word is bond. She handled all eight inches with ease as I fucked her slowly at first, savoring the feel and warmth of her body. I bit the back of her neck as I stroked her insides, making her moan—making myself moan as the base of my dick hit my clit. She pressed her hips back to meet my thrusts as I reached around her body and pressed on her slippery clit with two fingers. She reached back and grabbed my thigh, pulling me in closer as she worked her hot pussy on my dick.

She grunted. "Oh, God, this dick is good."

"Yeah, you like that shit?" I whispered in her ear.

"Oh, fuck, yes…nice thick dick…mmmph…"

"Yeah, you gonna nut on this dick…?"

"Yes, niggah…mmmph…make my pussy skeet…"

"Oh, you wanna talk shit, huh? You one'a them shit-talkin' freaks, huh?" I slapped her on the ass.

"Yeah, niggah…oh, shit…motherfucker…push my guts in, niggah…"

With one hand, I pinned her wrists to her back and started ramming her. I pressed her down into the seat, pounding her harder and harder. Her pussy was as wet as a river, soaking my dick, clenching my dick, milking my dick, calling my name over and over.

"Fuck my pussy, niggah…uhh…yeah, yeah…make my pussy spit, niggah."

Word is bond, yo, Kamisha was talking mad nasty in the back of that truck. We fucked hard, fogging up the windows. She even let me get up in that tight ass. By the time I finished gutting her insides out she climbed up outta that truck walking like she had just got fucked by a herd of horses. I tore that pussy 'n' ass up.

Now she's been pressin' me to slide back down there to hit that shit again. But I ain't with that shit, yo. I'ma hit it 'n' quit it kinda muhfucka.

"Yo, what's good, ma," I say, I unzipping my jeans and sliding my hand down into my boxers. "How's that fat, sweet peach doing?"

"Heeeeeey, boo," she sings into the phone in her syrupy Southern drawl. "It's sooo wet and juicy. You wanna taste?"

"Hellz yeah," I say, reaching for my lube and squirting some over my dick. I glide my hand up 'n' down the shaft, every down stroke pushing deeper into my clit. "Word is bond, ma, I wanna lick all up in that good shit, then give you all this dick." I stroke myself. "What kinda panties you got on?"

"Mmmm, you making pussy tingle. I have on a black thong."

"Oh word? Damn. I bet all that fat ass looks real sexy in them shits, too. I wanna suck on them panties, ma, while I'm hittin' that shit from the back."

"Mmmm. That sounds good. It's all yours, boo. So when are you coming back to Atlanta to get some more of this wet pussy?"

Yo, real shit. I have no intentions of going back to the ATL to link up with this broad. Yeah, she's mad sexy. Yeah, she had some good pussy. But unless she's down for another car fuck—from the back and we happen to run into each other, she prolly won't be getting another round of this dick. And that's real shit, yo. I mean, shit. It ain't like I can come out 'n' say, "Yo, ma...by the way that dick I fucked you real good wit' ain't no real dick. Oh, and another thing: ya boy ain't no real niggah." Nope, not gonna happen. So, nah, we definitely not linking up again.

See. Typically, when I hit up a straight club and score some pussy afterward, I ain't pressed for exchanging the digits. But there are always exceptions to my rule, like her. So when I'm outta state—or even here in the tri-state—and I link up with a sexy bitch, like Kamisha, I usually take their numbers knowing nothing else is gonna ever pop off between us. That I ain't gonna be checkin' for them after I get in them drawers. But, if a chick's from outta state, I still might hit 'er up to kick it, or—as in this case—get me a quick nut off since I dig a good phone-bone e'ery now 'n' then.

And Kamisha's freak-nasty ass is always down for hot, steamy phone sex.

"Soon, ma," I lie, gripping my dick tighter in my hand. "Word is bond. I wanna bury my dick deep in that shit."

"Oooh, I like that. Mmm. Hearing your voice always gets my pussy so wet."

"Oh word? You dig my voice?"

"Mmhmm. It's sexy as hell. Shit, you sexy as hell."

I grin. "Oh word? You think a muhfucka's sexy?"

"Mmhmm. My girls were saying how fine you was when they saw you in the club that time." She laughs. "I had to get you before any of them did."

"Oh word? You glad you did?"

"Yup. And I want some more of Daddy's big dick, too."

"And Daddy got all the dick you want. You got my shit hard as hell, ma."

"Oooh. What you doing to it?"

"What you think? Strokin' it, ma." I grunt, grinding my hips up into each hand stroke. I feel my nut building up inside of me. "Yo, ma, take them panties off 'n' let me hear you play in that fat pussy. Let me hear you get that pussy wet, ma."

It doesn't take her long to get wit' the program and start strumming her fingers over her clit, then inching them into her pussy. She starts to moan. "For real, Reggie. You need to come back to the ATL and let me get some more of that dick. It felt so good in my pussy, Daddy."

Her Southern accent is thick with lust.

"Damn…mmmph…Daddy wants to give it to you, too. Real good. So you want some more of this big dick, huh?"

"Oooh, yes. It's so fat. I loved the way it stretched the back of my pussy. I wish I coulda sucked it for you. Maybe next time. I ain't never been fucked in the backseat of a truck before. That was so hot, Reggie. I don't know what it is about you, but I can't stop thinking about you."

Yeah, I already know what it is. You can't stop thinking about this dick 'n' how well I served them holes up wit' it.

I grin. "That's wassup, ma. I can't stop thinking about you either." Yeah I know it's all game, but whatever. "Or that fat pussy. I wanna eat that shit, again."

She moans. "What else you wanna do, papi?"

"I want you to sit on my face and fuck my tongue. I love eatin' pussy, ma. And I wanna eat yours again."

"Mmmm. I love my pussy ate. And you ate mine so good. I ain't had a nigga eat my pussy like that in a minute, boo."

I grin. I know my tongue game is right. And I know how'ta eat a pussy inside out. "C'mon, ma. You got my dick real hard. Stick a finger in that pussyhole for me. And tell me how wet it is."

She moans in my ear. "Ooh, Reggie, it's so wet and slippery. It's like being in an ocean, waves and waves of warm juices all for you. I can't wait for you to put your dick back in it. Is your dick out?"

I grunt as the base of my dick swiftly brushes up against my clit. "No doubt. I'm stroking my shit imagining being balls deep in your pussy. Damn, ma. I wanna fuck."

"Mmm, me too. Stroke that big dick for me, daddy. I wish you'd send me a picture of it so I can have something to masturbate to."

I blink. She's sent me several pussy shots over the last few weeks, and has asked me on a few occasions to hit her wit' some flicks of my shit. But it ain't gonna happen.

"I really wanna see your dick, boo."

I shake my head. "Nah, I ain't with sending cock shots out, ma, unless you my girl, feel me? But I'ma come through and hit you with the real thing again."

"When, Reggie? When you coming back to Atlanta to feed my pussy some more of that good dick, boo? Every time we talk you tell me you're coming back out here, and I'm still waiting. Are you married or something?"

"Nah. I tol' you. I'm single, ma."

"Mmmph. Then what is it? Do I need to get a flight to come there 'cause I will?"

"Nah, you good, yo. But, dig. I ain't tryna talk about all that right now." *I don't know why the fuck I even called this bitch.* "I'm tryna bust this nut real quick, yo."

She sucks her teeth. "Then come out here and see me. You can bust all the nuts you want. I wanna see you, again. But if you're not interested in spending time with me then say so."

I sigh, letting go of my dick. Real shit, this broad done messed up my mood, for real for real. "Listen. I'ma bounce, yo. I'll holla at you later, a'ight?"

"Wow. I'm trying to talk to you about spending some time together and 'I'ma bounce' is all you gotta say? Wow. I tell you what. Don't bother. Delete my number." The line goes dead.

I shake my head. *These fuckin' broads stay trippin'! I'm horny as shit 'n' that dizzy bitch wanna be on some stupid shit.* I glance at my watch, then down at my lubed dick.

Fucking bitch!

10:38 P.M., it ain't no surprise when I'm in my whip, pulling up into the crowded parking lot to this spot, Club Scandal, in Paterson. It's my first time here so I ain't really sure what's gonna pop off. But some of the straight cats that I work with who've been here say that this spot always has some bangin' bitches looking to get their fuck on up in there. So here I am. Hoping to get up on some cutie who's liquored up right and horny enough to wanna fuck in the backseat of my whip, or on the side of the building.

I park. Then sit out in my whip for a minute and finish smoking my blunt. I slink down in my seat, gaping my legs open, grabbing at my dick. I get my smoke on. I'm horny as fuck. The only thing on my mind is getting this dick wet. It's an addiction. Chasing pussy. Straight pussy. Driving up and down the highway to straight bars and clubs, hoping to bang some unsuspecting pussy. It's a rush for me.

One I ain't tryna let go of anytime soon.

With my blunt dangling from my lips, I peep my reflection outta the rearview mirror. Real shit, I'ma sexy muhfucka. I reach for my brush, brushing my deep waves. My hairline is piped out, crisper than a muhfucka. My barber is real sick wit' a set of clippers, and he knows how'ta hook a niggah up right. All I need are some sideburns 'n' a mustache and you wouldn't be able to tell me a muthafuckin' thing, word up. Shit, you can't tell me shit now. So you already know what it is. I toss my brush over in the passenger seat, finishing up my smoke. When I'm done, I flick the roach outta the window. Then pull out a bottle of Marc Jacobs from outta the glove compartment, spraying it all over me. Real shit, as much as I dig blazin', I hate the smell of the shit in my clothes.

Let's see if I can make this shit pop tonight, I think getting outta my whip, setting the alarm, then making my way toward the club's entrance. I smooth my hand over my crisp white Polo shirt, tucking the front of it into my pants so that the buckle of my Gucci belt can show. Yo, fuck what ya heard. A muhfucka stays fly, feel me? I cock my Brooklyn Nets fitted up on my head, snapping it to the side, then step.

Two thick-hipped shorties walk by, checking me out. They look a'ight. But definitely nothing I'd wanna fuck unless I had no other options. I mean, real shit. They not mad ugly, but they ain't fine enough to get my dick hard either. Fuck what ya heard. I don't give this dick to anyone. You gotta be on point in order for me to wanna fuck you.

I give 'em both head nods. "Yo, what's good?"

They both speak, bouncing their asses mad hard in their tiny skirts. I stare at them asses. And they both got them fatties; word is bond.

Shit, niggah, what you stressin' about how them hoes look for when all you gonna be doin' is fuckin' 'em from the back? I scold in my head as I stand in the line to get in.

Chicks are free before eleven. It's after midnight. And a few bitches in back of me are poppin' shit about getting here late. Niggahs gotta pay twenty dollars to get in. "Bitch, you stay making us late for shit," I hear this chick say in back of me. "I swear. I knew we shoulda left ya stank-ass."

"Oh, bitch, please. Eat a dick. You know damn well y'all heifers wasn't leaving me no-damn-where. So shut the fuck up with them lies."

"Girl," I hear another chick say, "I know you ain't even stressing over ten-goddamn-dollars when you just sent Cedric a hundred dollars to put on his books. You stupid as hell."

Damn, I hope this spot ain't gonna be filled wit' a buncha ghetto-ass hood bitches. The last thing I wanna do is be someplace where a buncha bitches get to drinking 'n' tearing up the club if someone looks at 'em the wrong way. Although that hood pussy is good as fuck.

"Trick, don't worry about how much I sent Cedric. That ain't got shit to do with this bitch here making us late."

"Selena, shut the fuck up, okay. Damn. You stay fuckin' complaining about dumb shit. So, we late. Big fucking deal. If you pinching pennies then maybe you shoulda kept ya cheap ass home."

I chuckle to myself.

"Whatever, bitch. Think what you want. But watch and see what happens tomorrow night when ya ass ain't ready. We pulling the fuck out without ya ugly gorilla-faced ass. Two hours to get fuckin' dressed and ya ass still look like shit. Stank-ass."

"Bitch, hush," the other chick says. "I ain't hearing you."

"Damn," someone else huffs. "I wish both you bitches would shut the fuck up. It's ten fucking dollars. I'll pay your way in. I wanna have a good time tonight. And if I'm lucky enough, get fucked-down real good by one'a these fine motherfuckas up in here. Not hear a buncha whiny-ass bitches. I haven't had a hard dick in over three weeks and a bitch is real cranky. I might have to cut a bitch tonight if I don't get laid soon."

I chuckle, quickly glancing over my shoulder to see who's talkin' my kinda talk. *Damn, let her be fine.* All four of them look a'ight. But the broad wit' the mocha skin and greenish-colored eyes and big-ass tits busting outta a low-cut red dress catches my eye. I glance down at her big bouncy titties, then step forward in line.

"Girl, that nigga was looking all down your dress."

"Well, don't hate. Obviously he liked something he saw." She taps me on the shoulder. "Ain't that right, boo?"

I crane my neck, clearing my throat. Thanks to years of blazin' 'n' smokin' Newports I already have a raspy voice. But I deepen it, anyway, to add enough bass without overdoing it. "No doubt."

"Oooh, and you got the nerve to be a cutie, too. You gotta girl?"

I shake my head. "Nah. I'm good on that, ma."

She grins. "Good. Then maybe I'll save you a dance and let you buy me and my girls a drink once we get inside."

Oh, you'll let *me? Really?* I keep from laughing at that silly shit. These hoes got me confused. Her girls eye me, smirking. And I already know what it is. I'm fresh meat to 'em. They see me as an opportunity. They're probably thinking they can run my pockets all night. They look ready to pounce on the chance to get free drinks all night. Fuck what ya heard. If I'm coming up from off'a my paper, you're coming up outta them drawers, real shit.

"Maybe," is all I say, finally stepping inside the club's glass doors. After I'm frisked, I walk over to the glass window and hand the cashier, this sexy lil' brown skin cutie, my paper. She slides me my change, then stamps the inside of my wrist. I wink at her, walking off.

The music's on full-blast. Red Café's "Gucci Everything" is pumping outta the speakers. Mad heads are everywhere. Hands up, drinks up, muhfuckas are all pressed up on chicks' asses getting their dance on. The dance floor is in the center of the club and is mad packed. Although the lights are dim, so far, I don't see anyone I know, or who knows me. And I'm hoping it stays that way. As I make my way over to the bar, I peep a few broads checkin' for me. A few niggahs eye me. I give 'em all head nods and keep strolling by.

When it's my first time at a club, I usually post up at the bar, take everything all in. And tonight is no different. I'll hang around the bar, toss back a few drinks and hopefully catch the eye of someone worth spending my energy 'n' paper on. Getting some pussy is the only objective.

Two chicks eye me as they slide off their barstools. I ask 'em if they're coming back. They say no. "Not unless you want us to," one of 'em says to me. Her eyes all glassy 'n' halfway crossed. I smile. She's a'ight-looking in the face, and her body doesn't appear that bad judging by the way her jeans are wrapped around her hips. But I peep she gotta flat ass, which def ain't my thing. "Nah, I'm good, ma."

I take a seat up on one of the stools, glancing around the bar.

On the opposite end of the bar, a milk chocolate cutie is eyeing me. She has a drink in her hand. Sitting on a stool next to her is a tall, dark-skinned niggah all up in her grill. And whatever he's beating her in the head about she doesn't seem interested in. I order a shot of Henny and a Heineken. I glance back over at Milk Chocolate and she's still got her eyes on me. I give her a head nod and she smiles. The niggah she's with looks over in my direction, then turns back to her. He says something else to her and I peep her rolling her eyes. The niggah's rap game must be mad whack, I think, staring ahead at the bottles on the wall.

The bartender returns with my drink. I tell him to keep the tab open, then take a swig of my cold beer. A Meek Mill joint starts playing and I bob my head to the beat. Although I'm staring straight ahead into the mirrors along the back of the bar, I can peep Milk Chocolate glancing over at me outta the corner of my eye.

I take my shot to the head, then slide the empty shot glass to the edge of the bar, signaling for the bartender to hit me again. I concentrate on the colored lights shimmering in the mirror, steadily sipping my beer. "Yo, my bad, man," a brown-skinned cat says to me as he bumps into me trying to get off his stool. The niggah's lit.

I eye him, giving him a head nod. "It's all good, yo."

"Fuckin' Incredible Hulks. Got me ripped, fam."

"I feel you," I say, fighting back a chuckle, pleased that this niggah, like most, think I'm one of them. I've worked hard at achieving this look. Long hours in the gym to get this chiseled body, countless hours in the mirror brushing in these spinnin'-ass waves, and years of perfecting my swag. And it's all paying off.

Growing up, while all the lil bitches in junior high school were stressing 'bout pimples and periods and obsessing about the size of their titties and asses, I was embracing my tomboyish ways, hoping like hell that my A-cup titties didn't get any bigger than what they already were. I was praying that puberty wouldn't widen my narrow hips and turn them into dangerous curves, or that my ass wouldn't get wobbly 'n' bouncy like a chick's. That it stay muscled and firm like a niggah's. Being shaped like a chick wasn't what I hoped for.

While the young hot bitches in high school were obsessed wit' fucking and sucking the hottest niggahs. I was consumed wit' being one. Sometimes, nah...most times...late at night, I'd be lying in my bed—the base of my dick pressed into my clit—jacking off, stroking my shit until I popped off a hot one. I'd imagine what it would be like having a real dick. My silicone cock replaced by a long, brown fleshy dick with thick veins and a huge mushroom head. The base of my detachable cock would be where a pair of huge smooth-shaven balls would hang. And I'd imagine having one of them pretty bitches from school down on her knees sucking my dick, tea-bagging my balls...maybe even licking my ass, if she was freaky enough.

Her sexy soft lips would be wrapped around my cock. My leaking nut wetting her lips as she swallowed me down into her throat. She'd kiss the head of my dick, the head would glide gently into her mouth and my nut would spurt into her mouth as she cupped my balls. She'd lick my thick cock clean, then assume the position on all fours and take my dick, deep into her wet pussy.

My pulsing clit would vibrate through the shaft of my cock as I thrust in and outta her, until she cried out...and I cried out. And we both came.

For years, my mind constantly buzzed with erotic, freaky thoughts of fucking and getting sucked. And it was in those fantasies that I mastered beating my dick, that I learned how to bust my nut without ever touching my own self. So instead of using fingers, I'd get off with stroking my dick, my wetness coating the base of my cock. The tip of my clit became the head of my dick. And I'd nut, fast 'n' hard.

I was seventeen when I fucked my first *straight* chick. I was on the girls' Varsity basketball team. She was a Varsity cheerleader for the boys' basketball team, and the girlfriend of the captain of the team. She was one of them uppity light-skinned bitches with shimmering green-eyes and long, wavy hair who knew she was the hottest bitch on the yard.

Yeah, I ain't gonna front. I was checkin' for her like the rest of the niggahs in school, but I wasn't tryna press her. As far as I was concerned, she was outta my league. She wasn't down wit' the get down, so I knew enough to stay in my own lane. Along with the fact that she'd always had her lip curled up in disgust anytime she saw me in the halls, like me being who I was, was some kinda disease.

But one night after practice, she happened to be in the girls' locker room standing in front of the mirror as I walked outta the showers wit' a towel wrapped around me. Everyone else had already left the locker room. It was only the two of us.

Alone.

She eyed me through the mirror. But I igged her.

She huffed and turned to me. "So you're not gonna speak?"

I frowned at her through the mirror. "Bitch, please. For what, yo? Ya stuck-up ass sees me in the halls and you ain't never beat to speak so why the fuck should I speak now?"

"*Bitch*...?" And it was on 'n' popping. She started popping mad shit and before I knew it, I was up in her grill, finger pointing in her face, ready to punch her lights out. I could see that I had her shook, but I was heated...in more than one way. I was sexually frustrated. I wanted some pussy. And at that moment I wanted to beat the shit outta her for being such a homophobic bitch.

But then something flipped. I don't know if it was because she had tears in her eyes or if being up on her and breathing in her sweet scent had me all fucked up, but I stopped snappin' on her and stood there staring at her for what seemed like forever. She was staring back at me, breathing heavy. Before I knew it, I snatched her up and started kissing her, grabbing a chunk of her ass, and feeling all up on her titties.

It all happened fast. She didn't stop me. And I didn't want her to. I got her shirt off, then her bra. Then her nipples were in my mouth. And she was moaning. Then I was unbuckling her jeans and she was shimmying her way outta them. My fingers slid into her pussy. It was wet. *This bitch been wanting some of this*, I thought as I pushed my way into her knuckles deep, fucking her with fingers, first, then my tongue, then my strap-on. Yeah, she wanted me to fuck her. And I did. Right there in the locker room I banged her pussy up real good until her juices splashed out onto my cock.

Then I pulled out and bent her over one of the bathroom sinks, pulled open her buttery-soft ass cheeks and rimmed the shit outta her asshole. That was my first time eating ass. And it turned me the fuck on. Her wet pussy glazed my chin as I tongued her down. I stroked my dick and nearly nutted from the taste of her sweet, musky scent. "Ooh, yes, eat my ass, boo. You nasty fucker. Uh, yes…"

Ol' lil Miss Stuck Up was talkin' mad shit, eggin' me on. Urgin' me to keep going, to stuff my tongue chin-deep into her ass. She was an undercover freak like I thought she was. And it turned me on. But then she slipped and said, "Yeah, you nasty dyke bitch." Now my first response, as it has always been, was to hop up and push her wig back. But I decided to handle her another way. Instead of beating her face in, busting open her tight virgin asshole was a much sweeter way to get at her. And, at that moment, with my tongue in her ass and two fingers fucking her pussy I hoped someone walked in and caught us. I wanted someone to catch me ramming my cock into her ass.

Her coming outta her face calling me a dyke made me wanna fuck her hard and deep and fast until my whole dick slid out of her throat and my nut spurted outta her trash-talking mouth.

I spit in her hole, pushing my middle finger in. She gasped, wriggling her ass back and forth. I slipped another finger in, stretching her, working her open. She hissed and grunted, still poppin' shit.

I slapped her on the ass. "Is this what you want, stuck-up bitch?" She groaned. I stood up, bent her all the way over as she pulled open her ass. The tip of my dick popped in, and then I rammed everything in, causing her to yell out. I covered her mouth and she bit me, grunting. I could feel her ass spasming as I rapidly thrust into her. Rhythmic fuck-sounds, grunts, and moans and the scent of pussy and ass filled the locker room. I gripped her by the hair and banged the shit outta her, reaching around and playing wit' her clit. She glanced over her shoulder at me, pulling me into her by the back of my neck. She kissed me. A few seconds later, we were both nuttin'.

And when we were done, she walked out, like nothing ever happened. The bitch still didn't speak when she'd see me in the halls. But she didn't try to avoid me either. In fact, I fucked her on the low at least once a week for the rest of the school year. All the way up until she left to go to Spelman. And the crazy thing is, her boyfriend and I ended up the same university playing basketball. I'd see him on campus 'n' we'd speak 'n' shit, but I'd be laughing inside every time he spoke about his girl, knowing I'd been fucking her, too.

An old Kirko Bangz joint, "What Yo Name Iz?," starts playing, bringing me outta my thoughts. I toss back my drink. And order another one. Outta the corner of my eye, I peep Milk Chocolate glancing over at me. I grab my beer from off the bar, then spin around on my stool to check the happenings. Real shit, there's some bad bitches up in here, but the thirsty niggahs in the room are already sweating most of 'em hard. I glance over at Milk Chocolate. She grins at me. Again, the lame niggah she's wit' looks over his shoulder at me. I give him a head nod. He turns back to Milk Chocolate.

The bartender comes back wit' my third shot. I toss it back and I'm starting to feel right. Someone else gets up from the bar, leaving their stool empty. I half hope the seat stays empty or that some sexy ho inches her horny ass up on it. I peep Milk Chocolate dismissing the lame niggah who's been all up in her face, then making her way over to me. Looks like I'ma get my wish.

I spin around back toward the bar, fronting like I don't peep her. I sip my beer. "Hey, sexy man," she says, smiling. "Is anyone sitting here?"

"Nah," I say, eyeing her as she inches her phatty up on the stool. "It's all you." She's wearing a red, knee-length wrapdress. I watch as her slit spills open showing her smooth thigh. I lick my lips. *Yeah, she's fuckable.*

She turns to me. Her deep brown eyes taking me in. "You're too fine to be sitting here by yourself. Are you waiting for someone?" I tell her nah. Tell her I'm solo. Here chillin' by myself. "Mmmph. I tell you what. How about you buy me a drink, and we chill together."

"Oh word? And what about ole boy over there?"

She twists up her juicy red-painted lips. I squeeze my legs shut, imagining them thick dick suckers wrapped around my cock.

"Puhleeeze. That broke niggah was boring the shit out of me."
She waves the bartender over. "Hey, Frankie, let me get a Ciroc
and pineapple." Dude looks over at me. I order another shot 'n'
a beer. Tell him her drink is on me.

"Yo, you gotta name, ma?"

"It's Alicia. And yours?"

"Reggie," I say, placing my forearms up on the bar, then clasping
my hands around my beer bottle.

"So where you from, Reggie? I haven't seen you in here before."

"Yeah, it's my first time." I tell her I'm from Elizabeth, although
it's a lie. I don't ever tell any of these chicks I get at what town I
rest at.

"Oh, okay. So what brings you out here?"

"I heard this spot was live so I wanted to check out the happenings
for myself."

She grins slyly, lifting her drink. "Well, I hope you like what
you see so far."

I lean back, glancing at her ass, then back at her. "No doubt,
ma. So far, I'm diggin' e'erything I see. So where you rest at, ma?
Paterson?" She tells me she lives in Paramus, about twenty minutes
away from here. We go back 'n' forth wit' the small talk for a
minute. I find out she's twenty-eight. Single, but happily looking.
No kids. Has her own crib. And she works for the city. I tell her
basic shit. That I'm thirty, happily single, and no kids.

Real shit, I'm not sure how many drinks she tossed back before
she parked her ass up on the stool next to me, but after her third
Ciroc her tongue starts gettin' mad loose, talking about how she's
horny, how she came out hoping to bring someone home with her
tonight. And the more she flaps her jaws, the harder my dick gets.

I grin. *Them niggahs at work weren't bullshitting when they said
these hoes up in here are some easy ass.*

"Ain't that somethin'?" I say, eyeing her. "And I came here hopin' to slide my dick into somethin' real wet."

"You ain't ready for none of this wetness, boo," she teases, sipping her drink.

"Yeah, a'ight. That's what ya mouth says. I already know what it is. I stay ready."

She laughs. "We'll see."

"No doubt." I raise my drink, then toss it back.

Asap Rocky's "Fuckin' Problems" starts playing. "Aaah, shit." She snaps her fingers, starts winding her ass up on the stool. "This is my shit. You wanna dance?"

"Nah, I ain't tryna dance, ma," I say, leaning in closer. "I'm tryna fuck."

"Ooh, right to the point. I like that. A niggah who knows what he wants."

"No doubt. I ain't got time to be beatin' around the bush, ma. Life is too short for the dumbness." I grab my beer, holding it up. She clinks her glass against the bottle.

"Here's to knowing what you want. And knowing how to get it."

"And what you want?"

She licks her lips. "To get my drink on and have a real good time. And, hopefully, end the night with some real good dick."

"Yo, check this out, ma," I say, placing my hand on the small of her back and staring deep into her eyes. I'm not sure whether or not it's the drinks or the fact that the more I stare at her the better looking she is starting to look to me, but all I know is, my clit's throbbing like a muhfucka. And I wanna fuck. "You sexy as fuck."

She grins. "So are you." She tosses back the rest of her drink, placing the empty glass up on the bar. Her hand is on the inside of my thigh. "So now that we've gotten all that 'you're so sexy' shit out the way, now what? My place or yours?"

Nah, the backseat of my whip!

"I'ma make you nut, ma."

Her eyes widen. "Here? Now?"

I keep my gaze locked on hers. "No doubt." I lean into her ear, my horny hot mouth next to her ear. "I wanna finger your pussy, yo."

She laughs, almost choking. "Ohmygod, niggah, you crazy. I ain't never have no niggah tell me he wanted to finger-fuck me in a club, at the bar, around buncha people. OMG, you see all these niggahs in here? What if someone sees you?"

I shrug. "What that got to do with me and you, ma? Like I said, you sexy as fuck. I wanna have a few more drinks wit' you and feel ya pussy wrapped around my fingers while we sit here 'n' chill at the bar. You wit' it?" I take her hand and place it on the bulge in my jeans. "You feel that shit, yo?" She licks her lips, glancing around the club. "Yo, I tell you what. I'ma go wash my hands real quick. While I'm gone, I want you to peel them panties off for me."

She blinks. "And do what with them?"

I grin, stroking along the edges of her jaw. I lean back into her ear. "I'ma lick them shits, yo."

She laughs. "You crazy as hell."

"Nah, ma, I'm dead ass. If you aint wit' it, then I guess you'll be gone when I get back."

She tilts her head, smirking. One hand on her hip. "And if I'm still sitting here?"

"Yo, don't play, ma. You already know what it is. If ya sexy ass is still here when I get back, then you need to be peelin' them drawers off."

"Damn, niggah, you some kinda nasty." She glances around the bar to see if anyone is listening to us, then glances at her reflection in the mirror over the bar before bringing her attention back to me. I'm still staring at her when she looks me in the eyes. "Make sure you wash them hands good."

I smirk. "Oh, my hands will be clean. You make sure you have them panties off." I gulp back the rest of my beer and plop the empty bottle down, wiping my mouth with the back of my hand. I flag the bartender and order us another round of drinks. Leaning in, I tell her, "Real shit, ma. I wanna feel ya pussy. Then take you outside and pipe you out."

Eyebrow raised, she gives me an amused look over the rim of her glass. She takes a slow, deliberate sip as if she's tryna decide if she wants to indulge me, or turn up the 'tude and get it crunked for coming at her like this. She narrows her eyes, but doesn't start neck-rolling it like she's ready to crank up the 'tude so I already know what it is. She's a freaky bitch wit' it. I lick my lips. I can already see her dress hiked up over her hips, me in back of her watching my shiny, wet dick from her gooey cunt slide in and outta her. Her ass up, back arched, face pressed down into the leather seat, taking this dick like a pro.

Instinctively, I grab my dick. "Hope you're still here when I get back." I walk off in the direction of the men's room, feeling her eyes on me as I zigzag my way through the crowd. The club's mad packed. I have to practically elbow niggahs outta the way just to get to the fucking bathroom.

When I return to the bar, Milk Chocolate's still perched up at the bar. She's talking to some tall, lanky dark-skinned muhfucka wit' blonde locks. He dips off wit' a drink in his hand as I approach the bar. He gives me a head nod and keeps it moving.

I grin. "I see you still here."

"Of course I am. I'ma real bitch. I don't buckle, baby."

"That's wasssup. You got them panties off for me?"

She smirks. "Order me another drink and find out for yourself. You want 'em off, you take 'em off."

"Oh word? Don't think I won't peel them drawers off, ma."

"Then do it, niggah." I flag the bartender over and order her, like her fifth or sixth drink. Yeah, the bitch is tanked up. Her eyes are glassy. And I can tell she's feeling real right. I step in back of her, pressing myself up against her back. I slip my hand in the slit of her dress.

"You crazy as hell. You know that, right?" She says this over her shoulder, before glancing around the bar, then the club to see who's watching. "What if someone sees you?"

"Then let 'em watch. We'll give 'em a real live show." I inch my hand up her smooth thigh. "Open ya legs for me, ma. I see you ain't take them drawers off like I asked. But it's all good. I'ma slide my fingers in anyway."

"Ohmygod," she says, reaching for her drink the moment the bartender sets it in front of her. She tosses half of it back. *Damn, this bitch gotta long throat*, I think, inching my hand further up her thigh. *Fuckin' lush! Yeah, I'ma get some'a this pussy tonight.* "I can't believe I'm actually letting you do this. Right here."

"Why? I know you a freak, baby. Live on the edge a lil. Let ya freak flag fly." I press my hips into her back. My clit is pulsing through my cock. It's throbbing and I'm ready to nut, real shit, yo. I rub my dick over my jeans a few times, stroking it so that it pushes into my clit. My dick feels extra hard, even though I know it's all in my head. But the shit feels like it's coming to life.

"You gonna let me get up in this sweet, pink pussy, huh, ma?" She smirks. "Maybe."

"Yeah, a'ight, ma. Front if you want. I already know what it is."

"Oh yeah? And what is that?"

I lightly rub her inner thigh. "You want me to shove this fat dick into your pussy, and pound that shit real good for you, don't you?" I rub the front of her panties. I feel for her clit and massage it. "You gonna let me pound that pussy, ma?"

Her lips part, a breath escapes her, but she doesn't speak for a few seconds. She blinks, slowly having second thoughts about what's about to pop off. "Maybe…mmmm…we shouldn't. Not here."

"Yes, here. We good, ma. Relax. Let these muhfuckas do them while I do you." My lips are pressed up to her ear. "I'm spread ya slit wit' my thumbs, then run the tip of my long wet tongue from ya clit to ya crack, then skim ya slit wit' it before circlin' my tongue around your pussy. Then I'ma push it deep in you. You want that?"

She responds with a grunt.

"I bet you got some good tastin' pussy, don't you?"

"Mmm…sure do."

"I'ma 'bout to find out." I ease a finger into her panties, then dip a finger inside of her. Damn, she's wet. "Damn, ma…pussy's wet already, huh?"

She leans forward, places both hands up on the bar. "Ooh… you're a real nasty niggah. You got me doing some shit I ain't never done before." She locks her gaze on to me. "I hope you have a big dick 'cause I'ma wanna leave here and fuck after this."

The only place we fuckin' is outside!

I grin, already anticipating sinking my horny dick between her warm, wet pussy lips. "Oh word? That's wassup." I find her clit, circling two fingertips over it. "Want me to eat your pussy, ma?" I say into her ear. She's trying desperately to keep it together, but the way she's lifting up off the stool, grinding her hips, I can tell she's ready for more. She grinds her pussy over my hand in sync to Rihanna's "Love Song." "Ooooh, this…isssss…my shit… uhhh…"

"Yeah, work that shit, ma…"

She takes a sip of her drink, tryna play shit cool. She's fightin' hard to keep her composure, but the shit ain't workin'. She throws her head back. "Oh, god, yessss!" she yells over Justin Timberlake's "Suit & Tie" as it plays.

I slide two fingers into her pussy. And she almost topples off the barstool, choking a lil on her drink. With the exception of the dim blinking lights around the bar, the majority of the club is dark so no one standing near or around us peeps what's really going down over here. And if they do, they ain't beat about it.

"Yeah, ma," I whisper into her ear, "give me that wet pussy." I cup my hand underneath her and she pushes her pelvis down onto my hand.

"Oooh, yes," she calls out as Trinidad James' "All Gold Everything" starts playing. She bounces on my hand.

"Yeah, that's it. Nut for me in front of all these muhfuckas, baby." My thumb traces circles around her clit as my fingers rapidly slip in and outta her. "All these niggahs up in here, I bet they can smell ya wet pussy, ma." A moan escapes her mouth. She pulls in her bottom lip. "You gettin' ready to nut for me, ma?"

"Yesss…" I pinch her clit. "Ooh, yes, goddammit. That's my shit." She grabs the edge of the bar, and nuts all over my hand. She keeps grinding on my hand, her pussy pulling and gripping my sticky fingers. Her juices soak my hand. She's hot and wet. Her ass wiggling on my hand, her fingers clawing the bar as another nut sweeps through her pussy and onto my hand. Her body jerks. I wait a few seconds more, then slowly pull my fingers outta her gushy hole. She turns to face me, her eyes all lusty 'n' shit, and watches me slip my fingers into my mouth and suck them clean.

She eyes me, brushing her hand along the front of my jeans. "Let's get out of here. I wanna take you home with me."

She stands up, swaying a bit. *Yeah, this bitch mad tipsy. I'ma 'bout to get some'a this drunk pussy.* I grin. "Nah, ma, I ain't ready to go home wit' you."

"Then let me go to yours."

"Nah, can't take you to my spot, either."

She sucks her teeth. "Shit, niggah. You got my pussy all worked up. I want some dick. We ain't gotta go to my place or yours. But we gotta go somewhere. I wanna fuck. I can't take this."

"Then let's go to my whip," I say, signaling the bartender for the bill. I pull out a hundred dollar bill and toss it up on the bar. "You ready?"

"I ain't really into getting fucked in no car, like I'm some whore."

"Maybe you should try it. Step outta ya comfort zone, ma. Be my whore tonight. C'mon." I take her by the hand, leading her through the crowd.

She pulls back. "Wait. Let me go tell my girl, Elisa, I'ma go outside for a minute."

"Nah, text her. We're only goin' outside, ma. Tell her you'll be back in, like in, thirty minutes."

"Yeah, you're right," she says, pulling out her iPhone. She hits her peeps up, then follows me out the door.

"Damn, ma, you taste good." Alicia's on her knees, her head is pressed down into the leather seat, her ass cheeks spread wide. I swipe my tongue up and over her clit. Her body shivers as she moans. My tongue circles around her cunt, and she bucks against my mouth as my fingers find their way inside of her. My tongue swirls and caresses her clit while my hand 'n' fingers thrust in 'n' outta her. She surrenders to the sensations, and nuts against my mouth, grunting and groaning.

She cranes her neck over her shoulder. "Fuck me!" Her hips wind. "I want that dick, niggah." She reaches back and pulls open her ass. "Let me feel that dick."

I reach in my pocket and pull out a condom, tearing open its wrapper, then rolling it down onto my dick. Her pussy lips glisten. Her deep pink hole looks wet 'n' juicy.

I lean forward. She looks over her shoulder at me as I push through the tightness. Push through the wetness until I get to the bottom of her heated pussy. She gasps and hisses and whimpers as I ride her hips. I am lost in the idea of her thinkin' I'ma real niggah fucking her, lost in the fantasy of having my long, throbbing dick soaked in her juices. I close my eyes. Press my lips tight as I move inside of her. Fogged windows, my truck rocks as we get it in. Slow 'n' steady, I stroke her walls. Try to push in her uterus.

In.

Out.

In.

Out.

She moans, her nails digging in and grabbing at the leather seats.

I change my rhythm, pulling back a bit so I can spread open her ass and watch my dick slide in 'n' outta her. "Goddamn, that pretty pussy's grabbin' this dick, yo. Oh, fuck. Look at that shit. Tight-ass pussy all stretched open for this dick."

She grunts, bucking her hips, grinding her pussy up on my dick.

"Yeah, that's it, ma...nut on my dick. Coat my shit wit' ya juices..."

Her whimpering and moaning turns into chanting, "Yes, yes, yes, yes...ooh, ooh, ooh, ooh..."

I lightly bite the back of her neck. Grab a handful of her hair and yank her head back while plowin' my dick into her, fast 'n' deep. With each thrust, she grunts.

My whip smells of hot sex, wet pussy. My head starts to spin as I breathe it in.

"Ohhhh…fuck!"

"Yeah, that's it, ma…bust that pussy all over this hard dick…" she bounces her ass up on me. "Yeah, baby, give me that shit. Aaah, yeah…"

She twists her neck to face me. "I wanna suck your dick, niggah."

"Nah, baby, not tonight. I wanna keep it buried in this hot pussy."

"No, let me suck it. You can put it back in me. I wanna taste you."

What the fuck? As bad as I'd dig seeing her juicy lips wrapped 'round my dick, ain't no way it's about to pop off. Not tonight. I loop an arm around her waist, then use my other hand to reach up under her to play with her clit.

I groan into her back, feeling my own nut building up inside of me as the base strokes my clit. "Ohhh, shiiiit…pussy's good…" Yeah, I don't really know how good the shit is wrapped around my strap-on. But I know how it felt on my fingers, how it felt and tasted on my tongue. And I know what it looks like watching it slide in 'n' outta her. So I already know if this was a real cock guttin' her up, it'd feel good as fuck wrapped 'round my shit.

She grunts. "Oh, fuck, I'm cum…ming…mmmm…oooooh, yessss…"

I grunt along with her. "Yeah, baby… aaah, shit, I'm cummin' wit' you."

She screams out, and comes and comes and comes. My grunts deepen as I keep thrusting into, grinding the base of my cock against my clit. A few minutes more, and I slip outta her, then quickly plunge my tongue in, flapping it around her wetness, pulling her juices out, slurping her nut into my mouth. I do this as a diversion. As a way to pull off my condom and stuff my dick back into my pants before she can turn around and wanna see it, throat it. She rocks her hips, her pussy clenching my tongue.

"Ooooh, yesss…I'm coming again."

My mouth cups over her clit and I suck it as her body shakes. She rides my lips and tongue. Afterward, I climb into the front seat and crack open the steamed windows while she straightens herself. She climbs into the passenger seat.

"Whew, that was good." She runs a hand through her hair, then uses her fingers to fluff it out. "I feel like I need a cigarette now." She pulls her cell outta her purse.

"Glad you enjoyed it, ma," I say, cranking the engine.

"Yeah, you did that, boo." She hands me her phone. "I'ma need you to lock your number into my phone."

Shit. I hit her with one of my pre-paid jump-offs. I hand it back to her. She leans over and cups my cheeks. "Listen, ma. Real shit—" she smashes her lips against mine, tryna suck the air from my lungs. Her kiss is rough, real hungry, at first then softens. Her tongue slips inside of my mouth, swirls around mine. She sucks on it. Tastes her pussy on it.

She pulls back and we are both breathless. Her eyelids lift, and she looks me in the eyes. Hers are full of lust. I can tell she wants some more of this dick. Probably wants more than what I can give, or am willing to give, without her uncovering my secret.

"Thanks for bringing the freak out of me."

I grin, driving up closer toward the club's entrance. "No doubt, ma."

She opens the door, leaning in and kissing me quickly on the side of the mouth. "I'll call you."

"Cool." I eye her as she shuts the door and walks back toward the club. I pull off, tapping the horn, then peeling off, heading toward the parkway. I glance over and smile, grabbing the silky fabric she's left in the passenger seat. I reach for her panties. Bring them to my nose and inhale, holding the scent of her pussy in, committing it to memory. Yeah, she most def had some good pussy.

A few days later, me and some'a my bros, Prince, Scooter, and Jack—are down at the Fish Basket, a hot lil stripper joint flooded with hot femme bitches shakin' them moneymakers mad fast 'n' nasty. We're sitting in a booth, swag on ten, laced up in our Timbs, crisp white Tees, fitted caps, and jeans—poppin' mad shit 'n' tossing back shots of Rèmy XO, eyeing the action.

"Yo, this niggah right here," Prince says, flicking his thumb over toward me, "stays missin' in action."

Jack laughs. "You know that niggah stays on the prowl."

I wave 'em on. "Whatever, muhfuckas. I'm doin' me."

"Damn, that bitch is bad," Prince says, pointing to a big-booty, caramel-skinned cutie with tassels dangling from her long, dark nipples. Her tits are mad small, though.

"She's a'ight," I comment, tossing back another shot of Yak. Glad her ass has moved onto something else other than what I'm doing. "Them titties too small for me, though."

"She's 'a'ight'? Niggah, is your crazy?" She shakes her head.

I shake my head. "Nah, I'm dead-ass. She look a'ight."

She tisks. "You stylin', yo. That bitch is fiiyah, son."

I shoot her a look. "Yeah, a'ight. And she still got 'lil itty-bitty titties, muhfucka."

"I ain't checkin' for her boobs, niggah. You see the basket on that bitch, yo? That ass fat as shit." She grabs at her crotch. "Word is bond, yo. I'd run this dick all up in that juicy muhfucka."

Scooter throws a balled-up napkin at Prince, pulling out his cell. "Muhfucka, ya horny-ass stay tryna run ya dick up in sumthin'. Ya ass gonna fuck 'round and catch some shit you can't get rid of."

Prince gives Scooter the middle finger. "Catch that, pussy-whipped muhfucka. I ain't catchin' shit, bruh. I stays strapped. But you, on the other hand,"—Prince points at her—"'bout to catch another smack down if you don't have ya ass home by eleven."

Jack and I laugh.

"Yo, fuck outta here, muhfucka. Smack down hell. Queesha don't run shit over here."

Scooter is a five-six, baldhead, Hershey chocolate, masculine muhfucka with a mad thick neck, and seven-inch scar from her left cheek to her jaw compliments of her jealous-ass wifey. Three years ago, she caught Scooter grinding up on some other broad at a party and rolled up on her with her blade in her hand and did her dirty. The crazy-ass broad got her for about eighty-stitches, that time. Another time, she cut up all her shit 'n' tried to set a niggah on fire in her sleep. And you'd think Scooter's dumb ass woulda dipped on her nutty ass by now. Nope. She still with that crazy bitch.

Prince smirks. "Yeah right. Don't answer that phone, muhfucka, and let's see what happens. Tomorrow you'll be comin' out to the courts wit' two black eyes."

I crack up laughing. "Yo, real shit, son. Ya girl do be fuckin' ya lil ass up, yo."

Scooter sucks her teeth. "Fuck y'all muhfuckas." Her phone stops ringing, then starts up again. "Fuck! Let me get this shit before this bitch start buggin'."

We all laugh at her. "See. I tol' y'all her ass is pussy-whipped," Prince says, eyeing the broad with the big ass up on the stage.

Scooter gives Prince the middle finger, answering her phone. "Yo, what the fuck, Queesha…fuck! A'ight. I know, damn. Why can't you relax, yo? I'ma be home in a few. Damn. I'm sayin'… why the fuck is you buggin'…?"

We eye Scooter as she leaves the booth beefing with her girl. Jack tells us she 'bout to go to the other side of the club to shoot a round of pool over in the pool area. She grabs her drink and dips. Prince and I stay in our seats. I pour myself another shot.

Prince nods over at the stage. "Yo, son, I bet you that bitch got some good pussy."

"I ain't gonna front, bruh, she def caked up in the back, yo."

"Real shit, yo….I'ma bag that tonight," Prince says confidently, bobbing her head to the music and eyeing the stripper as she drops down to the floor and starts crawling on her hands and knees like a hungry panther on the hunt for her next mark.

I laugh. "Pretty muhfucka, you stay fuckin' with them strippers, yo. And you know most of 'em ratchet as hell."

She grins. "Shit, muhfucka. Ain't nothing wrong wit' a lil' ratchet pussy e'ery now and then; that shit be good as hell, son. And them ratchet bitches suck a mean dick."

I shake my head, laughing at her silly ass, eyeing this light-skinned broad, Peaches, with big bouncy titties just the way I dig 'em. She's rocking a shiny silver halter-top and matching thong. She shakes her jiggly ass in front of a few niggahs, then makes her way over to us when she see them niggahs ain't giving her no play.

She licks her lips at me. "What's good, Reg? Hey, Prince. Y'all lookin' like you could use a good time." She cups her titties, then slides a tongue over her nipples. "What can I do for y'all tonight?"

"Not a damn thing, ma," Prince says, shooing her outta the way. "I already got my eye on someone. But you can hook my niggah up wit' a lap dance, then maybe a lil extra, feel me?"

"Nah, yo, I'm good," I say, peeling off a few bills, then slipping them inside the front of her thong.

She smiles, leaning into my ear. "Reg, baby, you fine as hell. If you change your mind, let me know. I've been wanting to fuck you for a minute." She flicks my ear with her tongue.

I grin. "Oh, word? You wanna fuck?"

She nods, snapping her fingers to a Lil Wayne joint and popping her pussy up in my face. She smells like coconut oil and pineapple. "Reggie, you know I'm big on you, boo. All you gotta do is say the word and this pussy is yours?"

"Oh, a'ight. I'll keep that in mind." I slap her on the ass, then watch her move on to her next potential mark.

Prince eyes me, shaking her head. I frown. "What, muhfucka?"

"That biscuit's feelin' you, yo. I don't know why you don't get up off ya bullshit 'n' get wit' the program."

I wave her on. "Tsk. Man, I ain't thinkin' 'bout that broad. You know I don't get down wit' strippers like that."

"Yo fuck that. I heard that bitch got some good pussy 'n' can suck a mean dick."

I shrug. "Good for her. I ain't on her like that. All that broad's good for is a lap dance e'ery now 'n' then. But givin' her this dick ain't it."

Prince looks at me like I'm crazy. "Yo, ain't nobody sayin' you gotta marry the ho. Just fuck her. The bitch practically throws the pussy on you e'erytime we come up in this muhfucka."

I glance over at the stage, takin' a swig of beer. There's a tall, thin brown-skinned chick wearing a silver sequined bra and thong and a pair of high-ass platform heels up on the stage, twirling herself around one of the poles. Niggahs start throwing them dollars up when she drops to the floor, then starts doing back-bends and Russian splits, bouncing to the beat of Juicy J's "Bands

That Make Her Dance." She goes into a handstand, then starts popping her ass.

"Real shit, Reg, you stay buggin', yo."

I peel my eyes from the stage, looking at her. "Buggin' how?"

"All this pussy up in here and you ain't tryna fuck." She shakes her head. "Yo, keep it gee, son. When's the last time you stretched out butt-ass naked in a bed and fucked a shorty down real good?"

I blink, caught off-guard by the question. Real shit, I can't remember the last time I kicked back and got this dick sucked right, then rolled up into some pussy. I shrug. "Fuck if I know, yo. Why?"

"Shit, niggah." She points over at Peaches. "That bitch ready to fuck the skin off ya shit and you ain't goin' for it."

"Yo, I already tol' you. I ain't beat for none'a these broads, man."

She frowns. "Oh, what? They ain't straight enough for you, is that it? I know you gotta be tired of frontin'. You spend more time gettin' ass in the backseat of whips 'n' shit, misleading bitches…"

"Yo, hol' up, fam, you comin' outta pocket, now. I ain't even 'bout to have this convo with you, yo. I like what I like. You like what you like. Let's leave it at that, yo."

"A'ight, whatever, yo," she says, motioning for the stripper chick she's been eyeing practically all night over for a lap dance. "Yo, let me get a lap dance, ma?"

She grins. "Anything for you, sexy." She cuts her eyes over at me, and winks. "You wanna be next?" She introduces herself as Wet-Wet.

Prince grins. "Wet-Wet, huh? Why they call you that, ma?"

"'Cause I gotta extra wet pussy. You wanna feel how wet it gets?"

Prince slaps her on the ass. "Then grind up on this dick 'n' let me see how wet that shit gets, baby. Yo, Reg, you sure you don't want next?"

"Nah, I'm good. Do you." I toss back another shot, glancing at my watch. It's a lil after midnight. I feel like dipping up outta here 'n' hitting up a straight spot. But I know I'm all tanked up 'n' ain't tryna get pulled over by the Po-Po then end up wit' a DUI or some shit all 'cause I'm out prowling for some pussy.

Prince gives me the finger as Wet-Wet straddles her, then starts grinding into her lap. Prince cups both of Wet-Wet's titties in her hands, then starts squeezing them. "Yo, fam, you need to feel these soft-ass tits, yo." I tell her I'm good, watching as Wet-Wet rides Prince to the beat of the music, every so often glancing over at me and winking.

I pour myself another drink. Two songs later, Prince is seventy-five bucks lighter and ready to fuck. She grabs Wet-Wet by the arm. "Yo, how 'bout you hook me 'n' my boi up wit' sumthin' a lil more private?"

"Nah, I'm—"

Prince shoots me a look, cutting me off. "Relax, son. I got this." I shake my head, filling my shot glass with more Remy. Truth is I could use a good dick suck, and maybe some ass. "So what's good, ma? We freakin'?"

She looks over at me, then back at Prince. "It's fifty for the first fifteen minutes."

Prince flashes her a knot of paper. "I'm tryna wear that ass out. That shit you talkin' ain't shit."

She smiles. "Give me like five minutes," she replies, leaning into Prince's ear and whispering. Prince slaps her on the ass, opening and closing her legs. Judging by the way Prince is grabbing at her dick I know Wet-Wet musta said something mad nasty to her.

Prince nods. "Yeah, a'ight. Don't be frontin' either, yo."

"I don't front, boo. I do what I do. I'll be back in a few to show 'n' prove." We both eye her as she walks off, her fatty bouncing 'n' swaying as she moves through the crowd.

"Word is bond, yo. Her ass is softer than muhfuckin' cotton. We 'bout to bust that shit wide open, yo."

"Nah, fam. I ain't tryna fuck that broad, yo. I tol' you, I'm good."

"Fuck outta here wit' that dumb shit, yo. You ain't good, niggah. Lyin' muhfucka. Don't front, niggah. You not about to sit here 'n' gee me, son. You wanna fuck, don't you?"

I laugh. "Yo, niggah, you funny as hell."

"Funny hell, muhfucka. I know you miss havin' a pretty bitch down on her knees sucking ya dick. Tell me you don't miss that shit, yo."

I frown. "Muhfucka, I get my shit sucked."

She gives me a "yeah right" look. "When, niggah? When you ain't somewhere lurkin' around tryna scheme on some straight pussy? When's the last time any of them bitches sucked ya shit, yo?"

I shift in my seat, tossing back another shot. "I don't know. It's been a minute."

She laughs.

"Yo, I ain't tryna hear that shit."

"Whatever, son. Riddle me this: Why them straight bitches ain't suckin' ya shit?" She snaps her fingers. "Oh, wait. That's right. They don't know you ain't no real niggah." She starts laughing.

"Yo, suck my dick, niggah."

"Hahaha! You too busy eatin' the pussy from the back, then runnin' ya dick up in it. Yo, real shit. Ya shit's s'posed to stay wet, niggah. You s'posed to have a few cock-washers on ya team at all times. You gettin' you some ass tonight…on me. I'm let you hit that shit, first, then I'ma sink this dick way up in that shit, while you knock them tonsils out."

I laugh. "Yo, you wild as hell."

"Nah, muhfucka. I'm horny as fuck. I'm tryna get this dick wet. And you need to stop frontin' and get wit' the program and come let this bitch wet yours, too."

Twenty minutes later, I'm standing with my hands on my hips, my jeans wrapped around my ankles and my dick hanging outta the slit of my boxers as Wet-Wet is down on her knees spinning my top while Prince is on her knees in back of her eating her pussy. Prince is naked from the waist down, her Timbs still on her feet.

"Yeah, ma, suck that dick," I say, dipping at the knees 'n' thrusting my hips. "Yo like that shit, yo?" she grunts, taking my cock deeper into her mouth, then pulling it out and licking on it. "Spit on that shit, yo."

Wet-Wet spits on my dick, then licks around the base of it while jacking me off. She moans. She grabs my ass, pulling into her, my crotch against her face, the base of my cock rapidly pressing up against my clit as she takes me deep into her throat.

Prince stands up, her fingers now replace her tongue, pumping in Wet-Wet's pussy. "Yo, word is bond, fam, this bitch's pussy is mad juicy, yo." Prince slaps her ass cheeks. "Yo, you ready for this dick?"

"Mmmph. Uhhh…"

"Yeah, I know you want this big-ass dick, yo. I'ma give it to you real good, too."

I eye Prince as she pulls open Wet-Wet's ass and sinks her dick into her pussy. She grunts, sucking my dick faster and harder.

I groan as my clit and cock are being worked simultaneously. "Oh, shit."

Prince grins. "Yeah, muhfucka. I see she suckin' the shit outta that dick, ain't she? See, niggah. I knew you needed that dry-ass dick wet." She laughs.

"Fuck outta here, muhfucka," I say, grunting as Wet-Wet grabs me by the ass, pulling me deeper into her, my crotch against her face, the base of my cock pressing feverishly against my clit as she takes me down in her throat. She's sucking mad fast and hard, pulling it outta her throat every so often so she can spit on it, then take it back into her mouth. Her hand around the lower part of the shaft, she presses the base tight against my clit causing the right amount of friction to take me to the edge. "Oh, shit. Goddamn, yo. Word is bond. This ho's a freak. She can suck a mean dick."

Prince laughs. "You like that shit, son?"

"Aaah, shit. I'ma 'bout to nut, yo."

Prince grunts. "Yeah, muhfucka, get that nut, yo. You 'bout to spit that shit, yo?"

"Hellz yeah…aaah, fuck!"

Prince grabs Wet-Wet by the hips, pounding into her, giving this ho the fucking of her life. Wet-Wet moans. "Yeah, you got some nice wet pussy, ma. Got my dick slidin' in 'n' outta that shit. Freaky-ass bitch. Aaaah, fuck, yeah…"

The room is flooded with the sounds of slurping, moaning, grunting, and groaning. The air is thick with her musky excitement. Shit, maybe it's coming from all three of us. Fuck if I know. All I know is, I'm mad horny. And this bitch is spit shining and sucking my dick like it's the last dick she's ever gonna suck.

Prince pulls her dick outta Wet-Wet's pussy, then drops to her knees 'n' starts eating her out. The way she's moaning and wriggling her ass, Prince must be tonguing the fuck outta her with that long-ass tongue of hers. Her shit's so long she can touch her chin and the tip of her nose with it. Bitches stay braggin' about her tongue-work. And this lil freak's gonna be yapping her jaws about it, too.

"Yo, Prince, tear that shit, yo," I urge. "Is it good, fam?"

Prince lifts up. Her lips shiny from Wet-Wet's cunt-glaze. "Hell, yeah, yo. This muthafuckin' shit's mad juicy, yo. I'm ready to put this dick back up in this shit."

Prince stands up and pulls open Wet-Wet's ass cheeks, then

plunges her dick back in. Raw. Real shit, yo. Prince is a wild-ass muhfucka. She stay fucking bitches without using condoms. Wet-Wet gasps, inching forward. "Hell, nah, get yo' freak-ass back here. Take this shit, yo. Ain't no need in tryna run from this dick." She locks her arms around Wet-Wet's waist and starts speed fucking her, pounding the shit outta her.

"Yo, stick ya finger in her ass, yo," I rasp, staring over at Prince, feeling another nut building up inside of me. Wet-Wet's hands are squeezing my ass. Her soft hands feel good on my skin. Slowly, one of her hands glides along my crack. I usually don't let broads fuck wit' my asshole, but tonight I'm caught up in the moment and ready to flow wit' whatever pops off. She eases a fingertip over my hole, then presses in. "Oooh, yeah." I grab her by the head, and thrust. My ass cheeks clenching her hand.

"Yo, fam, you should bend over 'n' let this freaky bitch tongue that ass out for you." Prince slams into her pussy. "You wanna lick my boi's hole out? You wanna give my niggah some of that tongue work, don't you, baby?"

The only thing Wet-Wet can do is grunt since her mouth is stuffed wit' my dick. Prince eggs me on, and I give in to the moment, turning around, bending over and letting her tongue-fuck my asshole. I jack my dick as her tongue goes in 'n' outta my hole, then makes wet circles 'round it. My breath quickens. Real shit, yo. If I had a set a balls right now they'd be mad tight wit' excitement. I'm so ready to bust.

By the time I roll the condom over my dick and get up in her, the base of my dick is soaked from my own juices. Wet-Wet's cunt is mad messy and wet from her cum. I'm stroking her walls nice and slow, deep thrusting and snapping my hips into her. Her pussy's deep as hell and she's handling the thick eight-inches I'm pushing up in her guts with mad ease. She bucks her hips as she coats my dick with her juices, grunting and groaning while she sucking Prince's cunt-soaked dick.

"Yeah, bitch, suck that shit, yo. Word is bond. Gag, bitch."

Prince is holding her by the back of the head, face-fucking her while I'm hitting her walls. All you hear is gurgling. Prince eyes me, smirking. "Yo, son, that shit's good, right?"

"Uh, hell yeah. This shit's real wet, yo." I slap her on the ass.

"I tol' you this bitch was gonna have some good-ass pussy! Tear that shit up, yo."

Wet-Wet's moans get louder as I speed-fuck her pussy, sticking a finger into her asshole. She reaches in back of her and pulls open her ass cheeks, giving more access to her sopping wet cunt as she gives Prince hands-free throat work. I stare at my cum-coated dick as it rapidly disappears in 'n' outta her. The lips of her pussy slap and stick against my thick dick.

"Uhh…uhhh…ooooh…"

"Yeah, you like that dick, don't you?" Prince asks, pulling her cock outta her throat, then slapping her wet mouth with it. "You like the way my boi's fuckin' that juicy-ass pussy, yo?"

She grunts.

"Damn, son, you tearin' that shit up. See. I tol' ya ass you needed some pussy, niggah."

I shut my eyes 'n' try'n block Prince out. Try to imagine fucking some random straight broad who doesn't know that I'm a stud boi. A'ight, a'ight…real shit, I get off on deceiving bitches. There's something about not being clocked that really excites me, gets my juices flowin'. It's like having an adrenaline rush so powerful that ya heart practically stops beating, then skips two beats before it stops again.

"Yeah, bitch," I grunt, slamming my hips into her. "Take this dick. Uh, shit…"

I bang her guts up for another ten minutes or so, then pull my dick out leaving her sloshy hole stretched 'n' soppy. I finger her pussy. I can feel her getting wetter with each stroke. For some reason, I wanna eat her pussy. My mouth starts to salivate anticipating rolling my tongue up in her 'n' tasting her. I tease her pussy with my finger until I can no longer hold out from plunging my tongue into her juices.

A few seconds later, I'm squatting down and grabbing her by the hips, pressing my face into her ass, pulling open her cheeks, then darting my tongue into her tight, moist hole. It puckers. I flick my tongue over it, back and forth, up and down, then zigzag it from side to side. I reach for her clit and pinch it as I'm tonguing her ass. I slip a finger into the back of her pussy. Her juices splash out onto my hand.

"Uh…uh…uh…mmmmph…"

I don't know how long we're going at it—her sucking Prince off, me eating her out—before she stops sucking Prince's dick, glancing over her shoulder. "Bang this shit, niggah…make my pussy scream…I wanna feel the dick…"

I wanna push this dick back in her, give her what she wants. But I'm not. I won't. Not yet. It's been so long since I've actually fucked a femme chick or ran a train on one wit' my boi, Prince, that I'm actually tryna savor the shit.

Prince grabs her by the back of the head and face-fucks her. The harder Prince hits the back of her throat, the wetter her pussy gets. Prince fucks her throat in long, deep motions. Wet-Wet's creamy lips coat my lips as my mouth moves over her pussy.

Wet-Wet moans and grunts.

"Yo, I think this bitch's clit is in her throat, fam," I say, in between her cheeks. "You hittin' her throat 'n' her shit's juicier than a muhfucka, yo."

"Oh, word? That shit's nice 'n' wet, huh?"

"No doubt."

Prince lets go of her head, placing her hands up on her narrow hips. "This what you want? Two big dick muhfuckas handlin' ya holes, yo?"

She grunts. Loud gargling sounds escape from the back of her throat as Prince punches her tonsils up. While Wet-Wet's down on her knees sucking Prince's dick and lapping around the base of the harness, I go back to eating her pussy and stroking my dick, patiently waiting to feel her pussy lips around my big dick again. But not until she begs for it, not 'til she's weak with want, and can't stand the torture of not having her snatch pounded by this dick.

"Yo, I think she's ready for another round of dick," Prince says, pulling her dick outta Wet-Wet's throat. "You want some more dick in that pussy?"

She grunts. Bucks her hips. "Yessss, boo."

"Yo, fam," Prince says, grinning. "You thinkin' what I'm thinkin', yo?"

I raise a brow. "You tell me, yo."

"Let's give it to this freak in both holes, yo." She looks over at Wet-Wet 'n' asks her if she wants to get fucked in her ass 'n' pussy at the same time. Her eyes light up like she's 'bout to win the door prize for freak of the week.

"Oooh, yesssss. I love double-penetration. Thought you knew, boo."

Prince helps Wet-Wet up off her knees, then takes her by the hand and leads her over to the only sofa in the room. A red velvet joint that looks like it's been fucked on 'n' nutted on by mad muhfuckas.

I eye Prince as she grabs a white towel from off the table and places it down on the sofa. She sits, stretching her legs out and stroking her cock. "Yo, ma, get ya fine ass over here 'n' come sit up on this dick, yo."

Wet-Wet shakes 'n' gyrates her hips like she's 'bout to perform up on stage. When she makes her way to the sofa, Prince pulls Wet-Wet onto her lap. I stroke my shit as Wet-Wet straddles her, placing one'a her lil-ass titties into Prince's mouth. I keep my gaze locked on that fat, juicy ass as she lifts her hips, reaches in back of her 'n' guides Prince's dick into her pussy. She sits all the way down on it, grinding her pussy in Prince's lap. Prince grabs her hips 'n' starts thrusting her cock up into Wet-Wet's guts.

I watch as her pussy opens 'n' coats Prince's dick wit' each stroke. I lick my lips walking up behind her 'n' pulling open her ass. She glances over her shoulder. "Oooh, yes, put it in my ass, baby... give it to me good."

I stick a finger into her ass, then another, fingering her hole until it loosens before pressing the tip of my dick in. She gasps, pauses, leaning forward, then wrapping her arms around Prince's neck. Prince waits for me to push my dick into Wet-Wet's ass 'n' start fucking her before she starts fucking her pussy again. My pumping matches Prince's thrusting. Wet-Wet groans, yells out 'n' arches her back. I watch as her ass 'n' pussy stretch open.

"Goddamn, yo, this shit looks sexy as fuck," I rasp, feeling a nut bubbling up inside of me. Wit' each push into her deep, hot ass, I grunt. All you hear is squishing, slippery noises 'n' the slap-slap of skin against skin as Wet-Wet's juices sputter outta her pussy. She screams. Prince 'n' I are sweating and grunting and pounding into Wet-Wet's holes.

"Oh, yesssss, give me the dick, muhfuckas...ohgodohgod...fuck my pussy...fuck my ass...mmmmm...yesssss... Shit, niggahs! Y'all fuckin' me sooooo gooood...uhhhhh...ooooohhhh...I'm cuuuuu-uuuuummming..."

Prince 'n' I bang her senseless, fucking her ass 'n' cunt raw. It doesn't take long before we're both nutting at the same time, our bodies shuddering. I keep grinding. Prince keeps thrusting.

Four hunnid dollars later, Wet-Wet wobbles back out into the club and Prince 'n' I hit the exit door, popping mad shit 'bout how we bust that ho's ass open.

Two weeks later. And once again, I'm sitting up in a club—at the bar—on the prowl for some straight pussy. Tonight, I'm at this spot, Sensations, in Maplewood. The club is packed. And I ain't gonna front. There are some fine broads up in here, but most of 'em seemed booed up. And the others, from what I can see, are a buncha straight-up hood rats, like this thick, creamy, brown-skinned chick who sashayed her hips up in my face, sticking her bouncy titties out for me to peep. She's rocking a pink cat suit that's hugging every curve of her body and showing the print of her fat pussy lips. Real shit, she's a walking campaign for a yeast infection. No thanks. Not interested.

Besides, she's rocking a mouthful of gold. Where they do that at? This chick is all kinds of wrong. But I ain't gonna stunt on this hood booga's body. She's serving up a nice set of titties, a small waist, and ass for days. Still, there's something in her round brown eyes that spells crazy.

"Hey, boo," she slurs, swiping the bang of her pink bob weave across her forehead. "You fine as hell, niggah." She runs a finger over my bicep. "You need to let me take you home and fuck you down into my mattress. Give you some'a this good pussy."

I peep a few chicks in earshot laughing. "Dietra, girl," one of the chicks says, glancing at me. "I see you at it again, boo."

"Gurrrrrrl," Pinky Ghetto says over the music. "You know I

stay on dick patrol. Ain't no shame in my game. And this mutha-
fucka right here"—she shoots me a look—"can get it. Get it real
good." She starts thrusting her hips, then slapping her ass. And
of course them broads 'n' a few niggahs cheer her on.

*Bitch, please! If you don't take ya drunk, ho ass on somewhere and
have a seat.* Ain't no way I'ma ever stick my dick in a broad rocking
gold fronts. I grin. "Yo, you wildin', ma. But, nah. I'm good, yo."

"Uh-huh, I bet you are. You look like you got mad skills. I bet
you fuck real good, boo. Let me test ride that dick and see just
how good you are."

I laugh, shaking my head. "Nah, ma. Maybe some other time."

"Then how 'bout you buy me a drank?" She wobbles in her
wedge heels a bit, grabbing my arm for support.

"Yo, real shit. Looks like the thing you need is some water."

She throws a hand up on her hip, then starts snapping. "Mutha-
fucka, you don't tell me what I need. Who the fuck is you, telling
me I need to drank some water? Niggah, fuck you. I'll buy my
own goddamn drank. Cheap fuck."

Shit! Fuck! *That's what the hell I get for coming up in the hood.* I
put my hands up and step back. "Yo, ma. Real shit. I ain't tryna
beef wit' you, yo."

"Well, niggah, too bad."

"Dietra, gurrrrl," one of her lil cheerleaders says, grabbing her
arm. "Let this niggah live, gurrrl. Can't you see he ain't from
around here?"

She glares at me and grunts. "Mmmph. You right, gurrrrl. Fuck
him. He prolly gotta little-ass dick anyway." I take a deep sigh
when she lets her girl drag her away. Something tells me I should
bounce, but for some reason I stay instead of listening to my gut.
I want some pussy. And I know that there's at least one horny
chick in here willing to let me get up in between her hips.

But after almost two hours sitting at the bar, I'm almost ready to concede defeat when I finally manage to snatch up this lil dark chocolate thing-thing. She's about five-five 'n' thick in all the right places. And based on our conversation—after she's tossed back three Incredible Hulks, she's a freak looking to get freaked.

"Yo, ma," I say over the bar chatter and loud music, "how 'bout we go outside 'n' chill in my whip?"

She grins, showing off her straight, white teeth. I can't remember what the fuck her name is, but it don't matter. After I hit it, it's a wrap any-damn-way. "Why, you tryna get your dick sucked or something?"

I laugh. "Nah, I'm tryna eat that pussy real quick." I grab my crotch. "Then slide this hard-ass dick up in you, that's if you wit' it. So what's good?"

She bats her mink lashes. "Hopefully, all that good shit you talking."

I grin. "Only one way to find out. You ready?" She tells me to give her a minute so she can use the bathroom, then tell her girls she's gonna be outside. I see her when she steps outta the bathroom, then walks over to a group of girls. She says something to a thin, light-skinned chick, points over in my direction. They all look over at me, then say something to her. She laughs, then walks off. I bob my head to the music as she makes her way back over to me.

"Okay, I'm ready."

"Cool."

"But I told my girls if I'm not back in ten minutes to call the police."

I laugh. "Damn. You shoulda tol' 'em at least twenty."

She laughs with me. "Boo, please. All it's gonna take is ten minutes for me to have you nuttin' on ya'self."

"Oh word? It's like that?"

"I can show you better than I can tell you. You'll find out soon enough."

I lick my lips in anticipation. Then as we're heading toward the door, someone cuts in front of me, looping an arm through mine. My mouth drops open. It's Alicia. She looks over at Dark Chocolate. "Sorry, boo, *he's* with me." She tilts her head, ready for it to turn up.

Dark Chocolate looks from me to her, then back at me. She frowns. "Oh, no thank you, boo-boo. I don't know what kinda games you got going on, but I'm not the one." I watch as she storms off, popping shit about niggahs being on their bullshit.

I blink, bringing my attention to Alicia. "Damn, why you do that, yo?"

She smirks, brushing a strand of blonde weave outta her face. She's wearing a short faded jean skirt with a yellow low-cut blouse. I ain't gonna front, yo. She's lookin' mad sexy in her lil wears. "Umm, hello to you, too." I glance down at her smooth, bare legs, then down at her yellow painted toes peeking outta a pair of strappy sandals before looking back up at her. I can see it in her eyes. She's lit up.

"Yo, when'd you get here?"

She stumbles back a bit, placing a hand up on her hip. Seems like every broad up this bitch tonight is boozed up. "I've been here. And I saw when"—she points a finger at me—"you walked your slick ass up in here."

I frown.

"Yeah, niggah. I've been watching you all night, sitting ya fine ass up at the bar. Got all these bitches all up in your face 'n' shit. And I know you ain't hardly think I was gonna let you walk up outta here with some other bitch so you can play her like you tried to play me. Ohhh, noooo, niggah. Not tonight."

I can tell she's about to really get shit poppin' real quick if I don't spin off on her drunk-ass. "Yo, ma, you trippin'. But I ain't 'bout to stand here 'n' beef wit' you. I'm out." I brush past her, heading toward the exit. But her ass is right behind me still poppin' shit. And I'm like, "What the fuck?!" But I don't snap on her ass 'cause I really don't know who she's hear wit' or what the fuck she's all aggie about. I mean, a'ight, so I gave her a number to one'a my dead pre-paid joints. Big deal. I don't know her. She don't know me. And it ain't like I owe her shit.

I stop in my tracks and turn to her. "Yo, what the fuck is your problem? Why are you tryna be all up on my neck, yo?"

"I'm on your neck because you and me have some unfinished business, that's why, niggah. And if you wanna see me turn it up out here tonight, keep walking and see what I do."

Some niggah she must be cool wit' walks up on us, shooting me a look. "Yo, you good, baby?" He gives her a hug 'n' kiss on the cheek while eyeing me all reckless 'n' shit.

Alicia narrows her eyes at me, then looks up at dude. "Hey, Roy. Yeah, we good. Ain't that right, Reggie?"

I eye dude. He's about six-feet-something, and every bit of two-hundred-thirty-plus pounds. The niggah's arms are like tree trunks. Ain't no way I'm tryna rock wit' this niggah. Two of his boys are posted up in back of him. And it's just me out this bitch, so ain't no way I'm tryna get caught up in no drama, feel me? I shoot Alicia a look, clearing my throat. "Yeah, no doubt. We good."

She smirks. "Just what I thought." Dude says something in her ear. And she giggles. "Niggah, you stupid." He laughs. She playfully swats his arm. "You know how I do, boo. I gets hood when I have to."

Dude cuts his eyes back over at me. "Oh, I know how you do it, baby. And you know I got ya back, ya heard?" He raises a brow, then steps off wit' his boys in tow. I keep my cool, but inside I'm relieved that them niggahs ain't jump into their capes 'n' try'n play Captain Save A Trick.

I sigh. "A'ight. You got my attention. Obviously there's something you wanna get off ya chest. So what it is?"

"Let's go to your truck. What I have to say to you I don't wanna say it out here. I don't want everyone all in our business."

I blink. *Bitch, you was already about to let shit get live out here. Now you wanna be worried 'bout muhfuckas in our business.* We ain't got no business. But, whatever! As long as her ass ain't tryna turn it up, I'm good.

"You are a real fucked-up individual for how you did me, niggah. But, it's all good. I got something for your black ass, niggah."

I suck my teeth, stepping off. *Here we go wit' this shit.* She follows behind me. And the whole time she's walking up on the heels of my Timbs she's saying shit like, "Yeah, niggah, you did that. You played the shit outta me real good… But I got something for you, niggah… You think you can come up in my hood and play me? Oh nooo, boo-boo. You fucked the wrong one, hun."

I let the bitch keep talking. But I'm kicking myself for getting caught up in some dumb shit. I knew I shoulda never came up in this spot. I shoulda took my ass over to the city like I was gonna do from the rip.

"I feel like punching you in the back of your head, niggah."

I shoot her a look. "Yo, go 'head wit' that." *I shoulda knew her ass was ratchet.* When we get to my whip, I disarm the alarm. She opens the back passenger door and climbs in.

I frown. "Yo, why you sitting back there?"

"I don't wanna sit in the front. And I don't want you sitting up there either." A part of me is thinking I should snatch her out by her hair and throw her onto the ground, then back up over her ass and peel off. But I shake the idea from my head. I open the other backseat door and get in.

"A'ight, yo," I say, shutting the door and looking at her. "You got me. Now what you gotta say to me?"

She shifts her body toward me, staring me down. "Do you even remember my name?"

I give her a screw-face. "C'mon, yo. I know you ain't almost get me caught up in some dumb shit wit' ya peeps 'cause you wanna play the name game. Yeah, I remember ya name. So what's really good?"

"Answer the damn question. Do you remember who I am or not?"

"I already tol' you. Yeah, I know who you are, Alicia. I met you at that spot in Paterson."

She grins seemingly satisfied that at least I know who she is. "Yeah, and we fucked right here…in this truck, niggah."

"Sooooo, what? Now you wanna refund or some shit 'cause I didn't fuck you good enough?"

"Oh, you got jokes, huh?"

"Nah. I'm sayin', yo. What's good? I mean, damn. You comin' at me all kinda sideways and I ain't diggin' it, yo."

She huffs. "Whatever. And I didn't dig how you played me, either. Why you give me that bullshit-ass number, huh, Reggie? If you wasn't beat to stay in touch you shoulda just said that shit instead of giving me some wrong number. Who does that shit? This is two-thousand-thirteen, niggah. Be real with your shit. I'ma grown-ass woman, okay. Don't think I fucked you because I was drunk and didn't know what I was doing. I knew exactly what I was doing when I let you run your fingers all up in my pussy at the bar. And I knew exactly what I was doing when I walked outside with you. I fucked you because I wanted to. And I remember everything—and I do mean *everything*—about that night."

I glance at my watch. It's almost midnight. "Okay, so what is it you tryna say, ma? It's getting late 'n' I ain't really beat to be out here all night playing games wit' you, yo."

"Niggah, I ain't playing games. The only one who seems to like to play games is you, niggah."

I take a deep breath. I feel myself about ready to snap on this broad. "Look. It's obvious you pissed 'bout something, so say it so we can move on. I'm ready to—"

She catches me off-guard, pulling me into her by the back of my neck and pressing her lips against mine. Next thing I know, she's straddling me. And we're going at it. Our tongues are flicking against the others. She's biting on my bottom lip. I'm biting on hers. She grinds into me. And we go at it hard for what seems like forever, until she pulls back and says, "Ever since that night you fucked me outside in your truck, I've been thinking about you," she says breathlessly. "About this. About what I would do or say to you if or *when* I saw you again. I wanna slap the shit outta you, niggah."

I jerk my head back, staring at her. "Yo, you buggin' for real for real. Why you keep comin' at me all sideways 'n' shit?"

"I ain't bugging nothing. What you did was fucked up."

I give her a crazy-ass look. In my head, I know she ain't talking 'bout what I think she's talking about. Then again…nah, she ain't clock me. Or did she?

"I'm not the kinda bitch you play and think it's all good. Oh, no, niggah. I'ma *real* bitch. If you wanted to just fuck me, that's all it coulda been. But, no, you was all up in my ear talking about how you wanna spend time with me, how you wanna keep getting this pussy."

This ghetto bitch is fucking crazy!

"Yo, c'mon, ma. That was just some shit I was sayin' in the heat of the moment. I ain't mean nothing by none of that shit. It was talk."

"Mmmph. Then you shouldna said it, niggah. Say what you mean, not what the fuck you think a bitch wanna hear."

Damn, this bitch actin' like she needs a hug or some shit.

Before I know it, she slides down between my legs 'n' tugs at the buckle of my belt. I grab her wrists. "Nah, ma. Don't."

She narrows her eyes, sneering. "What, you don't like your dick sucked, Reggie? Huh, *Regggggie*? Or is that even your real name?"

I frown, tryna figure out how the fuck I'ma get this crazy nut up outta my whip so I can peel out before shit gets hectic. I can feel the hairs on the back of my neck start to rise. "Yo, I think you need to bounce, ma. You lettin' your liquor run ya tongue for you."

She yanks her hands away. "I ain't letting shit run my tongue, *Regggggie*. And I ain't bouncing nowhere until I see this dick, niggah." She reaches for my buckle again.

"Nah, yo. Chill." I grab her wrists again. I don't wanna take it to her head 'cause I already know it's gonna make shit pop hard out here. I already know this broad is the type of chick I'd have'ta knock the fuck out. And I ain't tryna go there if I can help it. "Word is bond, yo. You really comin' outta pocket, ma."

"No, niggah. You outta pocket for tryna squeeze my wrists up. Get the fuck off me." She yanks her hands back. I tell her I ain't tryna beef wit' her. That I ain't looking for problems. I keep calm. Try to reason wit' this bitch, but she ain't hearing it.

Next thing I know, she's back up in my lap, straddling me. "Niggah, you the one outta pocket. And you do gotta problem, niggah. *Me*. You thought you could fuck me in the backseat of your truck, like I'm some trick-bitch, then play me, huh?"

"I wasn't playin' you, yo. I was diggin' you *that* night. And I wanted to fuck you. It was sex, ma. So why is you buggin' like it was something more? I ain't put a gun to ya head. You let me hit it 'cause you was wit' it."

"Yeah, niggah, I was with it. That's already been established. And, yeah, I know it was only sex. So what? The point is, you shoulda kept it real. But, no, *Reggggggie*, you played me out giving me a wrong number 'n' shit." She grabs my face rough. I grab her hands. Try to pull her hands away. But she presses her lips into mine. And I ain't gonna front. The crazier she acts, the hornier I'm getting.

Without much thought, I grab her ass and squeeze. Real shit, this crazy bitch got me wanting to fuck her, again. She pulls back, stares at me for a few seconds, then she moves her mouth closer to my ear.

"You like to role play, huh? You wanted me to play your dirty backseat whore, didn't you? You thought it was okay to play games with me, huh, *Reggggggie*?"

I grimace. *Shit! She knows!* "Yo, ma. I don't know what you're talkin' 'bout, yo."

"Bullshit, *Reggggggie*. You know *exactly* what I'm talking about."
What the fuck, yo?! Why is this bitch draggin' the shit out? Why don't she just say what the fuck's on her mind?

She pulls her shirt off over her head, then lifts her skirt up over her hips. I try to keep from licking my lips, but the sight of her juicy titties peeling outta her lace bra is making it very hard. I ain't gonna front, buggin' or not, this broad got me going through it.

She snatches my hand and shoves it between her legs. "I want you to feel my pussy, niggah." She isn't wearing any drawers. Flashes of my tongue darting around her pussy shoot through my head as my fingers find their way to her slick pussy lips. She gasps. "Yeah, niggah. Put your fingers in." I push my fingers into her until they can't go any further. She's mad juicy 'n' hot. Real shit. I feel something shoot through me, pleasure ignites every fiber in my body and I feel my own shit starting to drip. I feel like I'ma 'bout to nut. "You feel that wet heat, huh, nigga?"

My voice dips real low 'n' husky. I'm horny as shit. Her aggressiveness got me clit aching. "Yeah, ma."

"You did that, niggah. That's how wet you got me. That's how hot you got my pussy."

I squeeze my legs shut. "Yo, c'mon, ma. What's good wit' you? Where's all this comin' from, yo?"

She gives me an incredulous look. "What's good with me? This pussy, that's what's good. You and me have some unfinished business, *Reggggie*. You fucked me in the backseat of your truck. Wouldn't let me see your dick, wouldn't let me touch it. Niggah, you wouldn't even let me give you head. What kinda niggah you know who ain't letting a bitch suck his dick?"

I blink.

She stares at me hard. Her nose flares. And she looks like she's ready to fist up. But I already know if she tries to go with the hands I'ma have'ta take it to her skull. I turn my neck tryna see who else is out here in the parking lot in case things get hectic. The lot is empty. I look back at her.

"Yo, I think you should bounce before shit gets outta hand."

"Ain't shit gonna get outta hand, niggah. I'm not bouncing nowhere until you fuck me right." She clenches her teeth. "I told. You. I'ma. Real. Bitch. And, tonight, I want you to look me in my eyes and fuck me like a *real* niggah. Let me be your backseat whore again." She reaches for my dick, grabbing at my crotch. "I wanna ride this dick, *Reggggie. And* suck it." She reaches for my buckle again. And I grab her hand. "Let me suck your balls, *Reggggie*." She presses her lips to my ear. Her tongue dips in, then out. "Let me run this tongue around them balls, niggah." She narrows her eyes, smirking. "I'm your backseat whore, remember?"

"Yo, c'mon, ma. Chill."

She tries to slide her hand up my T-shirt. I stop her. It's clear she's peeped my card. And instead of dragging this shit out any longer than need be, I decide to pull it for her. "Yo, ma. Listen—"

"Shut the fuck up." Her lips are back on mine. This bitch is crazy. But she can kiss her ass off. Her tongue goes deep into my mouth. My hands are back on her ass. My hips thrust up into her as she grinds down into me. "You want me to be your whore, niggah?"

I grunt.

"You wanna fuck me, again? Huh, *Reggggie?*"

She has me going through it bad, has me wanting to feel her heat on my tongue, on my fingers, all over my dick. "Yeah, ma. But I..."

"But nothing," she snaps, grabbing at my belt buckle again. "Then fuck me like one."

I stop fingering her. "Yo, ma ...listen, uh..." I try to grab her wrists, but she keeps pushing my hands away. "C'mon, chill...we need to talk, first."

"I don't wanna talk, niggah. I wanna be fucked." She presses her hands up against my chest, and I know there's no sense in stopping her now. It's obvious she knows. Or think she knows. *Shit! Why doesn't this bitch just say it, or ask it?*

She yanks my T-shirt outta the front of my jeans, then slides her hand underneath. "Put your fingers back into my pussy." My fingers go back inside of her. She leans forward, grinding onto my hand. She presses her lip to my ear. "I know what you are, Reggggie. I didn't at first." My fingers stop strumming in her cunt. She looks at me. "You gotta pussy like I do, don't you? You a bitch, ain't you, Reggggie?" She nips my ear. "Put your fingers back in my pussy. You ain't gotta say it. I already know."

I ain't gonna front. A part of me wants to ask her how she figured it out. But another part of me ain't beat to know. But fuck! My shit's hard as hell. And I'm wet all around the base of my dick.

She is pulling at my wife beater beneath my T-shirt. I close my eyes. Her hands snake their way up underneath. I swallow as she feels my chest binding. "Is this how you wrap your titties, niggah? Why didn't you just tell me, *Reggggie?*" My fingers stop diddling in her pussy again. I open my eyes. "Don't stop. Keep them fingers going. I'm going to nut on your hand, then I'm gonna fuck *you*. You wanna fuck with straight bitches, huh? I'm gonna give you this pussy the right way. Now answer my question, niggah. Why didn't you tell me?"

"Would you have still come outside wit' me?"

"I don't know. Probably not, then again...you're fine as hell... for a chick, pretending to be a dude, that is. But what you did was fucked up, *Regggie. You almost* had me fooled, niggah. Everything about you seems exactly like a niggah, even the way you fucked me. But I kept looking at your neck and I ain't see an Adam's apple. I kept looking, even when I held your neck while I was kissing on it. But I ain't pay the shit any mind. I thought maybe I had had too much to drink and that my eyes were playing tricks on me. I was horny. You made me horny, niggah. I ain't never have a niggah...well, uh, another bitch, finger my pussy in a club, then fuck me outside in the parking lot." I give her a "yeah right" look. "Yeah, I've been fucked outside in parked cars before with my man, or a niggah I was kicking it with. Not with some random niggah I only met at a club. That's not how I do mine. But you took me there. And, yeah, it's fucked up how you did it. But, I still can't stop thinking about how that shit felt. You fucked me good, niggah. You made my pussy whistle. Ain't no niggah ever hit my walls like that.

"And that's why when I saw you come into the club tonight I stayed in the cut and watched you the whole night. I wanted to see who else you were gonna try 'n' trick. I peeped how them horny-ass hoes were flocking to you. They didn't know, like I didn't. That you ain't no real niggah. Are you, Reggggggie?" She keeps running her gums, not giving me a chance to get a word in. "But you had your eye on that lil brown-skinned bitch. I watched and waited. I wanted to see how far you was gonna take it with her. Even though you didn't finger-fuck her at the bar, I watched you try to pull the same shit you pulled on me the other week with that bitch."

Damn, why she hatin'?

"I never kissed another bitch before you. But you ain't really a bitch, either. Are you, *Reggggggie*? I mean. You don't look like one. But that's what you are. Maybe not on the inside or from what others see on the outside because you hide it so well. But you have a pussy and clit and titties, too. Let me see 'em." She pulls at my chest binding. And I don't stop her. Not this time. Shit, what for?

I let her unfasten the pressure bandage and unwind it. When it unravels from my marked chest, she runs her hand over the marking where the binding had been. Her fingers lightly brush over my nipples. She kisses me, and I moan as I keep stroking her wet slit. Real shit, I've never had a straight chick flip the script on me the way she's doing it. My drawers are soaked, yo. "Yo, ma, I'm ready to fuck," I say, lifting her hips up. I take my free hand and unbuckle my belt, then unzip my jeans. Alicia watches me as I lift my hips 'n' tug my jeans down to my thighs. I watch her watching me.

Then before I know it, she's slinked her way down to the floor, yanking my jeans all the way down with her. Our eyes briefly meet before her soft hand rubs over the bulge in my burgundy boxer briefs. "Mmm, nice thick dick," she moans, placing her mouth over the front of my underwear and sucking.

She digs her hand into the flap of my boxers and pulls out my dick. She grins as it springs free. I peep her taking a hand and digging her fingers into her pussy while her free hand strokes my dick. She's got me mad juicy. My pussy has never throbbed the way it's throbbing right now. I keep my gaze fixed on her. She plays in her pussy and strokes my dick at the same time.

"I'ma ride the shit outta this dick, niggah. I'ma cum all over this dick, boi." She's stroking my shit just right. I cock my legs as wide as I can, my hips thrusting into the rub of the harness as it works my clit.

Oh fuck!

"I smell your pussy," she says, pulling her fingers outta her cunt and smearing her wetness over the head of my dick. I let out a soft groan as she strokes me, then lowers her head and slides her mouth over my dick, taking me into her mouth. She swallows my whole dick. She sucks my dick like a pro, her head bobbing up 'n' down as she sucks and strokes my shit. I grab her head, pressing it down into my crotch.

"Aaah fuck, yeah, suck that dick, ma."

She gags, but it doesn't take her long to relax 'n' take it all down in her throat. The sound of her sucking and moaning bounces off the steamed windows. She's giving me some real wet, sloppy head. Her nails dig into my thighs and I feel my clit harden 'n' swell. My head falls back against the headrest as I lose myself to the moment. My body shudders as I grunt and groan, then nut.

Alicia looks at me hungrily, licking her lips. "I ain't finished with you, yet, niggah." And with that, she straddles me again, reaching beneath her and pushing the tip of my dick into her pussy. She rides the head for a while, then sits all the way down on it. "Mmmm…you like fucking straight bitches, huh, niggah?"

I grunt, grabbing onto her hips as she rides me. She rotates her hips real slow 'n' seductive, then picks up her pace until she's riding me harder and faster. "Yeah, you all in my pussy now, niggah. Uhhh…oooh…you like that pussy, niggah…?"

I clench my thighs, moaning as I bust another nut. I swear it feels like my orgasm is shooting through my dick. She's got me going through it hard. I grab 'n' squeeze her ass, then slap it. "Yeah, ma, ride that dick, baby." I thrust up into her.

"Yeah, niggah…mmmm…make my pussy nut…uhhh…ooo-hooohooooh…mmmm…" She leans back, brings my hands up to her titties. I cup them. "You like them titties, niggah?"

"Yeah, ma…uh, fuck, yeah…"

She leans forward 'n' nips my bottom lip, eyeing me. "You want this pussy, niggah?"

I lick the tingling spot where she's bitten me. Another nut is building up inside of me. "Uh, yeah, give me that pussy, ma…" I arch my back, shut my eyes, and give into the racing heat that flows through my entire body as I cum again 'n' again. Digging my fingers into Alicia's soft ass, I let out a loud growl, rapidly thrusting up into her.

She's fucking my dick real good, her tongue slipping into my mouth. We kiss, hard 'n' long. And then she pulls away. Her lips move to my ear. "How you want this wet pussy, niggah…?"

My eyes flicker open. "Uh, shit…" I groan, staring into her gaze.

Her hips bounce up 'n' down on my dick. Her titties bounce in my face. I grab 'n' squeeze 'em, then suck 'em into my mouth.

She lets out a soft moan as my tongue twirls around each nipple.

Thrust for thrust, I give her the dick just as good as she's giving the pussy. "Yeah, ma, ride that shit, yo." I slap her on the ass. She's dripping into my lap. Her wet pussy's swishing and sloshing all over my dick. And I'm feeling lightheaded from the smell 'n' sound of her cunt.

"You real nasty wit' it."

"Niggah, this how a real bitch fucks. Now sit back and shut up. And let me get my nut." She groans. "You like fucking straight bitches, huh, Reggggie? You like this wet pussy, huh, nigga?"

"Uh, fuck, yeah. Mmmm."

I grip her hips and grunt as I bust another nut, enjoying the ride as Alicia fucks my dick, giving me the pussy the way I like it.

Straight no chaser!

ABOUT THE AUTHOR

Cairo is the author of *Big Booty, Man Swappers, Kitty-Kitty, Bang-Bang, Deep Throat Diva, Daddy Long Stroke, The Man Handler and The Kat Trap*. His travels to Egypt inspired his pen name.

T hree weeks later, with my new laminated membership card tucked in my clutch, I slip out of my apartment—scantily dressed in an ultra-short black dress with a cutout back and plunging V-neckline and a pair of black four-inch Jason Wu lace-up sandals—and creep my way back to The Stud Palace—the place where seduction and lust opened up a whole new world of being for me. The place where being fucked slow and deep by a *stud* unleashed a burning desire within me, unlocked inhibitions I'd kept repressed for far too long.

This time...alone.

Perched up on a leather stool in the section of the club called the CockTail Lounge. A decadent oasis, hidden behind thick mahogany doors, located on the top floor down a long dimly lit corridor. Upon entrance through the double doors, you ascend a flight of winding stairs onto the roof with its retractable glass ceiling, heated floors, and breathtaking view of New York City.

Gas-lit Tiki torches and flickering candles of enormous sizes and varying heights add to the seductive ambiance and décor. There's a gorgeous wraparound bar—where I'm sitting—in the middle of the stunning space with private leather booths along the glass walls and plush purple leather sofas and overstuffed leather chairs situated throughout the area. Huge go-go cages sit atop massive speakers, displaying the most succulent pieces of pelvis-thrusting eye-candy clad in wife beaters, colorful boxer briefs, and Timberland boots.

The CockTail Lounge is where discreet, horny women teetering on whoredom and tossing their inhibitions to the wind, releasing their inner freaks, like myself, can fulfill their carnal desires by selecting the stud of their choice off of ornate purple and red menus, along with any combination of drinks of their liking. There's a picture beside each studs' name, along with their stats: age, height, weight, nationality, and turn-ons. Delicious *boi* treats such as: Cocoa Bombshell, The Smack Down, Caribbean Breeze, Chocolate Pleasure, Cream de Cocoa, Dred Delight, The Red Dragon, Chocolate Thunder, The Incredible Hunk, King Kong, Stud Daddy, Whip Appeal, G-Spot, The Pussy Pleaser, and a list of others are all available for one's decadent pleasures.

Tonight, I am feeling slutty and bold, sipping on my second Pussy Pleaser—a mixture of Absolut vodka, blue Curacao, and grenadine with splashes of pineapple and cranberry juices.

I slowly slide the tip of my tongue over my glossed lips. I twist in my seat, discreetly grinding my pussy into the center of the leather stool as one stud after another swaggers out and into the middle of the room, flexing and profiling. Then saunter off. I have my sights on the Pussy Pleaser.

In her photo, she's the color of licorice. Dark. And, hopefully, just as sweet. Her stats state she's five-eleven, 157 pounds, brown eyes. Dreads. Her turn-ons: tight wet pussy. And squirters.

"Glad to see you came back, ma," a husky voice says in my ear; soft lips gently brush against my lobe, startling me. "You look good enough to eat."

My pulse quickens.

My whole body shudders, heated realization dances up and down the center of my spine, finding its way along the inner part of my smooth thighs, twirling along the seam of my pussy. There is no name, just the silken voice and the delicious memory.

I swivel slightly on the stool, bringing into view the one who changed my whole life three weeks ago. Tonight she's wearing a white T-shirt, baggy faded jeans and crisp white Nikes. She has a black Brooklyn Nets fitted pulled down over her dark brown eyes. Her bone-straight hair is pulled tightly into a ponytail.

Her heated gaze slides over my body like melted butter. My eyes lower to the bulge in her jeans. Instantly, her thick dick jutting out from its harness flashes through my mind, replaying the way she slowly fucked me in long even strokes, plunging deep on the in-stroke, then slowly pulling out until the head of her dick kissed the mouth of my pussy before plunging back in, hitting the bottom of my Honeywell.

The way she fucked me was…sweet torture.

She's handsomely beautiful—if that makes sense. Hell, nothing makes sense to me anymore.

A month ago I would still be home somewhere fighting my truth, hiding behind pretense, still surreptitiously masturbating to mental snapshots of naked women—the swell of their breasts, the dark, succulent ridges of their nipples, the smooth curve of their hips, the scented heat of their pussies and asses—stained into my memory as I finger-fucked one orgasm after the other out of myself.

But now secret fantasies have become a reality. The Stud Palace—in all of its opulence and decadent pleasures—is addictive.

From the moment I stepped through these doors—three weeks ago—I was hooked. Its debauchery has rented space in my head ever since. It has kept me craving more of its delicious, dirty deeds.

And I am here, again. Hungry for another round of seductive pleasure, craving the soft touch of a masculine woman, yearning to taste her steamed juices as they seep out of her womanhood and coat the base of her harness.

I press my thighs together, squeezing back want and desire. "Isn't this a nice surprise," I say, eyeing her over the rim of my glass. God, I'd love to feel her lips on my body again; the wet, warmth of her mouth capturing my cunt and clit. "If I didn't know better, I'd think you were stalking me." Amusement laces my tone as I arch my brows.

"Hey. I could ask you the same thing."

"I'm too classy to stalk," I say, teasingly. "But *you*, on the other hand…"

She chuckles. "Nah, never that, baby. But I'd like to stalk that sweet, tight pussy, again."

She licks her plump, pillow-soft pussy eating lips. I watch as she pulls out a piece of cinnamon gum and folds it into her lush mouth. A tinge of jealousy creeps up in me, wishing it were my chocolate nipples being rolled into her mouth instead of chewing gum.

I swallow.

I feel my smooth cunt starting to slicken as I imagine her long tongue flicking up and down on my clit as she pushes three slender fingers knuckles deep into my swelling river of juices.

"Let's go to one of the booths," she offers, her voice throaty and filled with lust. Salacious intent dances in her eyes, her attention completely focused on me.

I give her a coquettish grin. "Why on earth would I want to do that? A lady neverwalks off with strange women."

"Then don't be a lady. Be a tramp."